REIGN OF THE DEVOURER

Doom towered over Zargo, a shape stronger and more terrible than the mountains.

"Tell me what is here," said Doom.

"There are human memories here. And ones that are older. It keeps memories, and it… it consumes them."

"Where?" Doom asked. He leaned forward, eyes blazing behind the mask.

"Beneath us. Far beneath us. I think you should leave it alone," said Zargo. "It's dangerous."

Doom said nothing at first. His still presence, so powerful it filled the space between the mountains, invited Zargo to decide which was more dangerous, Doom or the call from below. Then Doom said, simply, "It will be mine."

Zargo understood that there wasn't a choice of danger. It was the collision of wills between Doom and the hunger beneath that he should fear.

ALSO AVAILABLE

MARVEL UNTOLD

DOCTOR DOOM IN:
REIGN OF THE DEVOURER

DAVID ANNANDALE

ACONYTE

FOR MARVEL PUBLISHING

VP Production & Special Projects: Jeff Youngquist
Associate Editors, Special Projects: Caitlin O'Connell and Sarah Singer
Manager, Licensed Publishing: Jeremy West
VP, Licensed Publishing: Sven Larsen
SVP Print, Sales & Marketing: David Gabriel
Editor in Chief: C B Cebulski

Special thanks to Tom Brevoort

Doctor Doom created by Stan Lee & Jack Kirby

First published by Aconyte Books in 2022

ISBN 978 1 83908 094 4

Ebook ISBN 978 1 83908 095 1

Cover art by Fabio Listrani

Distributed in North America by Simon & Schuster Inc, New York, USA
Printed in the United States of America
9 8 7 6 5 4 3 2 1

ACONYTE BOOKS

An imprint of Asmodee Entertainment Ltd

Mercury House, Shipstones Business Centre

North Gate, Nottingham NG7 7FN, UK

aconytebooks.com // twitter.com/aconytebooks

For Margaux, always.
For all that we have,
and for what is to come.

PROLOGUE

By such dread words from Earth to Heaven
My still realm was never riven:
When its wound was closed, there stood
Darkness o'er the day like blood.
PERCY SHELLEY, PROMETHEUS UNBOUND, I.99–102

They were here because of the scars. Doom knew that was why he had come. He wondered whether Grigori Zargo knew what had drawn him here as well.

Standing on the peak of a jagged claw of hardened lava over fifty feet high, Doom watched the priest move like a crawling insect over the tortured land. North of Doomstadt, and south of the Kanof Valley Dam, the dried lake bed had been wounded again and again over the course of the last year. The land here had the misfortune to be crossed by multiple ley lines. Where a node had formed, Doom had constructed an arena for his Midsummer duel against a champion of Hell. The duel had shattered the crust of the Earth. The molten blood of the plain had run incandescent red. And then, when Zargo had done as Doom commanded, and raised the lodestones that had been created by the agony of the ley lines, the land had bled again, had burned with the touch of Hell seeking a clawhold in the world.

The face of the plain had suffered greatly. It was scarred. Long ridges of black rock, like the spines of fossilized leviathans, crisscrossed the baked, glassed lake bed. They were the maps of the injuries. Where the blood had erupted most violently, the formations were congealed pain, shrieks of lava raising their twisted points to the sky.

The wind keened over the ruined land. The summer had been a cool one. On Walpurgis Night, April 30, Doom had activated the Harrower, the engine born of science and sorcery that he had created to pull his mother's soul from Hell. His mother, who had only ever sought to protect her people from King Vladimir, and whose good intentions had been used and twisted by Mephisto to trap her in Hell. Every Midsummer, Doom fought Mephisto or his choice of champion to free her. Every Midsummer, Doom lost the duel, its terms always predetermining its end. On Walpurgis Night, he sent the power of the Harrower into Hell instead. But the rebel Fortunov had sabotaged the machine, and the Harrower had unleashed a plague of demons on the city. Doom had destroyed the monster the Harrower became, and stopped the plague, but there had been a price to pay. He had come to the plain because of the personal cost he had suffered. His subjects had paid too. In the wake of the demons had come the rain of ash. It had spread far beyond Doomstadt to cover all of Latveria, as if the city had been the center of a massive volcanic eruption. The ash had fallen slowly, covering the sky and the ground for weeks. Even after the worst had passed, it was as if the sun had been shackled, unable to bring its full strength. So summer had passed, subdued and sullen.

The Midsummer duel had come and gone, and he had lost again, to the howling mockery of Hell.

Now it was September, and fall was as eager to make its presence felt as summer had been reluctant. The winds were stronger and more piercing than usual. Here and there, ash still fell instead of rain. The dried lake bed was one such place. The ash fell more often here than anywhere else. Eddies of black whirled, caught in a mournful dance with the wind. The air was gray, the entire region of the duel shrouded in limbo.

Gray wind and black scars, Doom thought. That is the fruit of my labors.

The landscape spoke to him of what he had lost. It was the image of the price he had paid. In his struggle against the Harrower, there had been a revelation, and then it had been taken away from him. All he could remember was that he had forgotten, and that what was forgotten was beyond price.

Gray wind and black scars. It does not end like this. I will not permit it.

Below, Zargo walked aimlessly, moving from ridge to ridge. The priest spent most of his days here, Doom knew. The days that he did not, were spent sequestered in the rooms he had taken in Old Town, in the near shadow of Castle Doom. Zargo had not returned to St Peter Church, whose vicar he had once been, since its destruction. He had not even gone to see the progress of the reconstruction. The church would be restored to everything it had been. Doom would not permit scars to deface Doomstadt.

He had fled the sight of his church, but Zargo could not stay away from here. Doom wondered if Zargo understood what was drawing him to the lake bed. Perhaps he did. Whether Zargo grasped the idea or not, this was a place where he belonged. This was where he had first truly flexed his powers as a geomancer. The scars of the land were part of Zargo's history. His actions had helped to create them.

The wind blew harder, billowing Doom's cloak. He looked away from Zargo and let his eyes trace the lava scars. Their shape was a memory in the most profound sense. The land remembered its pain, and showed it. What was here could not easily be erased. There was no forgetfulness here. That was important.

Scars could not be forgotten, Doom thought. They were the sign that there is no true healing.

No healing, no forgetting, no forgiving. Not when there were scars.

The scars on the land angered him. This portion of Latveria had been defaced, and to no end. The demons had killed hundreds in Doomstadt, and Doom's mother was still in Hell.

These were the marks of his failed work. They were the marks of the debt owed by those who made it fail.

Doom thought about Fortunov. He let anger wash over and through him in a molten wave.

Then he calmed himself. Scars were a goad, too. They drove him to greatness.

These scars would have their use. They would take him to power.

Zargo felt the gaze of Doom. It weighed on him, heavy as stone, and it bore through him, sharp as ice. He stopped walking again, exhausted by its strength, and stared numbly at the broken textures of the lava ridge he stood upon.

Why was Doom here? Zargo couldn't be of interest to him any longer.

Except, somehow, he was.

I did what he commanded. Because I obeyed, I helped unleash Hell. Because I obeyed, my church fell.

He didn't think he could ever go back to St Peter. He couldn't look at the construction site. He had gone by once, just once, and he had been unable to see the rising of a phoenix. He had only seen the evidence of destruction. His eyes had looked to where the towers should have been, and seen only absence in the sky. When the work was finished, he would not see the church whole again. He would see a simulacrum, a monument to his sin.

The ruined lake bed was another such monument, but at least it didn't look like the thing he should have saved. So his guilt brought him here instead, like a tongue drawn to the gap of a newly missing tooth. He found no comfort when he walked on the broken surfaces of the ridges. He found still less on days like this, when the wind blew hard and when the ash stung his eyes and throat. On days like this, the world beyond the lake bed vanished. The hills to the east and west were shapeless masses, a thicker darkness embracing the gray, slowly converging to the north. To the south, there was nothing, just the slow fall of ash erasing the horizon. Surrounded by pain, he became part of it. His breathing, gnawed by guilt, was heavy and rasping.

He was no good to anyone, and most certainly not to his flock. Their shepherd was absent, and that was another sharp fang of guilt, but he couldn't face them. Not yet. Perhaps not ever. He had lost all the certainty and peace he had known in the Nigerian seminary that had trained him and given him everything good about the priest he had believed he should be. The priest was gone, brought low because it was only as a geomancer that he had been able to protect his parishioners from demons. He needed to be alone, and so he came here, to wander the twisted lines, to indulge in a pilgrimage with no purpose or destination, and in a meditation without peace.

Now Doom had come. When Zargo saw the silhouette on top of the one of the tallest of the lava formations, he looked away, momentarily gripped by the delirious thought that he could pretend Doom was not there. He tried to walk on. Maybe he could go so far that he would not be able to see this formation.

The gaze held him. It stole his strength, and what sense of purpose he still had. He walked without seeing where he went, directionless. A new fear gripped him, a fear of what might come, and it wrapped its talons more and more firmly around his chest. Finally, it immobilized him. He stayed where he was, head down, vision glazed by gray, and waited for the inevitable.

Zargo did not hear Doom descend from the peak. He did not hear the thrust of Doom's waist-mounted jetpacks. All he heard was the crunch of stone beneath heavy boots. That was the sound of fate coming for him again. It made him turn around.

Zargo looked up. Ash fell around Doom, dancing around him as if it feared him. Inside the dark green of his hood and cloak, the gray of his armor was stronger than the gray about them. He was the shape of will, and that was a terrifying thought to Zargo. If Zargo was partly responsible for the pain of the land, he had also been just the tool of force too strong to resist, too great for Zargo ever to fully comprehend. Doom's will had directed him. Doom's will had been the engine of everything that had happened. There had been catastrophe, and it was Doom's will that had ended that too. Everywhere Zargo looked, he saw the physical traces of Doom's will.

"I have nothing left to give you," Zargo said. Despair gave birth to what was almost defiance. "What more do you want? You have broken my faith and my church."

"*Your* church?" Doom asked. The metallic voice was deep. Its rasp harsh as a prison.

Zargo said nothing. There were answers to the presumption in Doom's question. Zargo didn't have the strength to give voice to any of them.

"St Peter is being rebuilt," Doom said, his tone knowing. He paused long enough for Zargo to squirm in the guilt of his silence. "You could be ministering to your flock even now. Yet you are here instead."

"I am not worthy to be their priest."

"That is your choice. I am unaware of any edict declaring your unfitness." Doom shrugged. "The state of your faith if no concern of mine, nor do I find it remotely interesting."

"Why do you torment me?" Zargo pleaded.

"The torment is your choice to experience," said Doom. "Wallow in it, if that is your wish. I am here because you are my subject, and you are of use to me. Your powers are, that is."

"You are speaking to the geomancer once more," Zargo said dully.

"I always have. That you have split the geomancer from the priest is, again, your choice. As a way to suffer, it is so unnecessary that it borders on bad comedy, but that too is not my concern. Your obedience is."

Zargo tried to meet Doom's gaze. He couldn't. The eyes looking down at him were harder than the titanium mask. "How can I serve?" he asked. There had never been a question of choice.

"You will serve me by doing what you have come here to do. You are here because the land holds memories, and you can feel them."

"Anyone can. All they have to do is look or touch."

"Your sense of the memories is far more profound." Doom stretched his arm to take in the landscape, his fingers wide as if to grasp hold of it. "You think about what you did to create these scars. You think, too, that they are the expression of my will."

Zargo felt the blood rush from his face. He couldn't swallow. *How can he know?*

Because he was Doom.

"Will affects reality," said Doom. "The mind is energy. If this is so, the memories are energy too, and cannot be destroyed." Doom made a fist, as if pulling something up from the ground. "You will assist me in finding what is lost but not destroyed. You will unearth memories. Literally."

"What memories?" Zargo asked, wary of the answer, frightened of what he might have to do, and resigned to the knowledge that he could not disobey.

"All of them," said Doom. "And the power they contain."

The wind gusted against Zargo, shrieking with premonition.

PART 1

THE VAULTS OF REMEMBRANCE

I heard
Thy curse, the which, if thou rememberest not,
Yet my innumerable seas and streams,
Mountains, and caves, and winds, and yon wide air,
And the inarticulate people of the dead,
Preserve, a treasured spell.
  PERCY SHELLEY, PROMETHEUS UNBOUND, I.179–184

ONE

They gathered in the ruins of a fortified house. It was in a pass of the Malhela mountains, close to the border between Latveria and Symkaria. The pass was rarely used. It was too narrow, steep and crooked for any route for vehicles to have been built along its ancient path. On foot, it was treacherous, and too dangerous to be traveled at night. Crevasses cut across it, and there were long stretches where the path was an uneven ledge only a couple of feet wide.

There must have been a time, Rudolfo Fortunov thought, when the pass had seen more use. The house was evidence of that. Perhaps this route between the nations hadn't always been so forbidding. When the change had come, though, it had come long ago. The house had been disused for centuries. It was a boxy thing, almost a keep. Its roof had fallen in, and the upper portions of the walls were breaking down, as if chewed by giants. Mortar crumbled out from the heavy slabs of its masonry. Inside, it was hollowed out. There were no longer any divisions between the rooms. The house was a shell.

It was altogether too fitting a place for this gathering.

There were twenty of his partisans with him, and that number was close to being the sum total of the forces he still commanded. He had lost so many in the failed coup, and still more when the demons had come to Doomstadt. He had fled Doom's anger, and hidden for months in the wilderness. So had his followers, though still more had abandoned the cause. After the disasters, too many no longer believed the Fortunovs could ever be returned to the throne. Those who still believed, the ones with true iron in their souls, were, like him, ragged, hungry and exhausted.

"So you're abandoning the field, then," said Maleva Krogh. "You are running away."

"We are retreating," Fortunov told her. "That is not the same thing as flight."

"Is that what you tell yourself?"

Fortunov's jaw clenched. He fought with his temper and kept it down. He was too drained to rage anyway. But this was why he had always kept Krogh at arm's length, even though no one was more committed to the overthrow of Doom than she was. Her family was one of the oldest in Latveria, older even than the Fortunovs. Though the Kroghs had never ruled the country, they had been so integral to the old order, they might have been its spine.

Or maybe its skull. They were what lurked beneath the skin.

Doom had destroyed the power and the fortune of the Kroghs. He had burned their stronghold. He had broken their hold on what they knew to be theirs. Though Maleva Krogh had never had a military title in the old regime, as one of Fortunov's partisans, her fight to take that back was fanatical.

Her war was a cruel one. She was as set on punishing the people for their temerity in turning from the old order as she was Doom for having dismantled it. Her cruelty gave credence to the stories – half rumor, half folklore – that Fortunov had grown up hearing about the Kroghs. He had to be careful to hold her back, or she would do his cause more harm than good. But at the same time, no one could rival her adamantine commitment to the fight.

Krogh was in her seventies. She was tall and wiry as a mantis, walnut-hard and wrinkled by weather and bitterness. She had the narrow, sharp face of a mummified jackal. Fortunov had known her only from a distance in the days of his father Vladimir's reign. She and her family had been baleful presences in the court, powers on the sidelines and in the shadows rather than the center. They were the people his father spoke with alone, and whom other nobles feared. He did not think she would try to supplant him, though. The throne itself had never been for the Kroghs, he thought. How could they work in the shadows if they had to reign in the light? He felt confident in his estimation of her. She had never given him a reason to think he had been wrong.

Her defiance now, though, was troubling.

"What would you have us do, Maleva?" Fortunov asked Krogh. "We are as weak as we have ever been. Doom is strong. An attack of any kind would be futile. We'll be fortunate if we make it to Symkaria without being spotted by a patrolling Doombot, so forget about launching some sort of strike."

"A Doombot is not Doom."

"Isn't it?" said Fortunov. "Can you tell the difference between the machine and its creator? I can't. Can you stand up to one, when it fights with his weapons? I can't. And even if you could, what it sees, its master knows." He shook his head, frustrated with himself for even having such a pointless argument. But he couldn't stop. "And strike how?" he said. "At what? With what? Or do you want me to lead a useless charge?"

"Better that than useless surrender."

"Remember your place!" Leonid Kutuzov shouted.

Krogh glared at King Vladimir's former palace guard officer. Kutuzov rocked back and forth on his heels, torn between anger and the instinct to retreat from those cold, dead eyes.

Fortunov placed a calming hand on Kutuzov's shoulder. "There is no surrender here!" he said. "Our struggle is not finished. Doom has enemies outside Latveria who can help and might yet be convinced to do so."

"Like Advanced Idea Mechanics?"

Fortunov winced. A.I.M. had provided him with weapons, and he had used them all in the last attempt to take the castle. Things had not gone well. After the expensive disaster of the coup, he didn't think A.I.M. would look kindly on new overtures from him. "There are others. We need the chance to contact them, to rebuild. We need the refuge of Symkaria to start."

"*To start*," Krogh repeated, hissing contempt. "To start, to start, to start. Everything we have done for years has been *to start*, and we have begun over and over again, and every time we made a step forward, we've been sent back two." She jabbed a finger at Fortunov. "The Kroghs have backed you, as we backed your father, but Latveria has had other kings, from older bloodlines than the Fortunovs. The Kroghs remember the Haasens. We remember the birth of Latveria."

Fortunov snorted. "You are welcome to go looking for an heir to the Haasen line. I have no idea where you would find one without the help of a necromancer. And the Fortunovs are the rightful rulers of Latveria. *I* am the rightful king of Latveria. You would do well to remember that."

Krogh was undaunted. "You would do well to remember that the loyalty of the Kroghs is earned. It is not to be taken for granted."

What was the point of this? Fortunov wondered. *What a pathetic sight we must be, ragged beggars arguing over a crown. Doom would laugh to see us.* When he answered Krogh, he spoke softly, almost gently. "What Kroghs?" he said. He did not like pointing this out, but Kutuzov was right. She had forgotten her place. "What Kroghs?" he said again. "You are the last. Your bloodline is ended."

She said nothing, her face twisting with viper anger.

"You are skilled, Maleva," Fortunov went on. "I value you in our struggle. But this is the path we must take now. It is the only one open to us."

"Then you take it without me," Krogh said, raising her voice. "I will not leave Latveria, even if you will." She looked around, inviting the others to stand with her.

Kutuzov bent down to pick up his backpack. He shouldered it, then turned to Fortunov. "We do not have much daylight left, your highness," he said.

"Yes, you're right," said Fortunov. They had only a couple of hours before they would have to make uncomfortable camp. He was not going to delay any longer. He had spent two nights in this ruin already, waiting for this paltry group to gather. The house was barely a shelter at all. The wind blew through the breaks in the walls, shrieking and cold.

He picked up his own pack, and the rest of his followers did the same. "Farewell, Maleva," he said. "We will meet again, and we will march on the castle, once and for all."

Krogh did not reply.

The path went downhill from the house for several hundred yards before it angled around the mountain face and sloped up again. Fortunov looked back, just before the turn. Shrouded in black, Krogh was a silhouette against the stone wall, a raven in the wind. The overcast, late-afternoon light was already dim, and he could no longer see her face. He could feel her anger, though. It went with him, a deeper chill, as he left her behind and started on the road to Symkaria.

The last of Fortunov's troop disappeared from sight. Krogh was alone.

You are the last.

Fortunov's words stung. Until now, she had still had her small group to command, even if they were sworn servants of the Krogh, and not their blood. Those soldiers had left with Fortunov, obeying the higher authority of their king.

She was alone, and she was the last.

Krogh ground her teeth in anger. Fortunov was betraying the past with his cowardice. That, she could not forgive. The memories of the Kroghs were long. She felt her ancestors' memories as clearly as if they were her own. They *were* her own. They were her legacy, her birthright and her strength.

The family's history went deep in Latveria, deeper than the roots of mountains. The past belonged to the Kroghs. It was the site of their power. It was what gave their name its force of meaning and of fear, even now, even when there was no one left except her. The past belonged to the Kroghs, and the future must too, because the strength of the past was greater than parvenus like the Fortunovs could ever really understand. Continuity, tradition – those were just words, glosses. The unchangeable. The forever. Those were true concepts. With them came the ability to do what the Kroghs willed to the people beneath them, because that was what power and authority were for.

Krogh ran her hand over the crumbled wall of the ruin. She was touching the past, feeling in the roughness against her palm the past's abandonment, its fall into rubble, into oblivion. She touched the erosion that was forgetting, and it enraged her. She believed in the past, she remembered it, she fought for it, and it was slipping away, dragged across the horizon of forever to be lost.

She howled, hurling her anger in challenge to the cries of the wind. Let Fortunov turn his back on his duty. Let the masses forget their place. *She* remembered. She would be the champion of the memory of old Latveria and its righteous cruelty.

Her cry was hunger as much as it was anger. She *wanted* the past. She *needed* it, and all that it represented. The pangs of the hunger seized her, cutting off her shout. Krogh gasped, and doubled over in pain. She took a slow, ragged breath, and let it out as a high keen.

She would fight. She would destroy the usurper and all those who betrayed the glory of the past.

But she didn't know how, and she was old, and she was alone.

"*Tell me how!*" she pleaded, addressing nothing except memory itself.

And then, *Maleva.*

She held her breath.

Maleva.

The call was faint with distance, but it was unmistakable. She heard it between the wind, beneath the light. She heard it with her soul.

Maleva.

Something deep had heard her, and answered. It was the deepest of all memories. It was the dark heart that the Kroghs had always served, without ever truly knowing what it was. She did not know it now. It knew her, though, and that was sufficient. She had called, and it had stirred, and it had answered.

Krogh smiled. She straightened up, and turned back north.

"I am coming to you," she whispered.

There were dreams on the wind now, as she began to walk, old dreams, hungry dreams.

Dreams that would rend the day.

Doom walked slowly down the great hall of the library of Castle Doom. The floor creaked under his footsteps. It was a masterpiece of parquetry. Mahogany, oak, walnut and cherry formed an intricate dance of astrological and alchemical designs. Esoteric knowledge lived in the floor, never to be forgotten, the memories springing up whenever Doom glanced down.

The baroque vault of the ceiling, two levels up, was a riot of celestial conflict. Zeus felled the Titans, the Norse gods charged to the final battle of Ragnarok and Satan was cast down from Heaven. More than a dozen pantheons blended together in cataclysm.

Every fifteen feet, on either side of Doom, pillars marked the divisions between the long alcoves. In the recesses were the great bookshelves. The collection was two floors high, with a gallery running down the length of the hall at the upper level. Filtered light came in through the tall windows, the illumination inviting to read by, but safe for treasures on the shelves.

There were more than a million books in the library. Its holdings were more general and less esoteric than those of the great archive in the foundations of the castle. After Fortunov's attack on Walpurgis Night had destroyed part of the archive, Doom had had some of its materials transferred to the library while repairs were underway. The temporary additions did little to alter the character of the library's collection and its use. The library contained a wider sweep of the world's knowledge. Through it, Doom gained insights that took him beyond the specialism of the archives.

It was, he thought, as he moved through its hush, the representation of what he sought. He compared it to the thousands of books he had in his study. The smaller collection was to the library as the library was to the memories he was determined to unearth.

No, he corrected. The comparison was flawed. The finite, no matter how large, could not be matched beside the infinite.

He looked down the hall with pride at the march of bookshelves. Still, he was content with the analogy. It was a suitable symbol of his prize.

A large portion of the collection had been digitized. He

could access it and search it from anywhere, the results appearing on his mask's visor screens. That was useful, but he took pleasure in the space of the library, the tactile qualities of books and the serendipity of discovery.

He was hoping for some of that serendipity today, as the gears of his new work began to grind forward. He was not looking for any book in particular. He was curious to know, with his mind open, what would call to him. So he walked down the hall, stopping for a moment by each pillar to look left and right into the alcoves, then moved on.

Two thirds of the way to the end of the hall, he stopped. Intuition made him turn left. His gauntleted fingers brushed gently against the spines as he went by them. He did not read any of the titles until one book made him stop short, as if a dowsing rod had leapt to action in his hands.

Doom took the book down. *Phantasmus*. It was from the seventeenth century. It was a chronicle, presented as factual, of superstitious lore from the northern region of Latveria, particularly the villages of the Carpathian Mountains. Doom turned its pages, eyeing the snarling woodcuts, reading of the fears of the past. He felt a ripple of unease, which he thrust away.

That emotion was useless and unworthy. Enough of this. There was work to be done.

He replaced the book and stalked out of the library.

After her shift, Elsa Orloff made the long journey from the department of neurology to the office of the director of Doomstadt Hospital. Elizabeth Boehm presided over the operations of the hospital from the top of a squat tower that surmounted the center of the hospital. Orloff had met Boehm only a few times, and had never been to her office. Boehm's philosophy was that if she had taken on the best people to run each of their specialized areas, then she should let them do just that. Orloff appreciated that approach, and the freedom it gave her department and its head to do the best work possible.

Even so, Orloff had felt twitches of unease ever since Nikolas Steiner, her administrative aide, had poked his head into her office. She had been about to head home. He had made an apologetic face, and told her that Boehm wanted to see her.

"Do you know why?" Orloff had asked.

Steiner had not.

If all was well, then why was the meeting necessary? Then again, Orloff could think of nothing she had done that might put her in a bad light. She had plenty of time to go back and forth between the poles of worry and confidence between leaving her office and arriving at the door to Boehm's.

The reception area was sober. High-backed chairs upholstered in dark leather sat underneath the gothic vault of the room, their backs turned at a discreet angle away from the secretary's desk. The secretary, a young man with the careful courtesy and studied calm of a funeral director, stood up to greet Orloff as soon as she entered.

"Thank you for coming, Dr Orloff," he said. He stepped out from behind his desk and moved to the oak double-doors behind him. "Dr Boehm is eager to see you." He knocked, two soft, polite raps, then took hold of the brass doorknobs and pulled.

Orloff nodded to him and passed through. The secretary closed the doors behind her.

Boehm's office was huge. The ceiling's vault was twice as high as the antechamber's. A series of arced windows dominated the back wall, creating a panoramic view over thirty feet wide. The view was dominated by Castle Doom, its mass looking down from the heights of its mount, a reminder that whoever sat in this office did so at the pleasure of the king of Latveria.

"Do sit down, Dr Orloff," Boehm said. She was a short, wide woman, tiny behind her enormous desk. Her hair was candle-white, and she looked at Orloff through glasses so thick they magnified her eyes, making her gaze seem even more piercing.

Orloff sat in one of the chairs facing the desk. She was tall, but its back was higher than her head.

"I apologize for making your long day even longer," said Boehm. "I'm afraid this couldn't wait, though."

That sounded bad.

"Your work here has been exemplary," the director began.

"But…?" said Orloff. The defensiveness was an old reflex, cultivated through her adolescence outside Latveria, when she had encountered too many variations of that formulation as punishment for being trans. *You're good, but… You're smart, but… You're nice, but…* She had never expected to have the reflex triggered in Doomstadt Hospital.

"Oh no, you misunderstand," Boehm said quickly. "It's because your work is so exemplary that we are going to lose your services, and that grieves me."

"I don't understand," said Orloff, baffled. "I didn't think I was going anywhere."

Boehm looked grave. "You have been summoned to the castle," said simply, pronouncing the words as if they were the fulfillment of a prophecy.

Orloff was still confused. "I'm afraid I don't quite follow you," she said. Did Boehm think she would be terrified by the prospect? Many would be. "I have been there before." In fairness, she would probably have been terrified on that first visit, if she hadn't been married to the captain of the palace guard. She wondered why Kariana Verlak hadn't simply delivered the message to her at home.

Boehm looked down for a moment at the sheet of paper that rested at the center of her blotter pad. "The order to send you there," she said, "was sent to me. That means that the message was directed to me even more than it was to you."

"Implying that I will not be coming back?"

"I don't know. It isn't for me to know, just like it isn't for me to question. If your new duties turn out to be permanent, then I would like to take this opportunity to tell you that I wish you well. Though we haven't met often, I will miss you, because the work you have done here is good and important."

"Thank you," said Orloff. She felt as if the platform of her life, which she had believed level and stable, was shifting quickly, steeply and irrevocably. Part of her felt the desperate impulse to reach out and grab something, anything, that might stop the slide. The other part of her was eager to see where she might fall. She remembered the excitement of going to the castle for the masked ball in the spring, when she had seen and spoken with Doom for the first time. He had wanted her expertise then. He had told her to observe the other guests. They were the remnants of Latveria's old nobility, and as far as Orloff had been able to tell, Doom regarded them as having no purpose except as unknowing guinea pigs. She didn't know the nature of the experiment that had gone on that night. No harm had come to anyone, and so the evening was a dangerously exciting memory. Doom was a presence that filled awareness. She had felt the power of his intellect as if it were a physical force, like the pressure of an approaching storm. The awe she had experienced in her encounter had never really left her. Nor had the anticipation that she might be asked to do more.

She took a breath, fighting back a light-headedness the meaning of which she did not trust. The thought of leaving the hospital and her patients pierced through the vertigo, a sliver of pain. There was so much more she hoped to do for the people who came to her. So much was left unfinished.

This couldn't really be permanent. Could it?

She knew better than to say something about having a choice. "I understand my duty," she said. She understood very little else about this. "I know that what we receive comes with the duty to obey." She hesitated. "But I did think I was already doing my duty to Latveria."

"You were," Boehm said gently. "You did it extraordinarily well." Boehm licked her lips, nervous, and glanced over her shoulder at the castle. "Now you have a higher calling," she said.

The director sounded relieved that the greater calling was not hers. Orloff pitied her. Orloff's nerves jangled. She didn't know what to expect. She mourned what she was leaving behind.

But…

A higher calling.

That did feel right. That did feel thrilling.

TWO

The evening in the apartment on the top floor of the Old Town house was quiet. Dinner was paella, and Orloff and Kariana each had an extra glass of pinot noir, toasting each other in a deliberate celebration of Orloff's summons. They did not talk about what was coming with the dawn for the rest of the evening. Orloff retired to her study to finish the last of her paperwork. She wanted to leave Doomstadt Hospital without any loose ends. Kariana had her own reports to go through.

Later, they lay in bed, holding hands. They looked up at the slanted ceiling. A slowly shifting pattern of shadows and amber light moved over it, the reflection of the castle lights streaming through the circular stained-glass window over the headboard. Now, when the tasks were done, and all was quiet, Kariana said, "Are you ready for tomorrow?"

Orloff thought carefully, trying to find the truth of what she felt. She turned on her side, away from the amber dance, to look at her wife. Kariana did the same. Their foreheads were almost touching. "I don't know," Orloff said finally. "Am I ready?"

"If you're asking yourself that, then that's good," said Kariana. "If you'd said yes, I'd be worried." Kariana paused. "No one is ever ready for Doom."

"You smiled when you said that."

"Were you ready the night of the ball?"

Orloff laughed. "No, I wasn't."

"Was that a bad thing?"

"No. I think I might have been disappointed if I had been."

"There you go." Kariana turned serious. "I can't prepare you, because I don't know what's going to happen tomorrow either. I can tell you this. There will be uncertainty, there will be terror. You have to embrace them."

"I think I did, at the ball," Orloff said, remembering the strangeness, the grandeur, and the mystery. She had had the sense of being part of something much larger than she could grasp. Part of that had been because of Doom himself. His presence was too vast, as if the hall had tried to contain a thunderstorm.

"You did well," said Kariana. "But that was one night. This is different. You've been summoned. You have a greater duty now. That night was just a foretaste. You caught Doom's eye. You showed him that you could be useful. Now you're going to learn in what way."

Orloff laughed uneasily. "If you're trying to be reassuring, you're not doing it very well."

"I wasn't really trying to be. I'm being honest about what this means, Ellie."

"What was it like the first time you met him?" Kariana had been in the palace guard all her adult life, and its captain for more than five years now.

"I was frightened. Like any sensible person would be. But I came away from that meeting knowing the shape of the rest of my life." Kariana's laugh was a happy one. "That's a rare privilege."

Orloff thought about that. Her heart pounded a little harder. "All right, then. Coach me through this. What do I need to know?"

"Whatever Doom lets you know."

Orloff waggled a finger and gave Kariana a gentle tap on the nose. "That," she said, "is not what I meant, and you know it."

Kariana grinned. "I do. But what I said is true, too, and that *is* something you need to know."

"OK." Orloff took a deep breath, trying to make the lesson part of herself. "OK. Noted. What else?"

"Don't hesitate."

"I never do."

Kariana gave her a kiss. "I know, and that's why I love you. But I mean it. Whatever you're asked to do won't be easy, physically, mentally or spiritually." She was serious again. It was the captain of the palace guard speaking now. "Remember your duty to Doom. Our duty is our honor and our glory. So never hesitate."

Orloff thought about this. She glanced up at the amber light on the ceiling, and the play of shadows suddenly reminded her of Walpurgis Night. Too many things reminded her of that night. The horrors she had seen in the hospital rushed through her again, a wave that battered, and there were things in it that cut and gnawed. "Do you think about Walpurgis Night?" She hoped Kariana would understand what she was really asking.

"You know I do." Kariana put a hand on her shoulder. "I

still have nightmares. And you saw the demons in a way that I didn't."

"Is that…" Orloff broke off. The question was a hard one to ask. Kariana's loyalty to Doom was adamantine. Orloff tried again. "Is what happened on Walpurgis Night something that should worry me?"

"No." Kariana's answer was swift, sure, firm. "That was Fortunov's doing. He broke into the castle, and what he did caused the disaster. The horrors of that night are his doing." Kariana closed her eyes for a moment. "If anyone other than him is to blame for what happened, it's me. I wasn't able to stop him."

"You couldn't have."

"I should have."

"You were outnumbered. You have to forgive yourself."

Kariana's grimace showed how difficult she was finding that.

Orloff stroked her face gently. "You're too hard on yourself," she said. When Kariana opened her mouth to object, Orloff put a finger on her lips. "Shh," she said. She gave her wife the smile that meant *I love you and you're going to listen to me.* "I wish you would cut yourself some slack. You know? Just a little bit? Because Kariana Verlak is a worse taskmaster for Kariana Verlak than Doom is. If he was displeased with what you did that night, would you still be captain of the guard?"

"No," Kariana admitted, some of the pain draining from her face. She kissed Orloff. "Now. We were talking about you. And I'm going to say this again, because this is really everything you need to know. Whatever Doom asks, you must do. It's that simple. So your duty to act tomorrow will be no different from any other day, or from what is expected of any other citizen of Latveria. Got it?"

"Got it."

"You still have your thinking frown."

"I'm just wondering why me," Orloff said. That was the other question that had gone around and around her mind, a nagging refrain, since her talk with Boehm. *What does he want?* and *Why me?* would not leave her alone.

"Because there is something you can do that no one else can."

"He knows me that well, does he?"

"Probably better than you know yourself."

Kariana spoke as if this were the most natural, ordinary thing in the world, and a source of comfort. It made Orloff feel even more uneasy.

"You're not going to lose the thinking frown, are you?" Kariana asked.

"Probably not."

"Are you going to sleep tonight?"

"Probably not."

"Shall I stay up with you?"

"No," said Orloff. "You're here. That's what matters. You sleep. I'll fret. If I need you, I'll wake you."

"Promise?"

"Promise."

In the end, she did sleep. But the play of shadows followed her into her dreams.

Orloff walked up to the castle with Kariana in the morning, both conscious and proud of the portrait they made together.

"My troops call us 'the Hawk and the Blade,'" Kariana had told her one morning, not long after their wedding.

"I know why you're the Hawk," Orloff had said.

"You think my nose is that sharp?" Kariana teased.

"No! You're just... It's the way you hold yourself. It's your eyes. But why am I the Blade? Do they think I butcher people?"

"No," Kariana reassured her. "You're a different kind of sharp."

"You're saying I have a long face?" Orloff said, turning the teasing back on Kariana.

"Long and lovely," Kariana had said, brushing back her wife's dark hair. "But that's not what they mean. You look like you're always searching, like you're cutting through to secrets. I think that's a good thing, too."

Now they reached the main entrance hall, where Kariana had to turn off to head for the security center. Doom's elderly retainer Boris was waiting for Orloff. He was a big, bearded man, one of those men who seemed to have been carved from oak and clearly had never been young.

"Lord Doom awaits you," Boris said. "I will take you to him."

Orloff thanked him and followed. Boris did not speak as they walked, and she didn't try to engage him in conversation. If he did happen to know why she was here, he would not tell her, and it would be wrong of her to ask.

Boris took her through the great halls. They walked by sculptural tributes to Doom's inventions and the patents that brought Latveria its wealth, and by artifacts of the country's deep past. There were tapestries from the fifteenth century, perfectly preserved, though none bore any traces of the Fortunov dynasty. There were recent tapestries too, hand-woven with the same meticulous artistry as the ancient ones, made with recreated dyes of the same tints and colors. They blended in with the old ones, their representational style from the same period, but what they showed was the glory of Latveria's present, and its future forged by the monarch's will.

Boris took her up to the top of one of the high towers of the castle. He opened an iron door, showing her into a vast study, and then withdrew.

The chamber was circular and very high, with walls rising to a turquoise dome. Diamond clusters formed the constellations, and between them were inlaid silver runes. Orloff couldn't read them, but they left her with an impression of mysteries decoded and recoded, of knowledge older than she could imagine.

Narrow windows, easily fifteen feet tall, alternated with bookshelves on the wall. A raised platform occupied the center of the study. A colossal desk sat on it. Telescoping arms nestled at the desk's two outer corners, metallic snakes at rest, three-clawed hands closed. Orloff eyed the thin gap separating the platform from the floor and realized that the dais rotated. She pictured it turning to the view that suited its master's mood, their arms reaching out from the desk to seize whatever tome was called upon for that moment.

Doom stood in front of the desk, arms folded, looking down at her. The eyes behind the mask were unreadable. He was a giant, a monolithic arbiter of her future.

"Doctor Orloff," said Doom, and the voice reverberated in her bones. "Are you a scientist or a doctor first?"

Orloff hesitated. If anyone else had asked, the question would not have troubled her. She might have had to think about how best to answer. She wouldn't have been suddenly deeply worried about what was true.

"You find the question a difficult one?" Doom asked.

Orloff sensed time slipping through her fingers. She would be wrong to let it escape. "Science was my first love," she said. "Pursuing it is what led me to my calling as a neurosurgeon."

"You speak hesitantly."

"I wasn't sure what you meant by 'first.'"

There was a rasp of a grunt. It might have been of amusement. "So you answered chronologically," said Doom. "That is an evasion."

"I'm sorry, my lord," said Orloff. "That wasn't my intent."

"I don't think it was. Yet you did evade. Is that because you feel you should be a doctor first?"

"I have never looked at my patients as subjects of inquiry," Orloff insisted. "I have only ever seen people needing my help."

"Your record shows that is true," said Doom.

He let silence settle over the study. Orloff stood motionless, waiting for him to go on, more uneasy than ever.

Doom touched a folder on his desk. "You still have not really answered my question."

"I'm not sure that I can."

"Ah," said Doom. "Now you are being honest with both of us. Why this indecision, do you think? Why can't you decide whether the scientist or the doctor is your primary identity?"

"Perhaps because they aren't separate. I don't think there is a division between the two."

Doom did laugh now. It was the sound of amusement of iron and night. Orloff broke out in gooseflesh.

"That would be very convenient for you to believe, wouldn't

it?" said Doom. "That does not make it true. And convenience does not mean you *do* believe this." Doom paused. "You fear your curiosity," he said.

"I…" Orloff began, wanting to protest. The truth stopped her.

Doom nodded, apparently pleased. "Why do you fear it so much?"

Orloff took a deep breath. "It's something I've taught myself to be wary of."

"Why?" said Doom.

She had never spoken to anyone about this. She had barely articulated it to herself, even though the fear lurked at the back of her mind, waiting, and it had ever since she followed her calling. She had not even spoken to Kariana about this, as if to grant the fear words would be to give it shape and power. She felt a strange kind of relief to speak now, though, as if her fear, revealed, would wither before the greater terror that was Doom.

He already knows, she thought. *Kariana was right. He already knows.*

"My family has a troubled history," she began.

"The other Doctors Orloff," said Doom.

He does know. She almost laughed. She waited, but Doom gestured for her to go on. He was not going to do the work for her. "They are distant relations," she said. "But they *are* relations. One was based in London, in the 1930s. He specialized in insurance fraud and murder."

Doom nodded once, and she felt the depth of his knowledge even more viscerally. It was as if he was the one who had all the details of her family, and she was the student trying to recall them. "His standing as a scientist would seem to be incidental to his crimes," he said.

Was that a test? "Perhaps," said Orloff. "But some of what he did was medical torture."

Another satisfied nod. "Tell me of the other," Doom said.

"He was active in Paris, a bit less than twenty years earlier. He mixed murder with plastic surgery."

"A more direct application of his skills to atrocity," Doom allowed.

"So you understand my caution."

"Why are you wary of yourself?" Doom asked. "Do you think any Orloff who goes into medicine therefore also chooses to become a monster?"

"No," said Orloff. The answer came easily. She was proud of what she had accomplished. She was proud of what she had done for her patients.

"Then are you worried that your blood is tainted?" There was anger in Doom's rasp.

"*No!*" Orloff was horrified.

"That is fortunate. If I had even the slightest impression that you believed in the concept of a tainted bloodline ..."

"I *don't*," Orloff insisted, recoiling at the idea.

"That is clear," said Doom, the menace receding. When he spoke again, his tone was back to one of intellectual curiosity. "Then what is the source of your caution? Do think the Orloffs are cursed? Is it fate that bedevils your family?"

"I don't know." Orloff was frustrated by the weakness of her answer. Everything she had said was true, but it was also true that the example of the other doctors in her ancestry frightened her.

"Do you believe in destiny?" Doom asked.

"I'm not sure. It isn't something…" She stopped herself. She had been about to say, *It isn't something I've thought about.* But that wasn't true. Her fears proved that was a lie, even if she hadn't explicitly thought the word *destiny* when she looked back in horror at the other doctors. "It's not a concept I am comfortable with," she said. That, at least, was true.

"Yet you must confront it," said Doom. "It is cowardice not to. Destiny is not the work of fate or chance. Destiny is forged by will."

She wanted to believe that. There was strength in that belief. The past and the dead had no power over her destiny if Doom was right.

Doom stepped down from the dais. "Come," he said. His cape billowed with the force of his stride. "It is time to forge your destiny."

Orloff hurried to follow. "As a scientist or a doctor?" she asked.

"As both."

Doom took her to the other side of the study from the doorway. The stone of one of the arches rumbled aside at Doom's approach, revealing a small private elevator, the interior shining bronze. Doom glanced at the handrail, and though he did not take hold of it, Orloff caught the hint and grabbed on just as the door closed and the elevator dropped with stomach-lurching speed. Orloff felt herself grow lighter and worried her feet might rise from the floor of the car. Doom stood utterly motionless, as grounded and stable as a statue.

The elevator descended a surprisingly long time. Orloff

guessed they had dropped well below the ground level of the castle and were now deep into the rock on which it was built. The car finally came to a stop with a pneumatic hiss. The door opened, and Orloff stepped out after Doom.

Her eyes widened. She was in a laboratory, the largest she had ever seen, yet one that appeared to be just part of a network of such chambers. Doorways to the left, right and straight ahead opened onto short corridors that led to other rooms, dimly lit, in which she could see the shadows of equipment and machinery. The walls of the lab were banks of metallic blocks, deep gray and featureless. The way they interlocked with each other suggested they would, at a command from Doom, configure themselves into whatever architecture the work of the moment demanded. Twenty feet above Orloff's head, a grid of metal tracks was inlaid into the granite ceiling, paths of travel for clusters of servo-arms that rested, idle, next to the left and right doorways. Orloff realized that some of the metal in the ceiling was silver, not steel, and though it linked to and crossed the tracks, it was not part of them. The silver patterns were runes. She couldn't guess what they meant.

A place of wonders, she thought. She was suddenly ten years old again, and the world was revealing itself to her in grandeurs and mysteries. Then she gazed at what lay before her.

Dark wonders.

The temperature was cool, close to refrigerated. Though the chamber was a laboratory, it was also a morgue. In the center of the floor, slabs were laid out like the petals of a dark flower, radiating around a central machine that reached almost to the full height of the lab. It was black, its sides smooth. When

Orloff drew closer, she could see the switches built into it, and a central screen of glass. From a distance, the machine looked like an obelisk of black marble.

Corpses in varying stages of decay lay on the slabs. Some were fresh. Others were far gone into decomposition. A few were barely more than skeletons, bits of blackened flesh clinging to them like rags. All of them had wires connected to the skulls, as if they were hooked up to an electroencephalograph.

The bodies were a stark reminder to Orloff. *We all belong to him, even after death.* Unlike the other countries she had lived in, there were no organ donation cards in Latveria. Doom's subjects never ceased being his subjects. Death did not free them of their duties, and of their oaths of fealty. If their organs, or any other parts of their bodies, were required, then they were used. Burial and cremation were not rituals that could be taken for granted in Latveria. They came only when the dead were no longer useful, and some families regarded an immediate interment as a mark of shame.

Orloff knew this. The hospital had much cause to be grateful for Doom's edict of automatic donations. She also knew that there were the dead who did not wind up being used for medical or instructional purposes. They went to Castle Doom, to serve the purposes of the king. Their families would be given medals in the names of the loved ones, commending the dead for Exceptional Posthumous Loyalty and Service. The medals were treasured, and displayed in a place of honor on the mantles of the bereaved. Over the years, Orloff had seen a few of them, and spoken with their owners. The comfort and the pride the people took in the medals had eased her early qualms about the use of the bodies. It was something she had never encountered in her years outside Latveria. She had had to adjust to the idea.

What she had never seen, and never known, was what happened to the bodies that came to Castle Doom.

Doom moved to a machine at the center of the slabs and motioned for Orloff to join him. He touched the metal obelisk. It began to hum. Orloff smelled ozone, and the flesh of her arms prickled.

"Do you know what this is?" Doom asked.

"No," said Orloff. "I assume it can't be some kind of electroencephalograph."

"That is not far wrong."

Doom touched another control that Orloff could barely see, and the hum grew louder. Pressure built at the back of her eyes.

"What would you expect an EEG to register?" said Doom.

Orloff choked back a bark of shocked, disbelieving laughter. "Nothing," she said. *What else?* But why were the corpses wired up, and what was he doing?

She hadn't expected a demon to leap out of a patient's skull, either. Walpurgis night had taught her to rethink what was possible.

Doom touched another button. A faint, violet aura surrounded the obelisk. A screen in the side they were facing lit up. Green horizontal lines, one for each of the eight corpses surrounding the machine, crossed the screen. The hum began to sound like a muttered chant.

Orloff's flesh crawled. This was technology that she couldn't begin to understand. It was also something else. There were words for that, but she didn't think she could admit them to herself. Not yet. Not just yet.

"Watch," Doom commanded.

The order was unnecessary. Orloff couldn't look away from the screen. She was terrified about what she might see, and mesmerized by the prospect of seeing anything at all.

One by one, the lines began to twitch, then jerk up and down. The wave forms were unlike any she had ever seen. They varied in intensity. When Orloff checked the labels next to the readouts with those attached to the slabs, she saw that the intensity of the wave did not correlate with the age of the corpse.

"What are those?" Orloff whispered.

"Memories," said Doom.

She shook her head. "How? That's impossible."

"You have already seen the impossible," Doom reminded her.

"You can record the memories of the dead," Orloff said. She had trouble forming the words. Her face had gone numb.

"Yes. I can record them. This, though, is just the start."

Blood began to trickle from Orloff's nose. She wiped it away. She ignored the pressure in her head. "What is it that you want me to do?" she asked.

"Your task will be to amplify these results," said Doom. "And to decipher them."

The scope of what Doom commanded stunned her. It also excited her.

"A neurology of the dead," she said. She shook her head, amazed that she would utter such a phrase and not mean it as a joke. If anyone else had shown her this, she would have rejected it out of hand. Or she would have, before Walpurgis Night, before the hospital's halls had turned into things of flesh and blood. And this was Doom revealing this work to her. He made the impossible real.

"A kind of neurology, yes," said Doom. He touched the machine again, and it powered down. The chanting hum vanished. "There is memory in the inanimate. Something lingers in the brains of the dead. I wish to extract it."

"This machine," said Orloff, coming closer now that it was no longer radiant, no longer almost a living thing. "How is it able to do what I saw?"

"I will explain its principles to you in due course. They are not all from the realm of science."

No, they couldn't be, could they? There had to be sorcery here, the touch of things that she knew were real, but that were beyond all the realities she had studied and understood.

"Are you ready?" Doom asked.

"Yes," Orloff answered, without hesitation, just like Kariana had told her. The answer came eagerly. Her monstrous ancestors flashed through her mind, and she dismissed them. She was not them. She was sure of where she stood, and of the lines she would not cross.

It is time to forge your destiny.

She shivered from the touch of the sublime.

THREE

Zargo listened to the earth. It had been speaking to him all along, but he hadn't been consciously listening. He hadn't wanted to. Even wandering over the lake bed, and feeling the shared pain, he hadn't been tapping into the deep currents.

Now he did. Doom had commanded it, and there was no choice but to obey. After the encounter, he had returned to the apartment he had rented in Old Town and rested as much as he could. Now, the next day, he had come back with more purpose than he had had before. It was not his purpose. It had been imposed on him. But even a second-hand purpose made him feel a bit stronger.

It did not make him feel better. If anything, his guilt was stronger too. He was once again using the powers he had always felt were wrong. He had used them in Doom's service, and the results had led to the collapse of his church and of his vocation. Now he was going to use them again.

Doom had put a jeep at his disposal. He had assigned a

driver, too, but Zargo had begged him not to, and Doom had relented. Zargo wanted to be alone. "If solitude is what you need to do your work, then so be it," Doom had said. The jeep had a radio, and Zargo could summon aid at any moment. He also knew that he was being observed. Drones passed by overhead every so often, and Zargo assumed that he was seen even when he wasn't aware of a watcher.

The morning sun was warmer than it had been in the last few days. September was putting in a pretense that there were still traces of summer to be had. Zargo drove through the web of lava ridges, jouncing hard over the broken surface. He didn't really understand what he was looking for, yet. *You will when you find it,* Doom had said. He believed that. To his dismay, he believed Doom's pronouncements as fully as he had once believed that his destiny lay in the priesthood. He still held to his faith, but not to his role in it anymore. He didn't know what his destiny was.

Doom is going to show me, he thought, and he shivered.

Zargo stopped beside the cone that marked one of the greatest wounds. He sat for a few moments, listening to the ticking of the engine as it cooled. Then he got out of the jeep and climbed partway up the side of the cone. He lay down on the slope, pressing the palms of his hands against the stone, took a breath, closed his eyes, and opened himself up to the earth's pain.

He listened. He set aside his resistance. He had been coming here for some kind of solace, and he admitted now that he had incurred a debt, to the earth if not to Doom. He had injured the earth.

His awareness sank down through the cone. He dropped

into the cool darkness of the rock beneath the surface. He flowed through the veins of hardened lava. Zargo felt the twitching of the ley lines, still agonized from having been forced from their courses by Doom's duel with Hell. The earth cried out in its pain, and Zargo listened.

I'm sorry. I was one of those who did this, even though I did not mean to. I'm sorry. I'm sorry.

He wasn't looking for ley lines this time, though.

You will unearth memories. That was Doom's command.

Memories of what? How?

He sank deeper into the earth. His awareness spread wider. He became a net, a web, reaching further and further in every direction through the being of stone. He listened, and he meditated, and though it was difficult to admit it to himself, there was relief in exercising his geomantic powers. He was letting part of himself stretch and run and *be*. It was the part he had always tried to suppress. Doom had forced it to the surface, and now he had done so again, and through the act of using the powers, Zargo's guilt fell away. It would come back. He was certain of that. But, for the moment, in this flowing present, even as he listened to the earth and grieved with it, he also felt the first joy he had experienced in more months than he could count.

Scars were memories, but these wounds in the lake bed were new ones, recent memories.

What memories did Doom want?

All of them, he had said.

That wasn't possible. He couldn't find all memories. That was a meaningless demand.

Except Doom had made it, so it wasn't meaningless. If

Doom commanded it, then the universe had to alter itself to make nothing impossible and accede to his will.

Zargo dropped deeper and wider yet. No matter how far he reached in every direction, his sense of self remained whole. His identity did not waver or become thin. He saw more and more, became more and more a spirit of the earth, and he let himself feel the exhilaration of this being. He followed the lines of age, looking for deeper and deeper memories. He traced the folds of geologic change. He read the book of Latveria's formation. He moved through the upheavals of mountains.

Farther, and deeper, and deeper, and farther.

So much remembrance etched into the earth. These were not the memories Doom wanted, though. They were the simple facts of geology. Zargo felt their meaning acutely. They were not just a list of events, a survey in an academic text. They were as lived and experienced as war and birth. But they were the wrong memories. There was no power to be pulled from them. There was nothing secret about them, nothing forgotten.

What does he want? What does he want?

Deeper and farther, and farther and deeper.

The pull was sudden, yet distant. A thrum on the web of his consciousness, but not that of prey in a web. More a claw hooking around a thread of his mind and yanking. It was powerful, but thin, and so very much farther and deeper than he was. He focused on it, ignoring everything else. If he shifted even slightly, he would lose what he had found.

His eyes were closed, and he was traveling through the eternal night of rock by sense of being. Again and again, the pull almost slipped away, the signal lost to static and night. Again and again, Zargo just managed to keep hold, and travel a little closer.

No, not closer. That was wrong. He got a better fix, a stronger focus, on the pull. Or perhaps he gave it a stronger focus on himself. The hook went in deeper. He felt a sense of age, and of hunger. He hesitated for a moment, uncertain about letting himself follow the pull. But he had no choice.

Doom commanded it.

Night followed day, winter followed autumn, and Latverians followed Doom's orders. Disobedience was more than impossible. It was unthinkable.

Zargo followed the pull, and things stirred in his mind. Memories woke, memories long submerged but close to his core.

He was lying on his back. There were bars around him. He was in a crib. From another room came the sounds of grief. His parents, weeping. He didn't know why. He was too young to understand what grief was. But he felt an impulse that his adult mind recognized as the need to provide comfort. He wanted to help, to reach out to them.

The memory was as sharp as if the event had occurred minutes ago. It was one he had never recalled consciously. And it was one where he saw the drive that had been behind the joys he had had as a priest, those moments when he felt he had helped someone, in a way that really mattered.

The hook sharpened. It went deeper yet, far deeper than a memory of infancy. He brushed against deeper things. He couldn't make them out. They were too distant, and too vast, and too numerous. They were not his memories at all. They were held by the thing that was pulling him. And though the hook was sharp, the line that tied him to the force was too thin, too fragile. But it was there, so deep, beyond reach, yet unmistakable, now that he had seen it, and it had seen him.

Zargo pulled his awareness out of the darkness of the earth and returned to the physicality of his body. He blinked in the light and heat of the sun, a mole breaking surface. When his eyes cleared, Doom was there, a couple of yards above him on the slope of the cone. The sun glinted on his mask, making the eye slits seem darker, colder.

Though the day was still warm, the sun was now getting low on the horizon. It was less than an hour from setting. Zargo had been away from his body for most of the day. He was suddenly aware of being famished and thirsty. The slippage of time made him dizzy, and it worried him that he could vanish from himself for such an extended period without knowing it.

He wondered how long Doom had been there. He wasn't surprised that he was. It didn't matter that Zargo had been alone when he had begun his plunge into the currents of stone. Doom was always watching. Doom always knew.

"You have found something," said Doom.

"Yes, but I don't know if it's what you seek."

"We are looking for something we cannot define until we find it," said Doom. "But I believe you are more certain than you say."

Zargo could still feel the pull. It was faint, like a dream whose details he was trying not to forget. The need to follow the thread was as strong as the thread was fragile. His head buzzed with pieces of old memories. There were so many, it was hard to breathe. "Yes," he said. "Yes, you're right."

"Can you describe what you've found?"

"No. I don't have a clear sense of it. It's too far away, and too buried in ways I don't understand."

"Do you know where to go?"

Zargo closed his eyes for a moment. He focused on the pull, trying to map it to a physical space by remaining conscious of the force in the earth, and also of his body, of the stone under his feet, of the sun's heat on his head, of the wind against his cheek.

He opened his eyes. "North," he said. "It's to the north."

"Then go," said Doom. "Follow it."

Zargo turned to the jeep.

"No," said Doom. "That will be too slow."

Already, the rapid beat-beat-beat of a helicopter's rotors was growing louder.

Doom returned to the castle to wait for Zargo to contact him. He didn't think he would have to wait long.

The geomancer was better than he knew. He would find what Doom wanted. He was already hot on the scent.

Doom stopped to survey the reconstruction of the tower that had held his laboratory and observatory. The battle with the demons had destroyed it on Walpurgis Night. The damage had not created any setback for his research. The castle had many other labs. The disfigurement of the castle bothered him more, because of the loss it symbolized for him. That was one physical memory he wanted expunged. He was pleased to see that the work was almost complete, and the scaffolding would soon be coming down.

Outside the tower, he saw his new archivist. Georg Albers

had just completed his doctorate in library sciences at the Werner Academy. He came from a peasant family, in the northern village of Doomwinden. He had talent, and, even more importantly, he had loyalty, a quality that had been absent in Vassily Dubrov, the old archivist. Dubrov had waited fifteen years to show his duplicity, but when he had, he had let Fortunov's forces into the archives. Doom had looked carefully at Albers and his family. They were grateful to Doom for the educational opportunity Georg had been given. They were even more grateful for the overthrow of Vladimir.

Albers bowed deeply as Doom approached. "What progress have you made?" Doom asked.

"I have almost completed cataloguing what was destroyed in the archives, my lord," said Albers. The archives were in the foundations beneath the laboratory tower.

That was well done, Doom thought. The task of cataloguing in the midst of the rebuilding was not a simple one.

"I will have the complete list for you within a few days," Albers went on.

"How bad are the losses?" Doom asked.

"Considerable, but they could have been much worse. What I believe to be the rarest volumes in your collection have survived." Albers' left eye twitched slightly. He was showing some strain from being in close contact with dangerous books. But he looked no less determined than the day Doom had inducted him into the position.

He served as he should, Doom thought. He would adapt.

If he didn't, there would be others.

"Shall I begin the process of searching for replacements?" Albers asked, clearly eager for the challenge.

He *is* adapting. "Do what is possible," said Doom. "Leave the rest to me." There would be books that could be found through means that were unavailable to the likes of Albers, or to any librarian. There might come a time when Albers would have enough experience to delve more deeply into the hunt for eldritch texts. But not yet.

Albers bowed and withdrew. Doom lingered before the tower a bit longer, thinking about the priceless volumes that had been destroyed. The losses angered him, but they did not torment him the way the vanished memories did. The losses from the archive were a known, quantified. Albers could tell him what books were gone, and Doom would see that they were replaced. Even if some were gone forever, Doom would know what was gone.

I don't know what was taken from my mind. I don't know what is missing.

He might have lost the equivalent of a single volume, or the entire holdings of Castle Doom. The unknown ate at him. There was only one way to be sure he regained what he had lost, and that was to know *everything*.

The helicopter flew north. It was a compact machine, a Latverian design built for speed and agility. Zargo sat beside the pilot, an air force officer named Hagen, and kept his attention split between the call in the earth and the here and now. The thrumming of the engine shaking his bones helped keep him aware of his body. He was glad he hadn't tried to follow the call to its source by sending his being through the earth. He was still frightened by the loss of time. He was worried he might travel too far and not be able to return to his body.

Night had fallen when the helicopter reached the Carpathians. Moonlight bathed the landscape, and Zargo saw the mountains as hard masses, drenched in deep shadow, heaving their bulk against the dark of the sky. The pilot had been flying in a straight line since the start of the flight, following Zargo's direction. The call was growing stronger. It took little effort for Zargo to sense it now, but he still had to concentrate to keep the narrow line of the pull in his mental focus. He might yet lose it if he let go. He did not want to imagine explaining that to Doom once the monarch rejoined them.

They were deep into the mountains when the force sprang jaws of steel around him. He shouted, and the call yanked him against the side of the helicopter. If the door had been open, he would have fallen out.

"What is it?" Hagen asked in alarm.

"Here," Zargo gasped. "It's here." He could barely speak. He tried to pull his awareness fully into his body, but he couldn't. The grip was too strong.

Hagen began to take the helicopter down. They descended into a bowl between mountains, a cauldron of night.

Doom wanted to find memories. Oh, there was memory here. Zargo recognized the nature of the pull now, or at least part of what made it. He was caught by the gravity of memory that consumes, the memory one wants to forget, but refuses to die, that traps the mind with riptide strength. Every bad memory had this gravity. Zargo relived every memory over and over, feeling the guilt and the pain and the humiliation and the terror as vividly as the moment each memory was created. That was the flavor of the pull. Its full nature was something he didn't dare look at. He couldn't. It was a gorgon. And it ran deeper than anything he could imagine.

He wanted to flee. He wanted to forget. He wanted to be as far away as possible from this cauldron of memories. Only he had to get closer.

Doom commanded it.

The call grew stronger as the helicopter descended. Zargo's hands clenched as he struggled to free his mind from the grip. His nails cut into his palms. His breath was ragged, and he was suddenly drenched in sweat.

"All right," he managed. "All right. This is the place. This is close enough. Mark it and let's go. Let's *go!*"

Hagen kept bringing them down into the dark. "I can't do that," he said.

"Take me away from here!" Zargo pleaded. It was all he could do to keep the memories from overwhelming him.

"Lord Doom was clear. When we found the spot, he said we were to land and await his arrival."

"Please..." Zargo murmured. He wasn't really speaking to Hagen. The word was a prayer to Doom, and to the strength below, and to the God he had failed.

No one was answering.

The helicopter landed. Zargo fumbled with the door and staggered out. Mountain surrounded him, shaped blocks of night that blotted out the stars. He dropped to his hands and knees, and threw all his efforts into making a shield for himself. He focused on his self, who he believed himself to be. He was as honest as possible, but if he lied or erred, that didn't matter. It was the belief in a unified, coherent whole that mattered. "I am Grigori Zargo," he repeated to himself. "I was priest of St

Peter Church. I am a geomancer, may God forgive me." He concentrated on the present and near past, on the events that were most vivid and most responsible for defining who he was now, right now. The guilt was his, and he refused to share it with the force below. It wanted it from him. It hungered. It wanted his storehouse of memories, fresh and old, to add to its hoard. Zargo fought back, repeating his assertions of self, making them the brick and mortar of his defenses.

When Doom came at last, the exhaust from his jetpacks flaring in the dark, Zargo was shivering and drained. He couldn't stand. He could think more clearly, though, and he raised his head, drawing deep breaths. He could sense the call. It felt around his defenses, searching for a way in. He could keep it out, for now.

Doom exchanged a few words with Hagen that Zargo couldn't hear, then walked over to him. Arms folded, Doom towered over Zargo, a shape stronger and more terrible than the mountains.

"Tell me what is here," said Doom.

"I still don't know what it is."

"But there are memories." Doom spoke with an urgency Zargo had not heard before.

Zargo nodded.

"Not just the memories of Earth."

"No," said Zargo. "There are human memories here. And ones that are older. It keeps memories, and it… it consumes them, I think. It wanted mine."

"Is it something physical?"

"Like a lode stone?"

"You tell me."

"I don't know that, either. It occupies a physical space. I do feel that. I can picture it."

"Where?" Doom asked. He leaned forward, eyes blazing behind the mask.

"Beneath us. Far beneath us. It is deep. How far down, I can't say. I can't 'see' it." He shuddered. "I hope it can't see me."

Doom straightened, calm once more. "You have done well," he said, satisfaction in his tone.

"I think you should leave it alone," said Zargo. "It's dangerous."

Doom said nothing at first. His still presence, so powerful it filled the space between the mountains, invited Zargo to decide which was more dangerous, Doom or the call from below. Then Doom said, simply, "It will be mine."

Zargo understood that there wasn't a choice of danger. It was the collision of wills between Doom and the hunger beneath that he should fear.

Work began on the site the following day. It was September 23rd, the autumnal equinox. And the wind began to blow colder.

FOUR

Orloff didn't see Doom in the days that followed being shown her task. He left her to her own devices. Boris checked in twice a day, to see if there were any materials she needed. She was free to work as she saw fit, to bring help as and when she needed it. For the moment, she preferred to have the lab to herself. She was still processing the reality of what she was engaged in. That was easier to do without assistants to worry about. She needed time alone.

Her last exchange with Doom stayed with her. He was heading back to the elevator that would return him to his study, after showing her another lift, for her use, that would take her up to a hall that led to the ground floor of the castle. Orloff followed Doom and said, "Forgive me for asking the obvious, but I assume I am to keep the nature of my work to myself?"

Doom stopped and looked at her. "Why would you think that?" He sounded genuinely surprised. "You should speak with whomever might be useful," he said. "There would be no point in being coy with them. That will not get you the information you would need. I am concerned with the project's success, not its secrecy."

That exchange showed her again the extent of Doom's control. His absolutism was something she took for granted, but at the same time it took moments like this for her to truly understand it. Her memories of life outside Latveria were not that many years in the past. She knew how it was beyond the borders. This was not how things worked elsewhere. If she experimented with the dead in Manhattan, and was open about it, questions would be raised.

Should there be?

There wouldn't be here. Doom was the law of Latveria. There was no higher judge.

She had qualms as she moved from the astonishment of what Doom had revealed to her to the realities of the work itself. She had qualms about moving bodies around, of attaching electrodes to corpses and seeing what results she could conjure from places where no results of any kind should be possible.

She talked to Kariana about how she felt after the first full day in the lab.

"Doing this work or not isn't your decision to make," Kariana said.

"I know, but I can't tell myself I'm just following orders and move on."

Kariana took both her hands in hers. "I've never told myself that, either. That's not what I meant. Are you doing harm?"

"I don't see how. They're dead."

"But?"

Orloff sighed. "This is way beyond galvanizing a dead frog in biology. We're talking about neurological readings from corpses. That's an unusual thing."

Kariana smiled. "You'll get used to it. I'll always be here to listen, but you *will* get used to it."

"Is that a good thing?"

"I believe in my calling, and I believe in yours. So yes, it's a good thing."

Kariana was right. If it was the nature of her work that gave Orloff qualms, it was also the dark wonder of what she was exploring that overwhelmed them. During the day, at least. She was staggered by what Doom had done. She was staggered again when she got her first results.

She didn't get very far at first. She replicated what Doom had done with other bodies, confirming for herself that the phenomenon was real, and that it was not limited to a select few of the dead. She got readings with everybody she hooked up to the machinery. The results varied from corpse to corpse. Was she finding traces of a personality? Somehow still extant?

The possibility was intriguing and horrifying in equal measure, especially when the results came from the skeleton of a man who had, according to its records, been dead for more than ten years. She didn't like to think of herself going on and on and on inside a rotting shell.

She didn't know that that was what she was detecting. She didn't know what the signals meant.

The temptation to theorize was strong. That made it even more important to resist. She was working in a realm where it would be too easy to leap to the superstitious conclusion.

What she had was data. What it meant, she had no way of knowing yet.

The intensity of the readings varied from body to body. There didn't seem to be a correlation between the strength of the readings and how long the individual had been deceased. There was so much variation in the readings that more than a week passed before she spotted a pattern.

When she did, she told Boris that she needed to see Doom.

It was another two days before Doom granted her an audience. He was away from the castle much of the time, Boris told her. Another project was occupying his time and thoughts. But when she met him in the study again, she felt the laser focus of his attention on her.

I would never want to be on the receiving end of his focus as an enemy, she thought.

"Have you made progress?" Doom asked.

"I wouldn't say so, not yet. I'm still trying to understand what I'm seeing before I start trying to affect it."

Doom nodded and waited for her to go on.

"What I have found, though, is that regardless of the relative strengths of the individual signals, there has been an overall trend toward a rise in the intensity of the readings. Is this something that happened before you brought me in?"

"The research was in its early stages," said Doom. "But no. Can you pinpoint when the increase began?"

"It's hard to be certain," said Orloff. "The effect is gradual, and with all the variations, and the small sample size, I can't be as precise as I would like. But the increase seems to begin on or around September 23rd."

"Interesting," said Doom. "And significant. Go on."

"That fact that the increase is across the board astounds me," Orloff went on, becoming excited as she talked through the implications. They had been whirling dizzyingly through her thoughts since the equinox. "That there should be readings at all still beggars belief. But this... This is a reversal of entropy." She shook her head. "How many kinds of impossible is that? It simply can't be, unless there's something else that we're still overlooking, like some sort of current the dead are linked to. And even if that's so, then *how*?" She paused, acutely aware of Doom's stillness.

"I want daily updates of the level of the increase," Doom said. "Give them to Boris. He will relay them to me."

"You wanted me to amplify the signals," Orloff said. "Is that still the case?"

"Yes, to the degree that it is useful. The primary goal is to turn the readings into decipherable memories. Do not lose sight of that."

"I won't. I'm still a long way from that goal, though."

Doom regarded her steadily. "You'll reach it, Doctor Orloff. Of that, I have no doubt."

His confidence became her own. Doom decreed it, and so it would happen.

After meeting with Orloff, Doom returned to his study. Seated at the huge desk, he pressed a button in its side, and a screen, less than a millimeter thick and undetectable to the touch when flat, rose from its surface. "Lower laboratory, section theta," Doom said. The screen showed him Orloff at work. Doom monitored her for a few minutes. He nodded approvingly at the commitment and energy he saw.

She had none of Zargo's reluctance. The work itself drew her. The stranger it was, the better she liked it. She had promise.

Her intellect and her drive could be very useful. Doom suspected he would find a role for her that went beyond laboratory research.

He tapped the side button again and the screen lowered, vanishing into the desk. Just as Orloff vanished from his sight, Doom felt a bitter twinge of nostalgia. It took him a moment to place it.

She reminds me of me.

He did not often think of the good parts of his time at State University in Hegeman, New York. They were overshadowed by the disaster that had ruined his face and had set him on the course to truly becoming Doom. But there *had* been days, before that, when he had been lost in his research, caught up in the sheer excitement and joy of peeling away the layers of the unknown. Those days, when he had even forgotten his growing rivalry with Reed Richards, when only the purity of the work had mattered, were lost to him. But he saw some of that in Orloff. She was older than he had been then. She was long past her student days. She had reached the height of her profession, and now, delving into new mysteries at Doom's command, she attacked the challenge with the fervor of youth, and without the shadow that hung over Doom.

How curious. I envy her.

"You were dreaming again last night," Kariana said to Orloff. "I tried to wake you up. I couldn't."

They were having lunch together, sitting side by side on one of the palace ramparts. They dangled their legs over a fifty-foot drop. Below was one of the inner gardens of the castle, one that the staff was permitted to use. Gravel paths wound between meticulously cultivated rose bushes and formal hedgerows. From this height, it was easy to see the pattern of the garden. It was in the shape of Latveria. The roses were the cities and principal villages. The bushes were the mountain ranges and the river courses.

It was the day after her meeting with Doom. Orloff and Kariana had lunch together as often as they could manage it. For half an hour they ate bagged meat pies, kicked their legs over the drop, and giggled at the vertigo. And they usually managed, for more than a few of those thirty minutes, to be something other than a neurosurgeon and the captain of the guard. In those moments, Orloff was not experimenting with the dead, and wrestling with her excitement about doing so.

But today, Kariana was worried, and asking her about her dream.

"It was another bad one," Orloff said.

"Was it about what you're doing?"

"No. It was about Walpurgis Night again." She dreamt a lot of demons, and of the thing that had burst from a patient's head. The dreams had become more frequent and more vivid recently.

"That's happening a lot," said Kariana. She had noticed too.

"Are you going to say something about displacement?"

Kariana gave her a wry smile. "I was thinking about it. Are you worried about what you're doing?"

"The ethics…" Orloff grimaced. "I don't know. I don't *think* so. *If* this was futile, that would be one thing. But it isn't. Doom found something. If I manage to…" She couldn't quite bring herself to say it.

Kariana did it for her. "To read the minds of the dead?"

Orloff laughed. "Can you imagine? Can you imagine what that would *mean*, just that fact that there are minds to read, let alone being able to do it."

"I find the idea that there is still something in the corpses disturbing," said Kariana.

"You think I don't? What we're detecting might not be a mind at all, or anything remotely like a self. I hope that there's some other explanation."

"Like a glitch in the recordings?"

Orloff shook her head, emphatic. "No," she said. "In the first place, I know it isn't a glitch. And secondly, I don't want this to be futile. There *is* something there. And that's pretty incredible."

"There's the excitement back again."

"I *am* excited." She paused. "I'm also worried, and frightened."

"Good." Kariana squeezed her shoulder. "Those sound like pretty healthy responses to me."

"I need to understand what we're seeing, Kari. I *need* to know." She looked at Kariana, meat pie forgotten in her hand.

Her wife nodded slowly. "That's what's really worrying you, isn't it? That you need to know."

"Yes."

"Finish your pie," said Kariana.

"What?"

"Do as I said." Kariana took her own advice, finished eating and brushed the crumbs from her hands. She waited for Orloff to do the same. "OK," she said. She shuffled closer on the rampart so their shoulders were touching. She took both Orloff's hands in hers. "Tell me. Are you causing harm?"

"I don't see how." That was true, but it was also true that causing harm was one of the things she was afraid of.

"But…" Kariana prompted.

"It's what I'm brushing up against," said Orloff.

"Are you telling me that piercing the veil between life and death might be a little on the fraught side?"

Orloff smiled. "Let's just say I'd prefer it if my last words don't sound like I'm quoting a Boris Karloff character on his deathbed."

"That's why you need to do the job well," said Kariana, "so there will be no danger. And you will. I have faith in you. So does Doom, and that's more important than what I think."

"He has faith in my abilities."

"Rightly so."

"That makes me want to keep going. It makes me feel proud. But that's the thing…"

"The thing being mixing curiosity and pride."

"Exactly!" Orloff squeezed Kariana's hands and sighed, so grateful that Kariana understood, because of course she would, just like she understood Kariana's fears when they surfaced. "What if I go too far?"

"Who even knows what that means in this case?" said Kariana. "I'll tell you what not going far enough would be, though. That would be stopping before Doom is ready to stop, and that's not what you or I do. We're made of sterner stuff than that." She sounded stern then, too. "Besides," Kariana went on, "you've always pushed back the boundaries of your field."

"So have other Orloffs," she spoke quietly.

"You already talked about this with Doom."

"Yes."

"I doubt I can add anything to what he said."

"He knows a lot about me," said Orloff, "but he doesn't know *me*."

"I wouldn't be so sure about that."

"He doesn't know me like you do, then."

Kariana laughed. "I should hope not!"

"Don't be biblical," Orloff said, but she smiled too. "You know what I mean."

"You know I do."

Orloff leaned her head against Kariana's shoulder. "Just tell me the same thing again. Tell me I'm not like my ancestors."

"You aren't. That's a promise. Are you doing this for personal power or gain?"

"Of course not."

"Tell me why you're doing."

"Because Doom commands it."

"That goes without saying, but it also needed to be said. That's good, Elsa. That's important. And why else?"

"Because I need to know."

"Of course you do. You've always needed to know. That's always been who you are." Kariana dropped her voice to a tender whisper. "I'm grateful for who you are."

Orloff squeezed her hands again. The weather had turned cooler. The sun's rays felt thin, brittle, their warmth cast away by the slightest breeze. But there on the ramparts, held by and holding Kariana, Orloff felt autumn pull back a little and give her another few moments of summer.

"You can tell the difference between curiosity and

obsession," Kariana said. "You're not going to fall over the line. I guarantee it."

At the mention of falling, Orloff looked down at the drop below them. "I hope you're right."

"Are you going to make our lunch place all symbolic now? Are we going to have to talk about precipices and abyssal descents every day now?"

Orloff finally laughed. She let go of Kariana's hands, wrapped an arm around her and held her tightly. "Would that be OK?" she asked. "I was sort of hoping we could make existential crises a regular thing."

"You're seriously asking to be pushed, you know. I am the captain of the guard – I've had people executed for less."

"I'm not worried. I know you'll always hold on tight."

"Count on it."

FIVE

There weren't any nightmares that night, or the night after. Orloff had a few days' respite, and then they returned, sporadically, but more upsetting. The demons kept coming for her, and now they started taking Kariana away from her. The worst was one where Kariana was the patient on the table. Orloff woke up gasping and drenched in sweat.

The days were better. She felt newly inspired after her talk with Kariana. The doubts were at bay, and the drive to crack the secrets before her stronger than ever. Though there was no immediate measurable progress, she felt she was on the verge of a breakthrough. She found her attention shifting from the corpses to the machinery that recorded the signals. It wasn't a conscious turn of thought at first, but when she realized what she was doing, she followed her instinct.

She was grappling with the impossibility and the fact of sorcery. She lived in Latveria, and so she knew that sorcery existed. That was a given as inescapable as the sun rising in the east. The Werner Academy had entire wings devoted to its study and practice. It was, though, something that Orloff had never encountered in her work at the hospital. Knowing abstractly that sorcery coexisted with science, and seeing it happen in the machine Doom had created, were two different things.

Once she realized what she was struggling with was a paradox, she decided that what she needed to do was embrace it. She was no witch. She had no powers of her own. But the obelisk operated as it should when she used it. Maybe other machines imbued with magic would too.

That thought was the first part of the breakthrough. The second part flowed from the first, and was the result of mental experiment.

If I could add magic to another piece of technology, what would it be?

As she walked around Doom's machine, a new set of corpses connected to it, her eyes fell on the electrodes connected to the skulls, and she suddenly thought, *God helmet.*

The experiment had been a sensation in the early 2000s, and had still been a fascinating footnote during Orloff's university years. The God helmet generated light magnetic fields when worn. The contention was that the experiences reported by some test subjects so closely mirrored religious experiences that, ipso facto, religious experiences were themselves simply neurological events. The problem was, no one else was able to replicate the results, and the generated fields were so weak that they were unlikely to have any effect at all. *Magnetic placebo*, Orloff remembered having thought after reading one of the critical responses to the helmet. She had thought the device and the claims for it were too simplistic, too prone to confirmation bias. Yet its conception had appeal.

What if the fields were stronger? she thought now. *What if they were… supplemented?*

She felt a surge of nervous excitement. Transcranial magnetic stimulation *did* have real effects. And if something else with real effects was working in conjunction with it…

She wrote down what she needed for the lab and gave the note to Boris. Three days later, he brought a large case for her. *Like magic.* She didn't know how the logistics for the supplies worked, and if Doom vetted her requests or not. She put them in, and they were fulfilled. A researcher's utopian dream.

Orloff opened the package after Boris had left. Inside was a helmet. She lifted it out of the metal case and placed it on the work table next to one of the corpse slabs. It was surprisingly light for something that appeared to be forged of bronze. It was inlaid with silver, forming lines of runes that ran down from the crown in three lines, one on the back, and the other two on the left and right. The front of the helmet would cover the face down to the nose. A bronze shutter could snap down over what looked like a glass pane at eye level.

Why do the dead need to see?

Orloff examined the helmet in growing wonder. Three days. That was all it had taken to turn her written words into a reality. How many other labs were there in the castle? How many researchers were working on how many tasks for Doom? She thought about asking Boris when he next checked in, then realized she already knew the answer.

As many as necessary.

She placed the helmet on the nearest corpse, then thought

better of it. The man had been dead only two days, and with the helmet on he gave the impression of someone taking a nap.

"Bravo, the hard-headed scientist," she said, the sound of her voice hollow and very alone in the morgue. "Good, rational decision, that." She removed the helmet and placed it on another body. The flesh on this one was green-gray. "Much better," she said, fixing the helmet in place. "Everybody's doing better, aren't we?"

She was glad there was no answer.

There was a note in the case, handwritten by Doom. His cursive was regimental in its precision on the unlined paper. The style seemed old-fashioned to her, as if it belonged on a contract for her soul. It didn't ask for that. It outlined briefly how the helmet worked, how she could open it to modify it, and where to take it in the castle for further work, as needed. The lab she was directed to was on the same level as the morgue, and a short walk away.

She was amused and a little ashamed by how pleased she was to know that there were other people working in close proximity to her. It felt good not to be alone.

She stopped herself and took a breath. "OK," she said, trying to be stern. "Talk to me. We weren't jumpy like this until just now. What's going on?" She turned to the helmeted corpse. "You have any insights?"

The body reserved judgment.

"Great help. Thanks for your contribution." She tapped her fingers on the helmet. "You know what I think it is? I think it's this thing. I think we're about to make some real progress. And that's scary exciting. You get me?"

The body did not contradict her.

"Glad we're on the same page."

There was a set of controls on the right-hand side of the helmet. She turned it and the obelisk on. They hummed at different registers. A violet aura surrounded the obelisk, and a brighter one formed around the crown of the helmet, the halo of a dark saint. The pressure behind Orloff's eyes was stronger than it had been before.

There was a dial on the right side of the helmet that controlled the strength of the magnetic field. Keeping an eye on the readouts of the screen, Orloff slowly turned the dial up. The EEG spikes on the readout shot up at once. Between the highest peaks, where the line had appeared flat, now there were smaller variations.

After a minute, she turned the machines off.

"Friends and colleagues," she said, "we have amplification. A polite round of applause, if you please."

She grimaced into the silence. "No, I'm not clapping either," she said. "Doesn't really feel like that big a deal, does it?" She had succeeded in one of the tasks Doom had given her, and it was the least important of the two. She was no further along toward deciphering the signals.

She pulled up a stool and sat down next to the helmeted corpse. She steepled her fingers and tapped them against her lips several times.

This wasn't why she had had the helmet made. Admit it.

She removed it from the corpse, looking at the eye slit.

Why would the dead need that? They didn't. That was for someone else. Doom knew why she needed this before she did.

She took the helmet over to a sink on one side of the

morgue and sanitized the interior. "Are we doing this?" she asked aloud.

Of course they were. Stop delaying. The whole point of having a God helmet made was for her to put it on.

Technology and sorcery. A magnetic field to stir things up, to create the sense of a presence. The sorcerous factor that she could not understand, but knew to be genuine. The helmet wasn't for amplification. It was for connection.

That was why she had asked for the ports to be built into the helmet.

She thought about everything she and Kariana had discussed on the ramparts. She thought about her family history. *I'm doing my duty,* she reminded herself. *I'm not going to hurt anyone.*

What about yourself?

She would be careful. She would stop if things seemed to be going wrong.

How will you know?

"Because I'm good at what I do," she declared to the silence. "And I'm not going to try this on anyone else."

She carried the helmet back to the slab, her heart pounding. She was scared. She was also excited. She didn't know what she was about to experience. She was sure she was going to experience something. She was pressing against the veil, ready to tear it.

Ready to do more than step into the unknown. Ready to leap into it.

She linked the helmet to the electrodes attached to the corpse's skull. Then she put the helmet on.

...

The machine in the bowl of the mountains was complete. Doom circled the site slowly, examining the construction for flaws. Workers stood to attention, heads bowed as he passed, waiting to make any corrections he commanded.

The sky was overcast and low, dark clouds concealing the mountain peaks. The wind blew with the confidence of fall, flapping Doom's cloak and plucking the cables of the assembly like a harp.

The base of the construction was two giant, concentric frameworks, the outer one twice the size of the interior. The inner assembly closely resembled an oil derrick, which it was in many of its essential components. The derrick housed a massive drill, one designed not to extract oil, but to pierce a hole down which it would be possible, if necessary, to travel. It was going to create a shaft fifteen feet wide. The framework that surrounded the derrick was of much more massive construction, and made of adamantium-reinforced steel. The structure had to be strong to support the pyramid it held suspended over the derrick. Doom had had the pyramid built of obsidian and silver, and its base and its peak inscribed with occult runes. It was a hundred feet on a side, and a bit more than sixty feet high, its proportions conforming to the golden ratio. It was hollow. At Doom's command, it would drop, swallowing the derrick, and containing whatever might have been released from the depths.

Doom circled the outer framework, then went inside to examine the derrick. Zargo went with him, his reluctance plain. As they walked around the derrick, Zargo kept looking up at the dark mass of the pyramid, as if he expected it to fall and crush them.

It would not. Doom's construction specifications were exacting, and there would have been no deviation from them in even the smallest particular. The speed with which the construction had been completed would have been impossible almost anywhere else except Latveria. Few other places had the resources to devote to the task. And nowhere else had Doom to demand the work be done. He saw his will made manifest in the form and in the time he had required, and he was pleased.

He looked down at Zargo's stricken face. "We are about to begin the dig," he said. "If it will salve your conscience, you may plead with me not to do what we both know I shall. I will not have the time or the patience to listen to your fears once the drilling has started."

"The thing beneath us is dangerous," said Zargo. "I don't know what it is. But I do know it is strong. It's pulling me, and it's pulling at my memories." He paused. "It's pulling at my identity. That's what it feels like. I'm afraid of what it will be capable of if it's in the open."

Reassurance was needed. How tiresome. But if it would keep the priest focused on his tasks, then he would have it. Doom pointed at the pyramid. "Nothing will be released. That containment is stronger than any natural formation or mere depth of stone can ever be." Zargo opened his mouth to object again and Doom silenced him with a gesture. "You gave voice to your concern, and you have your answer. Any further conversation on this matter will be circular, and therefore futile. It will cease. Now. From this moment forward, all that I will hear from you is the information that I require. I trust that is clear."

Haggard, his eyes hollow with fatigue and worry, Zargo nodded. Doom had no sympathy for the man's fatigue. He was giving in to his weakness.

"Then we will withdraw," said Doom. His inspection was complete. He was satisfied. He strode out of one enclosure, then the other, Zargo hurrying to catch up. The priest's fears were irritating. His resistance to embracing the fact of his own power was irritating. Zargo was one of the most naturally gifted geomancers Doom had ever encountered. There were few human beings on Earth who could have found what Zargo had. He had found it so quickly, too, and Doom was certain it was what he had been seeking. There were memories below. Memories and the power behind them. The rise in the readings that Orloff had detected coinciding with Zargo's discovery was not a coincidence. It couldn't be.

Outside the pyramid's supporting framework, a group of technicians was standing by the controls that would activate the drill. Doom nodded to them. "Begin," he said.

They obeyed. The derrick vibrated as the drill powered up. The head spun, the rotation creating a whine like the warning of a gargantuan hive. Then the drill plunged into the ground, chewing through the grass and dirt and hitting the rock below. The initial scream of metal against stone sounded as if the earth were crying out in pain. Beside Doom, Zargo flinched. The noise became deeper after that, a grinding thunder as the drill also went deeper. Constant tremors shook the ground around the derrick.

Soon, fragments of rock were being sent back up the waste tubes and piling up on either side of the derrick, creating new hills. The access to the drill's shaft, though, was clear.

How far down? Doom wondered. Zargo had no idea. No matter. Since he had found his target, Doom was prepared to be patient. He was closer to his goal than he had expected to be. The commands he had given Orloff and Zargo had been vague, because he didn't know exactly what he was looking for.

He had gained and lost knowledge on Walpurgis Night. Memory had been taken from him, but a trace of it remained, though only in the awareness of its loss. Knowledge was power, and memory was the structure of knowledge. The knowledge of incantations and gestures was the basis of sorcery, an energy that only apparently came from nowhere. The truth was that memory was energy, and energy could not be destroyed.

Memory that was lost went somewhere.

The more he had searched, the more Doom became convinced that what he was searching for was a form of embodied memory. Its existence was dictated by traces in the earth and traces in the dead. Ordering Zargo to look had been a speculative act, but not an uninformed one.

Traces in the earth, traces in the dead and traces in Doom's mind too. He was following the scars of knowledge taken from him. The traces had guided his decisions. They showed him where to look, and how.

Now the search would bear fruit.

The drill went deeper. The mounds of earth grew. The ground vibrated with the strength of Doom's will.

"Why here?" Zargo said.

Doom looked at him. Zargo was frowning, his expression one of puzzlement rather than dread. This might be a conversation worth having, then. Instead of silencing him, Doom said, "What do you mean?"

"Why is what you wanted to me to find here, in Latveria?" said Zargo. "Is that luck? Chance? Doesn't that feel unlikely?"

"If this were the only one, it would be," said Doom. "I do not trust luck. I do not rely on chances. I shape them." He stretched his hand in toward the site of the dig. He closed his gauntlet as if he could pull memories out of the ground. "Let us call what you have found a memory node. Is this the only one on Earth? Does that seem likely, even if we do not know precisely what it is that lies below?"

Zargo shook his head. "I don't think so."

"No, it is not likely. I believe this is the node of Latveria. It is where the memories shaped by this land gather." He paused, thinking of what he hoped the node would be – specific to Latveria, but also universal. Why shouldn't all memories be gathered in multiple nodes? But even if they weren't, even if this was the Latverian node and only that, then that would be enough, because surely it would have what had been taken from him. And there was another possibility. "It may be, though, that the node exists only in Latveria. There may be only one. Why here? Because of Latveria's unique history. It is a tortured one. This land has been shaped by sorcery just as much as it has been by geological forces.

"One way or the other, we will know what you have found soon," he said to Zargo. "We will know it, and we will capture it." *And I will make it mine.*

Orloff saw wind. She saw its movement, its lines of current blowing through a shifting, fluid kaleidoscope of fragments that only seemed to be colors. They were, Orloff knew at once, memories, or the memories of memories, the broken shards of a lost stained-glass window. The image was gone, but what remained announced that an image had once been here.

The wind threw itself against Orloff. She had no body in the swirl, only an identity, and the wind tried to pry her apart. She resisted, and it pushed harder. Her bodiless self tried to breathe, and the wind reached inside her. It wanted to hollow her out, to take everything that was her and break it down, blast it into dust.

She clamped down hard on her being. It was hers. She would not surrender her identity to anything. She fought back, and in fighting realized that the wind did not blow *from* somewhere. It blew *toward* something, something powerful. Her mind conjured images of vortices, of maelstroms, of black holes and terrible gravity, and also of presence. The wind blew towards a being. It frightened her. She wanted out.

She blinked, momentarily disoriented to find herself back in the lab, the helmet in her hands. She had not had any sense of removing it, but her body had clearly responded to her will.

OK. That was a good sign.

Her heart was pounding, her forehead was drenched in sweat, and her breath came in quick, frantic gasps.

"How are we all doing?" she said, to hear the sound of her voice. "I think I'm in fight-or-flight mode." She did her best to steady her breathing. "Little bit freaked, I don't mind telling you. How about the rest of you?"

The dead had no reply.

"No answer means no bad news," she said to the bodies. "We're good, then." She took a few more breaths, grounding herself, disconnected the helmet from her first test subject and went back to the fresh corpse. "Your turn," she said, trying to sound casual for her own benefit. "I'm going to be in your head now. Thanks for not minding."

I can do this. I can do this. The hard part was over. She had already crossed the threshold and come back. Right? Right. Piece of cake. Piece of pie. Piece of mind…

Stop that.

She waited until her hands stopped shaking and her curiosity gained the upper hand on her fear.

She hooked up the helmet and put it on.

Braced for the wind, she withstood it more easily. Once more, she was caught up in the storm of fragments. She sensed differences between these shards and those that belonged to the other body, but she couldn't make out anything more precise than that. The pull was just as strong here. Ready for it, she resisted, a rock unmoved by currents, and she turned her attention cautiously toward the source of the pull. The moment she did, it became stronger, its attempts to crack her open and take what was hers more persistent. She fought back without panicking, and the attacks themselves began to give her an idea of the being that was linked to the dead. The wind was a scouring, like a tongue licking hollowed-out shells of the dead for traces of flavor. Having eaten what had once been there, it would never let go. Its hunger was infinite, its grip eternal.

It devoured. That was the core of its nature.

But what did it devour?

The pull was growing stronger. The thing was getting to know her too. Each moment that she stayed in this realm, the risk to her identity increased.

The temptation to understand was strong. She stayed. *Just a bit longer.*

The afternoon wore on, and the drilling continued. The hills of ejecta climbed higher, until the derrick was close to being hidden in a valley of its own creation. The roar of the machine was muffled, coming up the depths it had pierced. Doom stood close to the derrick, listening to the vibrating rumble in the ground and willing the drill to go faster.

"How deep is the shaft?" Zargo asked.

"More than a hundred feet by now," said Doom.

"How much further can the drill go?"

"As far as it has to." And how far was that? When would it reach the goal? He had waited long enough.

"I don't even know if what I'm sensing occupies physical space."

"Then your fears are without foundation," Doom said sharply, his patience with Zargo at an end. "And what I have commanded to be done here is a waste of time. But you do not believe that, and neither do I. You were pulled to this spot. What we are drilling for no doubt has a being across more planes than the physical, but the physical is still one of them."

Doom turned away from the derrick for a moment to look down on Zargo. The priest was hunched in on himself and shivering.

"You feel that we are getting closer," he said eagerly, taking hope from Zargo's misery.

Zargo nodded. He wrapped his arms tightly around himself. Good. Good.

"All those memories," Zargo muttered. He shook, as if trying to cast them away.

Doom would have reached out to snatch them for himself if he could have. He envied Zargo. *You do not appreciate your gifts, geomancer.* His was a power Doom did not have, and Zargo had already tasted what he desired. He felt the memories that were stored below. He knew them. "What kind of memories?" Doom asked, barely able to hold back his jealousy.

"Every kind," said Zargo. "I saw many of mine, ones that I had forgotten. Ones that I wish had stayed forgotten. Others, too, that don't belong to me. I don't want them either."

Zargo was a fool. A pathetic, blinkered fool. Doom did not even know what was taken from him. Only that it *was*. Did Zargo understand that kind of pain? Did he even understand what a scar was?

Doom's mask pressed hard against the map of old pains that was his face.

No, Zargo did not understand. Because he would throw away what Doom would shatter mountains to retrieve.

Doom looked back at the derrick and the rising mounds of earth.

And I will. I will split the Carpathians apart if I have to. If that shaft must pierce the Earth to its core, then so be it, and I will descend to its final reaches. Zargo moans about unpleasant memories. What does he know of the past and its tortures? I know more than he can ever fear. I know that Hell lives in memories. But so does omnipotence. I will face the worst of hells. I will take back more than what was stolen from me. I will take *everything*.

A sharp tremor shook the ground. The derrick groaned and

swayed. The roar of the drill was sharper, and lightning flashed up from the shaft. Zargo cried out in pain. He collapsed, hands clutching his head, ears bleeding.

The flash cut through the psychic realms. The mountains trembled, and so did the sorcerous ether. Doom stepped forward, driven by the need to take what had escaped and make it his. But the lightning was momentary, an outburst of bottled energy, not the thing itself.

You want to be free. You will not be. You have revealed yourself to me, and that was a mistake.

He was drawing closer to capturing that which was hidden.

A scream filled the space of wind and fragments. It shot at Orloff from the unseen heart of the hunger, a surge of force that staggered her. The devouring thing was closer, stronger, and its wind was as fierce as claws.

I want out.

The wind of the dead howled, the driven fragments slashed at her, sandblasting at her being. The thing that gripped would not release her.

I want out!

Devourer. She perceived the nature of the force with terrible clarity now. Devourer. It had consumed the memories of the dead and wanted hers now too.

Devourer.

OUT!

The helmet crashed to the floor, and she fell against the slab, gasping. She doubled over, hands clutching her chest, holding her self in, holding her soul in.

When Orloff could breathe again, she straightened. She

tapped her leg, her stomach, her shoulder, reassuring herself that her body was still here, still solid, still hers. She held her fingers against her temple, as if she could touch her mind. "I'm still here," she murmured. "I'm still here. All of me."

She rifled through memories, skipping from childhood to adulthood, of her parents and of Kariana. "I haven't forgotten anything." It was the most needful declaration she had made all day. She hoped it was true.

The memory of the Devourer was there too.

She feared it would remember her also.

It knew her now.

SIX

Boris put Orloff on a helicopter to the dig site as soon as she told him that she needed to speak with Doom. He didn't ask any questions. He didn't require a reason from her. He must have seen in her face how important it was. Though there was no need to, she took the helmet with her, clutching it as if it were a talisman. She was not religious. There had never been icons in her family's home. But this thing that she had helped design had taken her to places she had never imagined, and to revelations beyond what she had, until today, felt comfortable accepting.

The helicopter raced north, and she shivered with wonder and fear. Now that she was away from the lab, and not immersed in the work, the realization of what had happened was sinking in.

She had seen past death.

She didn't know the meaning of everything she had seen. She believed a lot at the intuitive level, and that was unnerving too. That wasn't who she was used to being. She wasn't about belief. She was about evidence, the empirical, the provable.

She had seen past death.

She knew that for a fact. That was provable, when it should be the least provable of all things.

Her sense of the world and how it worked and where she fit into it had been cut loose from its moorings. She was adrift, and a gale was brewing. At its center, the Devourer waited. With a few hours of distance between now and her encounter with its existence, she was able to think about it a little more calmly. Only a little. She dreaded feeling its presence again, and she knew she would have to. It was part of what she was learning.

She had had a breakthrough. It wasn't exactly the one that Doom wanted, but she had to tell him what it was. And it was a breakthrough that was forcing her to reconsider everything she thought she understood.

She ran a hand over the contours of the helmet. It was a technological device. It was also a sorcerous one. She still couldn't reconcile the two. She was having too much difficulty processing the reality of magic. The visceral experience of wearing the helmet wasn't helping. It only amplified the immensity of her new reality.

She arrived at the site after dark. Arc lights pierced the night, illuminating the work area with a painful, stark white. The helicopter descended to a pad constructed several hundred yards up the western slope of the bowl, higher than the new hills that had been created on either side of derrick, level with the base of the pyramid. Orloff stared at the pyramid during the landing, and had trouble taking her eyes off it after she alighted from the helicopter. She stood on the landing pad, helmet held tightly to her chest, and tried to take in what she was seeing. She only gave up the attempt when one of the site workers came up and asked her to follow him.

Above the landing pad were prefab dormitories for the work crews. They were long, low structures, the metal lighter, more solid and better insulated than the military huts of non-Latverian forces. Above them was Orloff's destination, Doom's quarters. The building was made of black metal, and so monolithic it looked as if it had been discovered in the hillside, a monument hidden there for centuries. It frowned, a building as stern as Doom's mask, its presence and position so pronounced, it was an architectural overseer. It would stand sentinel over the work even in its master's absence. It was two stories high. The upper floor bulged out over the entrance with a panoramic one-way window. In the harsh illumination of the site it was a cyclops, the single eye shining like a black mirror.

The worker brought Orloff to the open doorway and then excused himself. "Please go in," he said. "Second floor. Lord Doom is expecting you." He bowed quickly and hurried off, eager to be out of sight from the building.

Orloff paused, watching him go, and then turned his attention to the dirt and rock being ejected by the derrick. A low, steady tremor ran through the ground beneath her feet.

Someone else was coming up the slope, heading for her. As he drew near, Orloff recognized the priest. She had seen him once or twice, in passing, on the steps of St Peter, a man with a careworn but kindly face. Kariana had mentioned that Doom had singled him out too. He introduced himself, and they shook hands.

"Elsa Orloff," she said. "I'm pleased to meet you, Father."

Zargo grimaced. "Grigori, please. I'm not sure that I'm a priest any longer." He glanced curiously at the helmet, then waved at the dig site. "He has you working on this, too, then."

"I'm not entirely sure what *this* is," Orloff told him. "But no, this is not my field. I'm a neurosurgeon."

Zargo looked even more worried when she said that.

Orloff tried to reassure him. "My work is back in Doomstadt." She held up the helmet for a moment, as if it explained things.

"If you're here," said Zargo, "then you are working on the same project."

"I don't–"

"He wants memories, and you're helping him find them."

Orloff said nothing, unsure what was permissible for her to say.

"This," said Zargo, pointing up at the vastness of the pyramid, "and this," pointing at the derrick, "and the rumble in the ground, it's all about memories too. You're part of it. As am I."

"I should go," said Orloff.

"I asked him to stop," said Zargo. "I asked him not to do this. It's dangerous."

"He's expecting me," said Orloff. If Zargo was hoping to conscript her into trying to convince Doom to end this project, she was going to disappoint him.

Zargo must have read her thoughts on her face. He nodded sadly. "Yes. You shouldn't delay. Listen. I'm not asking you to change his mind. It can't be done. I knew that even when I tried. Just, please, be careful of what you do." He looked down at the vibrating ground. "There's something down there," he said. "Doom thinks he can contain it and control it. Remember that he might be wrong." He paused, seeming to think about what he had just said. "I'm sorry. That isn't very helpful advice, is it?"

"Not really."

"I had to give it, all the same. I had to try."

"Thanks, I guess," said Orloff. She appreciated that he meant well, but he was talking to the wrong person. The work she was doing for Doom frightened her, but it compelled her too. She was as committed to seeing it through as Doom was. She left Zargo there, looking at the pyramid, and entered the quarters. They were dark. Only the stairs were illuminated, a path of light showing her the way. She went up the steps, and another path of light took her into the chamber where Doom waited. The lighting here was dim. Doom was seated on an elevated throne, looking out of the hemispherical window. Between the throne and the window was an obsidian five-sided table. Symbols of crimson and gold marked its surface. Orloff recognized some of the symbols as astrological. Most of them, like the markings inside the helmet, were strange to her. They felt very old. Along the entire edge facing the throne was a complex of controls. Orloff couldn't begin to guess what they were for.

"You have news for me, Doctor Orloff," Doom said. He did not take his eyes off the dig.

"I do." She brought him up to date. He listened without interrupting. When she described the sudden spike in the power of the unknown force's pull, he leaned forward.

"When, exactly, did that happen?" he asked.

"At 5.13PM today."

Doom nodded. "At the same moment," he muttered. He sounded satisfied. "Yes. Good. That is in line with what Grigori Zargo experienced at the geomantic level. I detected the ethereal disturbance too." He was quiet for a moment, pensive. "Describe to me again your sense of what the force was doing."

Orloff obeyed. When she was done, Doom nodded again. "Devourer," he said, trying out the word. He spoke then, at first in a tone of interested speculation, and then with growing conviction. "Yes. Yes, why not? If we lose memories, but they cannot be destroyed, where do they go? To this being, if we can call it a being, this hoarder. It takes what it can, and at death takes all. But it is *only* at death that it can take everything."

"Why only then?" Orloff asked.

"Because there is no fight left. You say that you fought it."

"That's right."

"And you withstood it, though it tried to take your memories."

"Not my memories, exactly," said Orloff. "It tried to take *me*. All of me. My memories are part of that, but not its totality. I didn't feel them being taken. It felt like a hunger for something much more profound."

"I see," said Doom. After a thoughtful silence, he went on. "Your essence, then. Interesting. Truly the Devourer." He paused. "If it tried to take your essence," he said. "Then the memories it takes are a symptom of that theft. So is the name we have agreed upon so easily and so naturally. What trace of memory has its presence left in all of us? The fear of losing everything that makes up what we are. At a level deeper than

I had thought, we have always known what is down there."

Orloff felt the touch of vertigo again that came when Doom so easily opened up colossal implications before her. Fear and excitement wrestled, neither retreating an inch. "Given this," she said, "is the Devourer still what you're looking for?"

"As long as the memories are there, then yes. And I see no reason to think that they are not. I see every reason to believe that they *are*. What you have found tells me more about its nature, and what I must do to take from it what I need."

Orloff looked out at the dig. The walls and floor of Doom's quarters thrummed faintly. "If the Devourer is able to exert the force that it does, sealed away in whatever way it is, what happens if you release it?"

"I will not." Doom pointed at the pyramid. "This will be its new containment, and I will wrest its secrets from it. You have found the way forward there. A refinement of that helmet is the next step."

Orloff looked at the helmet, then at the table.

"Science and sorcery, doctor," said Doom. "The mix confounds you."

"I'm still trying to grasp what that mix means. I don't even know what sorcery *is*."

"Language is a form of it," said Doom. "Let us begin there. Consider that language is the imperfect analogue of meaning, like a three-dimensional representation of a four-dimensional object. Sorcery uses language of a special kind. Through it, the representation of a reality *becomes* reality. Sorcery's language and reality are thus much closer together, but the fusion is still imperfect. If sorcery's language were perfect, it would be omnipotence. It is not. But if I am right about the Devourer, it holds all memory, all knowledge. It is the key to perfection."

He did not use the word *omnipotence* again, but Orloff sensed it in the background. Gooseflesh ran down her arms, but not with alarm. Everything she had learned through all her years of study and research seemed insignificant beside what Doom had revealed to her in a few seconds. *I think I'm starting to really get it now, Kari.* She understood why Kariana told her never to hesitate. *When Doom tells us to jump, it's because we're going to fly.*

"How deep is the shaft?" she asked.

"More than a thousand feet now."

"How much further…" Orloff began, and then a violent tremor hit. It shook the building like a dog with a rat, hurling Orloff against the table. She dropped the helmet and it scraped over the surface, coming to rest in the middle, upright and facing the window as if it were bearing witness also. Searing light of violet and green, a violent aurora, erupted from beneath the derrick. Orloff staggered under the onslaught of light. She clutched the table to hold herself up.

Something howled inside her mind, hungry and raging. For a brief and terrible moment, claws sank into all that was precious and *her*. She fought back, ferocious. Essence or being or soul or mind, no matter its name, it was hers, and she would keep it. She held the claws at bay, and then the moment passed. She could see again.

Doom had left the throne. He was at the table's controls, the fingers of his right hand dancing over switches and sliders like an organist, his left hand making complex gestures over the table. Its runes glowed in rising and falling intensities, musicians responding to their conductor. Outside, the runes of the pyramid's base pulsed in echo to what Doom commanded of the table.

Orloff took a step back from the table, its power crackling the air. She started breathing again.

"There," said Doom. "It is contained." Satisfied, he folded his arms and walked over to the window.

"What was that?" Orloff asked.

"A burst of energy from the Devourer. That is to be expected as we draw nearer. You fought back well."

"You experienced that too?"

"Everyone in Latveria did, to some degree, I expect."

Doom did not sound concerned. That threw Orloff a bit. *Everyone?* she thought. She found it hard to dismiss an event of that scale.

"The touch of the Devourer will have been felt most strongly in the Carpathians," Doom continued, "and most acutely at this site. As you can testify, the moment of the Devourer's predation was brief. It may have tasted, but it has not fed."

"So nothing has escaped." Orloff wanted reassurance.

"Some small seepage of energy is inevitable, given the nature of the Devourer. It has always been reaching out, and always been feeding. What little surplus may have escaped will be too diluted across Latveria to be significant." Doom held up a hand. "Listen," he said. "What do you notice?"

"I can't hear the drill engine," said Orloff. There was no longer earth being added to the derrick's hills, and the vibrations had stopped. At the base of the derrick, there was excited movement, and one of the workers was running up the slope toward Doom's quarters.

Doom turned from the window. "Come," he said to Orloff. "You have arrived at an opportune moment. Let us go and see what we have broken through."

SEVEN

Maleva Krogh made good time for someone traveling on foot. She had made her way from the south of the country to the north, from the Malhela Mountains to the first rise of the Carpathians, without being caught. The call she followed was growing stronger. *Maleva.* Her name spoken by a voiceless presence, and by vows as ancient as her family. It was the summons to worship, the promise of darkness. The command had to be heeded, and she was glad to obey. In obedience, she intuited the promise of a hope fulfilled, of vengeance, and of the past restored.

The journey had been hard, though. She kept thinking about why she was being called to the Carpathians. There was only one possible destination for her in the mountains. As things now stood, the truth was that it was the only destination for her in all of Latveria. But it was a dead end. There was no reason to go there except to die, and she wasn't ready to die. She wasn't ready to give up the fight, even if she was the only one left to fight Doom.

The sense of the call, that there was purpose in her steps, was all that kept her from despair. She was alone. She was hungry and cold. The weather had turned, and she felt fall in her bones. She ate what she could scavenge in the woods and at the edges of settlements. She had a rifle, but she didn't dare hunt. She had to travel silently, not call attention to herself by using the gun. So she passed the edges of farms and the outskirts of villages like a ghost, gnawing on leavings and rotting vegetables.

The humiliation was worse than the hunger, the humiliation of having to steal what peasants threw away, when all that they had, even their bodies and their labor, should be hers.

In the foothills of the Carpathians, Krogh walked along the banks of the Zal. It was late afternoon, the temperature was dropping and mist was rising from the stream. She drifted with it toward the village of Zalbach. Still a couple of miles from the cluster of houses, the Zal ran out of the forest and past the outbuildings of a small farm. She stopped, staying in the shadows of a large oak, looking into the yard. A farmer was pouring corn into a trough for his pigs.

Krogh watched him, and hated him. Her hand clutched the pommel of the dagger. She had to will herself to keep the blade in its sheath.

Be calm and wait.

But why should she wait? Would she even be able to sneak away any of that corn without being seen? Why should she not demand what was hers?

Her breath became hard, almost a growl.

And then the flash came, a powerful burst of hunger and energy that shot through her brain like a red-hot poker through flesh. The distant call became a shout, MALEVA, and the unknown thing to which her family owed fealty seized her. It chained her to itself, and it held her too with something that felt like a promise.

Her hate and hunger fused. They were one, and they were supreme.

She flew out of the woods, rushing at the farmer with raptor speed, knife drawn. He turned at the last second, his eyes widened, and she plugged the dagger into his throat before he could yell. Warm blood flowed down her wrist. The man choked and twitched. She pulled the dagger free and he dropped, crashing back against the trough, and then down on to the ground.

The pigs milled around, snuffling and grunting. They ignored Krogh.

She stood motionless for a few seconds, thrumming still with the energy that coursed through her. Her relationship with the being behind the energy had ancient roots, yet its touch was new, and newly strong.

MALEVA. Calling, pulling, commanding.

She walked through the open door of the stone farmhouse and into its kitchen. A woman knelt before a wood-fired oven, reaching in to take out a loaf of bread. She had her back to Krogh. "Finished already?" she asked without turning around.

Krogh padded across the kitchen floor, yanked the woman's head back and slit her throat. She took the bread and a ham she found on a table, and refilled her canteen with water. She had enough supplies to see her to her destination now. She thought for a moment about staying the night, about sleeping in a real bed for the first time in months.

She couldn't risk it. She mustn't be foolish. Not now. Not after making it this far. Not when the call had become so strong and urgent.

She fled the farm as quickly and as quietly as she had come, returning to the shelter and the gathering gloom of the forest. Shadows and mist welcomed her, coiling around her legs and embracing her with concealment. She walked on for another few hours, eating as she went. The bread was hot, the ham succulent. It tasted good, and was even more satisfying for being hers as the result of the violent assertion of her rights.

Her stomach was full, but the deeper hunger was even worse.

When it was too dark to go on, she curled up between the thick roots of an oak that felt as old and angry as she. Krogh shivered under her cloak, with fury as much as she did from cold. And she shivered with the deep hunger, the hunger for everything denied to her, for the power that should have been hers, and for the glory that had been her family's.

The flash of energy still throbbed in her blood and through her limbs. The tips of her fingers pulsed. Her temple beat a heavy rhythm. When she fell asleep, she felt that she was falling *into* the power.

The dream came then.

No, not a dream. It was greater than that, more important, more commanding. It was a vision, a revelation, a conviction. The call became precise. When she woke, she woke suddenly, her eyes snapping open with old knowledge and the resurrection of ancient memories.

In the dawn, through new mist, she marched with purpose. Her destination was not a dead end. It was a beginning, the start of a reckoning for Latveria. She was marching toward triumph, and toward a legacy that she, the last of the Kroghs, would finally claim in its entirety.

She was going home.

It was almost dawn before the drill was removed from the shaft. Doom stood beside the derrick for the entire procedure. He did not expect the Devourer to escape from the shaft. That burst of psychic energy had felt like a build-up of the faint leakage from whatever its prison was, which had to be something more than simple rock. Even so, he had the pyramid ready to trigger at a moment's notice. If he had to activate the prison with himself and all the crews still within the shadow of its base, he would. There were ways of extricating humans from its confines, if it came to that.

He did not think it would. But he stood guard, ready and watching for anything he might learn about what lay below. He was tense with eagerness. He resented each second that passed without revelation. Soon, he told himself. Soon, soon. He hid his impatience, though, standing motionless, apparently impassive, before the hole.

Orloff was with him for the first hour, and then went off to get some rest when it was clear how long the wait would be. When the drill finally emerged from the shaft, he had Orloff sent for. She was at his side before arc lights were repositioned to shine down into the abyss. He was pleased by the fascination he saw in her face.

"You wish to descend too," he said.

"I do."

"Good."

"I would like to go as well," said a third voice.

Doom turned around to see Zargo staring past him at the shaft.

"You surprise me," said Doom.

"I need to know. I cannot hide from the knowledge of what I have helped uncover."

"Very well."

A foreman and the work crew who had raised the drill had approached to within a few discreet yards, waiting for new orders.

"Prepare two transports," Doom said to them. "Then make ready to come at my summons."

The work crew brought hover platforms to Orloff and Zargo. The devices were simple in their design, consisting of a disc five feet wide with a steering post mounted at one edge. Doom made himself wait while Orloff and Zargo learned how to use the transports. Now was when patience was most needed. The risks of eagerness would only be more severe in the time ahead.

When Orloff and Zargo had both mounted and activated their vehicles, the platforms rising silently a few feet into the air, Doom fired up his jetpacks and dropped into the shaft.

No more waiting. Now to see what will be mine.

The drill had left smooth walls in its wake. Doom flew down through a perfectly formed straight tunnel. The arc lights at the surface provided illumination for the first hundred feet or so, and then it all was darkness.

Doom activated the light sphere he had brought with him and sent it on ahead. The sphere flew on magnetic currents, as did the hover platforms. It was fast. Responding to the commands transmitted from his armor, the sphere stayed fifty feet ahead of him, illuminating the shaft with a clear white light.

Doom could have achieved the same result with a simple spell. He had decided not to introduce any further sorcery into the etheric atmosphere of the hole until he had a clearer sense of what he was dealing with. The Devourer was dangerous. Despite what Zargo might believe, Doom did not underestimate the power it represented, and the risk involved in seizing it. Zargo, however, was underestimating Doom's power. He would capture the Devourer. There could be no doubt of that.

For much of the descent, Doom dropped past the flysch of the Carpathians. After the first thousand feet, the geology around him became more complex, a concatenation of strata less and less natural to the Carpathians, or any single region. More and more, Doom saw the full memories of the Earth.

Anticipation grew, and so did the sense of imminent triumph.

This was a vault of memories. They had gathered here, and Doom would harvest them.

As the geology changed, light began to shine from below. Doom extinguished the sphere. It returned to him and flew just behind his shoulder, waiting to be used again. With the artificial illumination off, the glow in the depths became clearer. It was a multi-hued phosphorescence. The colors shifted and the intensity fluctuated, a subterranean aurora.

Doom dropped another half mile. The drill had gone even deeper than he had supposed. Then the shaft ended, and he emerged into an immense cavern. It was hundreds of feet high and thousands of yards wide. Huge gems covered the walls and vaulted ceiling. There were garnets, amethyst, apatite, opals and topaz. There were sapphires and emeralds ten feet across, and diamonds the size of skulls. The cavern was a fever dream of riches, the walls extruding luxury so extreme it became phantasmic. The light ran between them in veins, active and pulsing, colors chasing each other in an endless hunt.

Doom looked away from the gems. They were interesting as a phenomenon, but not what he had come for. They were not the riches he needed.

Twin rows of columns held up the vault where the gems gleamed like a galactic core. Doom landed and looked up at the nearest pillar. It was not natural. It had been carved from a single block of marble. So had the others. The designs on the pillars were not from any culture, ancient or modern, that Doom knew, yet there were echoes in them that he did know. He saw traces of the monumental work of ancient empires of Egypt, of the Khmer, of the Aztecs, and the Romans, and of Babylon, and more. The memories of all the great builders had gathered here too.

Memories, Doom thought. These were the true riches of this cavern.

Bridges linked the pillars at a multitude of levels, creating gossamer-thin webs of stone. Though the bridges were fused to the pillars, they were natural formations. Stalactites hung from them like so many icicles.

On the bridges, and on the floor, lay artifacts. Doom stood in the center of a ruined museum. Statues, altars, paintings, thrones, manuscripts, scepters, weapons, musical instruments and more surrounded him in heaps. He nodded to himself as he gazed at the hoard. *The sum of human endeavor*, he thought. The sum of memories. He touched one of the thrones.

This was real. This had been given form by the power that lay in this vault.

He breathed the very air of victory.

Then he looked up to watch Orloff and Zargo drop slowly through the cavern and bring their hover platforms to a halt on the floor. They stepped off their transports and stared, open-mouthed, at the cavern and its holdings.

Doom saw now that the rows of the pillars were not quite parallel. To his left, they marched off forever, each pair slightly further apart. The other end of the cavern vanished into gloom despite the rushing light. To his right, they drew together gradually, leading the eye to a blank, black wall. The artifacts washed up against it in frozen waves.

Doom walked toward the wall. Orloff and Zargo hurried to keep up.

"How is any of this possible?" Orloff asked.

"The question is an interesting one," said Doom, "but it is not the important one. That this exists is what matters. The question to ask, then, is its meaning."

Zargo stopped to look more closely at a statue leaning precariously from a heap of sculptures, its head almost touching one of the columns. "Is this the meaning?" he said.

"What is?" Doom asked. The statue, of what appeared to be a Roman statesman, did not look more remarkable than any of the other artifacts near it.

"The work is missing something. It feels hollow. Don't you think?"

Doom looked more closely, and he saw what Zargo meant. "The details are missing," he said. It wasn't that the statue lacked eyes or a nose. The features were all there. Their distinctiveness was not. There was nothing that marked the figure as representing a particular human being. Nor was there a recognizable style, no hint of the artist behind the piece.

"On this too." Orloff had picked up a painting. The suggestion of a ship was tossed in a dream of snow and waves.

"Turner's *Snow Storm*," said Doom. "*Steam-Boat off a Harbour's Mouth*."

"But it isn't, is it?"

"No." Like the statue, it lacked distinctiveness. It was missing something essential. It was art that was dead.

Orloff put the canvas down and wiped her hands on her trousers, as if she had touched something unpleasant.

Not the sum, Doom thought. *The dust of human endeavor.*

Orloff opened a film canister and pulled out a reel of celluloid she found inside. She extended a strip and peered at the frames. "*London After Midnight*", she read. When she replaced it in the canister, it shed flakes. "I can't make out the images," she said. "They're too faded."

They started walking again. The indistinguishable ghosts of terracotta statues stared blankly at them.

"How can any of this be here?" Orloff wondered. She wasn't letting go of her initial question. "Who built this?"

There were pieces from all eras, from every culture, though Doom saw more that was clearly Latverian.

"These are memories," said Doom. "Memories, or what remains of them, in physical form."

The closer they came to the wall, the more Doom felt an undertow of psychic power pulling them forward. He whispered a few syllables and gestured, summoning mental shields for all three of them.

"No human hands have placed these works here," he said. "But because the originals were created, and human senses beheld them, then memories of the works were also created, and the Devourer has called those memories to itself."

"And killed them," said Orloff.

"Indeed it has."

They reached the wall. "Keep back," Doom said. Orloff and Zargo obeyed, with some strain. They looked as if they were standing waist-deep in a strong current.

"What stone is that?" said Orloff.

"I don't know that it is stone." Zargo's breathing was harsh. Sweat droplets stood out on his forehead.

"What do you sense about it?" Doom asked.

"Nothing. I can't reach it. It's a discontinuity in the earth."

"And beyond it?"

"I can't sense what's there any clearer than before. This close, it's stronger, but not as much as I had feared."

"The barrier is a strong one." Doom reached out to the wall. He placed a gauntleted palm against it. He felt the hunger on the other side. It sensed his presence and hurled itself against its prison, a thing of all memories yet mindless in its need to feed. He understood its eagerness. He was so close now. He wanted to end all waiting and punch through the wall.

I have my own hunger, Doom thought. *I am the one who will feed, not you.*

He contacted the crews on the surface and gave them their new commands.

On his farm just outside the village of Kroghstein, Ewald Lang brought the last of the sheep into their pen for the night. His land was on a slope, bracketed by steep cliffs below and above. From the pen, at the downslope end of the farm, he could look down on the closely packed stone houses with the maze of crooked and narrow streets threading through them. Kroghstein huddled against the mountainside, trying to hide from the shadow of the ruined castle far above.

The clouds were coming in low, and the wind had grown cold and strong. It was going to be a bitter fall, and the temperatures had dropped noticeably in the last two days, since the night of the brain lightning.

Ewald didn't know what else to call the flash that had come behind the eyes. Everyone he knew had also experienced it. The flash had made them turn in fear toward Castle Krogh. The fortress' walls were crumbled, huge rents in them visible from the village. It had not been inhabited since the coming of Doom. The Kroghs had resisted, and Doom had smashed them. Then the people had looted it and burned whatever they could not carry.

Ewald was seventy-five. Too many of his years had been spent living in fear of the Kroghs. He had been part of the mob that set fire to the castle. He hadn't taken anything, though. He didn't want any reminders of the place where his brother had been killed to amuse the Kroghs. But he had wanted to feel some sense of justice, and it had felt right to feel the crunch of their ornaments beneath his heel.

A small thing. He wished the satisfaction he had felt had lasted longer. He wished he didn't still feel anxious every time he faced the cliff on the other side of his land and saw the castle frowning back at him.

He closed the pen, and the back of his neck prickled. He turned around and looked up, in the deepening gray and the start of a fine mist of rain.

There was movement at the base of the castle walls. He saw a crow in human form.

He rubbed his eyes and looked again. There was nothing now.

"Ewald?" Nina had come out of the house. "What is it?"

Ewald stared at his wife, his throat dry. "I thought I saw her," he said. He didn't speak the name. No one had since the night of the fire. It was bad luck to conjure the worst of the Kroghs.

"No," Nina whispered. "You didn't. Say you didn't. Promise me she hasn't come back."

More than anything in the world, he wanted to make that promise.

Terror kept him silent.

EIGHT

It took a full day for the equipment to be transported down the shaft and set up. More supplies were airlifted in from Doomstadt as the focus of Doom's project shifted from the bowl in the Carpathians to the cavern. Work crews established generators and rows of tents on the cavern floor. They pushed back hundreds of artifacts to clear enough space, and the new hills of objects all seemed to Orloff to be leading toward the black wall, pulled by the hunger of what lay beyond. By the end of the day, there was a full encampment.

Doom, Orloff thought, was preparing for a long process.

Doom had also seen to it that more than machinery was brought down. There were standing stones, too. They fascinated Orloff. They were of a polished, black labradorite. They seemed to pull the light of the cavern into themselves. To look at one was to be pulled into depths, as if the surface of the stone were a starlit sheen over a bottomless pond. Each stone bore a single ward in silver. Doom ordered them arranged in a wide semi-circle around the wall, the wards facing in.

During the preparations, Orloff had a chance to get a bit more rest, but her excitement kept her from grabbing more than a few hours at a time. The black wall was, she felt, the physical manifestation of the veil she had pierced with the helmet. She needed to know what was beyond it too. She had come this far on the journey. She couldn't turn back now.

Doom spent hours standing still before the wall, studying it. Sometimes he touched it, and he would lean forward as if it were speaking to him. Sometimes halos of blue and red lightning surrounded him as he tested the wall with sorcery. Orloff admired his methodical approach. He was close to his goal, and he was not going to lose it through reckless haste.

Zargo maintained a vigil, and he seemed to be getting even less sleep than Orloff. He prayed and he meditated, and Orloff was careful not to disturb him. Sometimes he knelt with his hands on the ground, his eyes open but blank. He didn't see Orloff when she walked past. Kariana had told her that Zargo was a geomancer, and she wondered what he saw during these communions, what veils he was crossing.

Orloff had plenty to keep herself busy. "You must refine the helmet," Doom had said as the encampment was being set up.

"I agree," said Orloff. "But I'm no engineer…"

"You do not have to be. Your task is to determine exactly what the helm must do. You must decide what neural functions it must be capable of."

"What it can already do is dangerous. I couldn't stay long on the other side."

"Of course it is dangerous," said Doom. "The risk is the marker of the task's importance. Remember that you fought against the pull of the Devourer, and you succeeded."

"Barely. And only by removing the helmet." But Doom's words struck a chord. She had crossed over, she had resisted, and she had returned. Did she realize what she'd done? This was *huge*.

"What tools, then," said Doom, "must the helmet provide so that you can fight harder, with greater facility? What protections must it have?"

"With respect," Orloff said carefully, "that sounds like it must become a weapon."

"If it needs to be," said Doom. "That is for you to determine."

Since that conversation, Orloff had been working on the helmet, starting at the most basic level, with the most important concerns.

What did she want, the next time she crossed the barrier?

She wanted to feel safe.

What would make her feel safe?

Being able to resist the current.

She thought about the helmet as a *helmet*, as armor. To resist the Devourer, the sense of self had to be strong. Embodiment on the other side would reinforce the self.

An armored body.

For the first time, she considered the need for more equipment than just the helmet.

Towards the end of the second day in the cavern, after a long stretch, she looked up bleary-eyed from a laptop screen crowded with windows and made herself stand. The table in her tent was littered with sketches and notes, and they were blurring into nonsense. She needed a break.

She blinked when she stepped out of the tent. Leaving its artificial, steady light to enter the shifting glow of the cavern always took a moment of adjustment. Then she climbed onto her hover platform and rode it up to the surface for some fresh air, and to check in with Kariana over the phone.

"How is it going?" Kariana asked.

"Everything you told me was right."

"You haven't hesitated, then."

"Not once." She laughed. "I don't know where this is leading," she said, and laughed again.

"But you have to find out."

"Kari, I can't even begin to tell you."

It was Kariana's turn to laugh, and that was a good sound. Doom set the tone for the work site, and the atmosphere in the cavern was serious. There was not a lot of laughter among the crews. There was still less around Zargo.

"I want to thank you for something," Orloff said.

"What have I done for you lately?"

"You haven't asked me if I'm safe."

"You've always known not to ask me that," said Kariana.

"And you knew it wasn't because I didn't care."

"I knew it was because you loved me and cared for who I was, and my duty is a big part of who I am. The same is true for you now. This is what you need to do, Elsa, and you're loving it."

"I am," Orloff admitted. "It's frightening sometimes, but I'm crossing barriers I didn't even know existed."

"How are your Orloff family worries?"

"Much better." She hadn't given much thought to her ancestors in the last few days. "I know my motivations are different from theirs." It crossed her mind that she had already accomplished more than they had ever dreamed of doing. She could be proud of that, she thought. That was OK. She hadn't harmed anyone. This was a good thing to take pride in.

"You are also performing your duty to Doom," said Kariana.

"Exactly." She was not following the path of her own megalomania.

"Go on, then. Breach the wall, Ellie."

"I will, my love."

On the third day, the work began in earnest. Her stomach a knot of tension and excitement, Orloff left her tent to witness the first attempt to break through the wall. She worried about what might come from the other side as much as she wanted to know what it was.

Doom had created a circle of containment within the standing stones. They glowed as the adamantium drill was brought to bear. The machine was much smaller than the one that had pierced the shaft, but it was large enough. As its heavy framework rumbled forward on treads, it made Orloff think of a battering ram approaching a castle gate. It spun up, its powerful whine filling the cavern. When it touched the wall, the whine became piercing, and Orloff's eyes watered from where she watched, a few yards outside the ring of stones.

Doom stood very close to where the drill touched the wall, observing the way it bit into the dark matter. After a few moments, he held up a hand and the drill wound down.

"Do you wish to see, Doctor Orloff?" he called to her.

She hurried over to join him at the wall. It was just as blank as ever.

"It's unmarked," she said. Tentatively, she reached out to the wall. When Doom nodded, she placed her palm against the surface. It was smooth, like obsidian, though it had none of the shine. It seemed to absorb light almost completely. "What kind of material *is* this?" she wondered.

"One that I have never encountered before. Its name will be what we decide to call it, should naming it prove to be useful. My interest is in its properties and how to overcome them." He gestured to one of the drill operators, who approached Orloff and offered her a face mask. When she had it on, Doom said, "Look closely."

At his command, the drill started up again. It bit into the wall. Orloff saw it make a hole, and the hole vanish as quickly as it was created.

The drill stopped.

"The wall is remaking itself," she said, awed. "Is it even stone?" She was trying to force this wall to make sense. Maybe it didn't.

"It resembles stone," said Doom, "but it is not. I do not believe it is matter at all. Not in the normal sense, at least."

"I kept thinking of this as another veil."

"Then you were right. The one you confronted fell. So will this."

Doom ordered the drill pulled back and the area within the protective circle cleared. Orloff withdrew. On her way back to her tent she saw that Zargo was observing the process too. He nodded to her, and seemed open to conversation. She stopped next to him.

"How are you holding up?" she asked. He looked exhausted.

"I'm managing and doing what I can. I know that wall is going to be breached, so I'll do what I can to make things safe."

He was helping Doom to the full extent of his powers, then.

Orloff wasn't sure he would appreciate being told that, so she kept her thought to herself. Instead, she changed the subject. "I keep wondering about this cavern. Who made it? Who built that wall? The artifacts here are both too ancient and too new."

"I don't know if anyone made all this," Zargo said.

"What do you mean?"

"Do you think a human hand touched anything we see here?"

"On the face of it, yes."

"Except we know that isn't true. That painting you picked up the other day, that wasn't really a Turner. I think it manifested itself here, like everything else."

"Including the wall?" Orloff asked.

"Maybe, though not in the same way. The artifacts seem like the results of the Devourer's hunger, don't they? They're called to it. The wall is its prison."

"A prison implies jailers as well as prisoners," said Orloff.

"It does," said Zargo.

They shared silent unease for a moment.

"What I'm sure of," said Zargo, "is that the thing beyond the wall would not have willed its prison into existence."

"You're implying intention on the part of the Devourer," said Orloff.

"I don't know to what degree it's sentient. You've felt it too. What do you think?"

"I can't decide if the hunger is anything more than an instinct," Orloff admitted. "But I do think it's something more than a force like gravity."

"I agree. So if there's even a vestigial form of sentience, I don't think it would trap itself."

"No, it wouldn't," said Orloff. "Then who built the wall?" The question kept bothering her.

"Maybe the Earth itself," said Zargo. "Its memories are here too. It was its scars that led me here. Maybe it defended itself in this way."

Orloff thought about that. "I'm having trouble imagining how that could be."

"You don't feel the earth the way I do. The ley lines, the currents of power... It's hard not to think of it as a living thing, at least as much as the Devourer."

"If you're right... If the earth somehow made that wall..."

"Then the idea of breaching it should frighten us."

She didn't disagree. She *was* frightened. But she still wanted to know what was on the other side.

She went back to her tent and lost herself in the work on the helmet. Time lost meaning quickly in the cave and its perpetual twilight aurora. Orloff was startled when she looked at her watch and realized it was after nightfall. She grabbed a ration bar for a quick meal, and barely got a mouthful down when the air seemed to change.

Something was going to happen.

She rushed out of the tent. Zargo was again where she had been speaking with him, halfway between the tents and the standing stones.

Doom had ordered a wider area cleared, with everything pulled back at least ten yards from the outside of the ring of standing stones. The drill now started up again, and the crew withdrew, leaving him alone within the protective circle. Facing the wall, he began making gestures. They hurt Orloff's eyes, and she looked away. The air crackled with gathering power. The pulsing light of the cavern grew sharper, and it gathered around Doom, vibrating with higher frequencies.

The power in the air rushed suddenly into the circle. Orloff gasped, buffeted by the force of a tempest. Spirals of shifting light gathered around Doom. They turned around each other, faster and faster, and then suddenly they were gone, replaced by sorcerous beams that blasted out of his outstretched hands. They struck the wall where the drill ground against it.

Long seconds passed. The intensity of the power kept growing. Orloff wiped a trickle of blood from her nose. Beside her, Zargo shook uncontrollably.

The wall cracked, and there was a flash like there had been three nights before. Orloff jerked as if from an electric shock as something shot past her, another fragment of power escaping. The wards on the stones glowed more brighter, and she had a sense of a seal being closed. Nothing more would get out.

The cavern hissed. The crack in the wall glowed an angry red, like incandescent blood.

When Doom lowered his arms and stepped away, the crack remained, ugly as torn flesh.

"We have begun," said Doom.

For the first time since Doom had seized the throne and shattered her family, Krogh crossed the blackened threshold into the castle. She had dreamed of returning so many times, for so many years, but the demands of survival, of living in hiding, had forbidden it. The last part of her journey had been agonizing. She had feared discovery, and resented the fear.

From the other side of the mountains that overlooked Kroghstein came the deep rumble of work, and the sky flashed with unnatural lightning that shot up toward the clouds. Doom was not many miles from here. She knew he was, because it could only be his actions that had led to the stirring in the depths. She had been called because of him. He made the calling possible, but he was also a threat.

He doesn't know I'm here. He can't know.

But his eyes were everywhere. She would have to work quickly.

Krogh entered the castle, and all the memories were gone. All her family's possessions, vanished. All their paintings, tapestries, carpets, furniture, busts. Everything. Only the walls were left, their ruin the trace and reminder of what had been. Ivy had overgrown the walls inside the castle as well as out. The roof was gone, and the rooms were open to the starless sky. The beam of Krogh's flashlight played over stone blackened by fire.

Her breath became a low growl, a subterranean expression of the anger she felt at the desecration. Fury sharpened her purpose, and she swore retribution.

At the center of the ruins was what had been the chapel of the Kroghs. The lurid stained-glass windows were all shattered. Tree branches had begun to reach inside. They shook in the wind, scraping fingernails against the stone frames.

The altar had been stripped of its adornments. That bothered Krogh less than the other thefts. This altar had always been an ornament, nothing more. The real one was below.

At the back of the chapel were the stairs to the crypt. She descended them, and found less damage there. The mob hadn't dared deface the graves of the Kroghs, and there was less to steal. She passed the tombs set into the wall, going deeper into the crypt, until she came to an iron door waiting in the gloom of a deep recess. It was strong and had resisted the assaults of the villagers. It was still locked.

Krogh carried its key on a chain at her waist. She had kept it as an act of faith, and as a mark of her will to return to reclaim what was hers. Even so, the prospect of ever being able to use it again had seemed more and more remote with every passing year that Doom remained on the throne of Latveria.

Beyond the door was a small, vaulted chamber. The walls and ceiling were unadorned. The Kroghs' true altar sat in the center of the floor. There was nothing else.

The altar was more ancient than the castle. It was more ancient than the Kroghs. It was their foundation stone. Carved out of dark granite, it was circular. There was a depression in the middle, edged with points, like the mouth of a moray eel. The sign of the Devourer.

The Kroghs understood hunger deeply. They consumed, and the more they took, the more they hungered for power. And the more power they gathered to themselves, the more they consumed. That had been the way of things until the coming of Doom.

There was another, deeper hunger, though. It was one that even the Kroghs only half knew. The legend of the Devourer was passed down through the generations, losing its shape and detail. By the time Maleva Krogh heard it, it was barely a half-remembered rumor for her, a vague conception of embodied hunger. It was also as important as her family name. The Kroghs bowed down before it, and to nothing else. It was the true object of their allegiance.

The Devourer had called her, and she had obeyed.

Now what?

She didn't know.

Krogh knelt and pressed her head against the altar. "I have come," she said. "Show me what I must do next."

The call was still there. The pulsing hunger and fury were still there, but nothing answered. She waited and she prayed, swearing her fealty to the thing that hungered.

She did not know how long she knelt. Her limbs ached, and the hunger of her soul grew. "I am here!" she cried at last. "I am here! What would you have me do?"

She jolted. Another strand of energy struck her, another faint but powerful touch of the Devourer. Her flesh burned, her breath came hard and fast, and the pain was the promise of transcendence, and she knew what she had to do.

Krogh stood up. She leaned over the altar, pulled back the right sleeve of her coat and lowered her arm into the darkened maw. "I am here," she said. "I am yours."

The darkness held her. Teeth bit her, though not through her skin. They sank deeper than that. She shuddered, and the withering of flesh and being began. It felt as if her blood were being siphoned out of her, though the loss was more important, and more profound.

Her self rushed into the altar, and something rushed to meet her. It was imprisoned except for this faint tendril, but it was enough for her being and the other to touch, and once they touched, the essence of the Devourer surged out of the dark and into her.

Her body changed. Her fingers lengthened. Her nails became claws.

Her teeth grew, sharpened and multiplied.

Held and captured, freed and rewarded, herself and Other, she screamed in pain and triumph.

She ended, and she began. She died, and she was born.

When Krogh ascended the steps from the crypt, she had gained another name. It was an identity, a calling, and a threat. It defined her hunger, which was greater now than she had ever known. It defined the power she had, to sate that hunger. The name had haunted Latverian folklore for centuries. It was the name for a feral nightmare, the undead devourer of souls.

From the well of the night, Maleva Krogh, first and queen of the returned urvullak, emerged to feed.

PART 2

THE WITHERING PLAGUE

Dear sister, close thy plumes over thine eyes
Lest thou behold and die: they come: they come
Blackening the birth of day with countless wings,
And hollow underneath, like death.
PERCY SHELLEY, *PROMETHEUS UNBOUND*, I.439–442

NINE

The process of breaking down the wall was slow, and it was exhausting. Doom had to draw upon sorcerous resources hour after hour, and that was draining. He had to stop for a few hours each night to sleep and regain his strength.

On this night, Doom did not sleep. Premonition, vague yet sharp, came over him as he stepped away from the wall. He recognized the flavor of the unease. He had felt it before, back in September, in the library of Castle Doom. When he had held *Phantasmus*.

This was a warning. *Do not ignore it this time.*

A warning of what?

Doom flew back up the shaft to his quarters. He sat down in the throne and called up the digitized reproduction of the book. He flicked through the pages, turning them with eye-blink commands. He read steadily, studying the fears and shadows of centuries past. Some lived on as superstitions in the present. Some had been forgotten, perhaps gratefully, in even the most mist-shrouded valleys.

There was no mention of the Devourer. There was no connection that Doom could see between it and the monsters that capered through the pages of *Phantasmus*.

Perhaps there is none. Perhaps the warning is of a completely separate threat.

That didn't seem right either.

Every instinct, crying out with alarm, told him to read.

You must learn this. You must.

So he read. And he did not sleep.

The storm began an hour before dawn. A crack of thunder jolted Nina awake. She lay there, eyes wide, heart hammering, breath coming too fast. She had come out of a nightmare of watching herself being sacrificed on a desecrated church altar. The image stayed with her, refusing to lose its clarity with consciousness. She kept seeing the hand raising the blade, and the blade plunging into her heart. She knew whose hand that was. She knew who was killing her. Because she knew, being awake was no comfort.

Maybe Ewald was wrong. He had to be. She couldn't be back. She wouldn't dare be so bold.

Nina glanced at Ewald's sleeping form beside her. She almost reached out to wake him, to ask for reassurance, to get him to say that he must have made a mistake, and how could he have possibly recognized Maleva Krogh from that distance anyway? She left him alone and took deep breaths, working on slowing the beating of her heart. They had both had a restless night. Ewald needed what sleep he could get. And there was nothing he could say that they hadn't already said to each other hours before. They had gone around and around with their fears, taking turns convincing each other that Maleva Krogh had not returned, and then losing all peace of mind in the next instance because… what if she had?

Lord Doom would protect them.

But did he know?

Doom knew all.

But he wasn't here. And Ewald saw her.

No. Please no. She couldn't be here. Nina couldn't go back to that time.

That time of random terror. That time of never sleeping soundly. That time when anyone could be taken away to the castle. Nina's elderly father had been taken away in the middle of the night. Not because he had done something to anger the Kroghs. He was taken, Nina learned later, because he had been chosen in a game of chance.

She wasn't here. She wasn't here. She wasn't here.

The rain was hard. Nina usually found the sound of its rattle on the roof comforting. It made the bed feel warmer, more enveloping. Not now, though. The wind was strong, and the water struck the window with the brittle clack of nails. With every gust, she heard the insistent scrabble of something that wanted into the house.

Stop it. Stop being foolish. Breathe. Get some sleep.

The creak and slam from outside frightened her so badly, it took several long, gasping seconds before she understood what she was hearing. The wind had caught the barn door and was swinging it back and forth.

She listened to the long screech, and the angry bang of the door. For the space of a minute, she tried to ignore it. She didn't want to go out in the rain. But with this wind, the rain would be driving into the barn, getting the feed wet. It wouldn't take much to turn the floor into a stream.

She sighed. She wasn't going to sleep anymore tonight anyway.

Nina got up, felt her way out of the bedroom and into the kitchen. She grabbed a flashlight off the counter, shrugged into her raincoat and shoved her feet into boots. Then she stepped out into the deluge.

The wind whipped rain into her face. She squinted and wiped water from her eyes. The rain came down in streaks through the flashlight beam. Nina shuffled forward through puddles, careful not to slip in the muck. She couldn't see more than a couple of yards ahead. The barn was invisible in the darkness, the uneven rhythm of the shriek and slam of the door her only guide through the downpour. The water ran in torrents at her feet, and the sheep in the pen made petulant sounds at her as she passed.

In spite of her coat and its hood, she was soaked before she was halfway to the barn. Water trickled down her neck and under her nightdress, chilling her. The discomfort was almost welcome. The nightmare receded before it.

The flashlight finally picked out the weathered wall of the barn. Nina hurried over the rest of the distance, risking a fall to get this over and done with. She took hold of the door mid-swing, mentally cursing Ewald for having failed to secure it before bed. The wind hurled its own curse against it, trying to knock her off her feet for having dared interrupt its game with the door. She staggered and slipped, clutching the door to keep from falling.

A scrape came from inside the barn.

Nina froze.

The scrape came again, long and deliberate.

The wind buffeted her again, as if mocking her. *It wasn't me! It wasn't me!*

Nina hesitated. She looked back in the direction of the house. She thought about the shotgun just inside the door.

Scraaaaaaape. Then *tap, tap, tap against metal.*

Go back. Get the gun. Wake Ewald.

She shone the flashlight into the barn, moving the beam back and forth. It was pitch dark in there, and the beam was too narrow. It passed over stacks of feed and tools hanging on the wall. The shadows jumped, jagged with the shapes of blades.

She wasn't going in there. She was going back. She let go of the door.

A clawed hand snaked out of the dark and grabbed her wrist. Nina screamed. She tried to pull away, and shone the light on her attacker.

Maleva Krogh snarled at her. If it had not been for the years of her cruelty, which had implanted her face permanently in the nightmares of every resident of Kroghstein, Nina would not have recognized her. She was transformed, yet still herself, the hate and the greed and the sadism as visible in the lines of her face as they had ever been. Krogh's hairless skull was longer, its dome risen to a point. Her flesh had tightened around her bones, as if she were a withered mummy. Her skeleton was long and angular, and her dark clothing hung too loosely on her frame. Her joints stuck out like incipient horns, tearing through the cloth over her coat sleeves and trousers. Her open jaws bristled with needle-like teeth.

Her grip was iron, and the feel of her skin was rough and cold, a lizard's hide.

Nina screamed again and pulled.

"No," Krogh hissed. "You are going nowhere. I have come to reclaim my rights. You are mine."

The feel of the grip changed. Krogh's flesh squirmed like maggots, and it scraped against Nina's wrist. Her scream caught in her throat. Krogh was suddenly inside her mind, and a will like claws seized her being and pulled it out of her. She spasmed as her memories and her loves and her hates and her fears and her joys and everything that defined Nina Lang were torn from her. She was being devoured, and she knew she was being devoured. That was the last thing she would ever know.

But the pain of the loss was only beginning.

When there was nothing left to feed on, Krogh released Nina Lang. She licked her lips. As she had consumed the final portions of Nina's self, her hunger and her anger had become so acute that she had sunk her teeth into Nina's neck, tearing out a chunk of flesh, splashing her face and tongue with blood. And so she tasted all that was Nina Lang.

Krogh looked down at the fallen woman. She knew everything about her. She had the memories that Nina had long since lost in her subconscious. Krogh knew every detail of her infancy. She knew every detail of Nina's great-grandmother's face, seen only once as she leaned over the crib. She knew every day of Nina's life. She knew every one of her fears. She knew how Nina had thought of her with terror in the years before Doom. And she savored Nina's final memory, and final horror.

Krogh had played an important role in shaping the identity of Nina Lang. And Nina Lang was a citizen of Kroghstein. That meant she belonged to Krogh. It was fitting, then, that Krogh lay claim to what was hers.

Nina began to move again. The shriveled husk of her body shivered and jerked. Her fingers hooked into claws and scratched in desperate fury at the air. Her skull lengthened, pressing hard at the taut, withered leather of her flesh. Her hair fell off in a single clump. Her lips pulled back over teeth that narrowed and sharpened. Hunger remade her in Krogh's image.

The urvullak that had been Nina Lang jumped to its feet. It swayed, head jerking in sharp, rapid movements, as if searching out a scent. She snarled, eyes wide and blank and mindless. There was instinct there, but no memories. Krogh had them all, and, through her, the Devourer. Nina had only their trace, and the need to replace them. The need to feed.

Nina loped through the rain on her longer, angular limbs. Krogh followed, the darkness limpid before her transformed eyes. Nina reached the farmhouse just as Ewald, alerted by her scream, stepped outside. She fell on him, teeth snapping and tearing at his flesh. The attack was frenzied, rabid. As Nina pulled away hunks of flesh, her hands shredded Ewald's shirt and clutched his arms. Through her grip, his self flowed into her. It did not stay with Nina. What respite the urvullak experienced from her hunger was short lived. As surely as the truth of the divine right of monarchs, the essence of Ewald flowed out of Nina and into Krogh, and to the Devourer in its prison.

Krogh hissed in satisfaction. She no longer breathed. Her lungs served no use except as a means of expression. They did so now. She uttered the sound of the hunter pleased by the kill. She was not satisfied, though. She never would be. Not when there were billions of souls to consume.

Nina fed, and Ewald transformed. Now there were two quivering, growling, ravening husks. They ran through the night and the rain, down the slope of the land, toward the village. Krogh stayed close behind, watching and learning, and eager for the new prey that would come her way. They scrambled down the cliff face, agile as spiders, and then they were twisted shadows rushing through the narrow streets of Kroghstein.

The village was hers by name. This night, it would learn that truth again.

Krogh knew where the Langs were going. She knew the village as they did, and she knew where their adult children were living. The Langs knew only hunger, and the instinct, driven by the echoes of what they had been, driving them to feed on what they had known.

Once they were properly in the village, Krogh stopped following the first of her urvullak. They would feed, and in so doing, they would feed her. She did not need to guide them to their prey. Nor did she need to guide what would happen after that. Hunger would make its way through the village.

She made for another destination. She walked the deserted streets, in no hurry now that more and more selves would soon be coming to her, answering the call of her hunger, and the gravitational pull of growing power. Water poured down in cataracts from overflowing gutters. It rushed over the cobblestones. There was no one outside, and there was no light behind the shutters of the blank-faced houses that she passed. The gray facades were heavy with the sleep within the walls. The streets were so narrow, they were wells of night, and would hold the darkness long after the sun had risen. Krogh was a phantom, the dark within the dark, the shadow of the end that came through the shutters, touching the slumber of the people inside with the premonitions of the feast.

Krogh made her way to the center of the village, to the cramped square before the town hall. The steep gables of the building lowered over the square and its wrought-iron fountain. The wind caught the spray from the mouths of the entwined salamanders, undulating it like a whip.

Krogh crossed the square and stood for a moment before the heavy wooden doors. In the past the doors had always been opened at her approach. No one dared risk the caprices of her anger, not until the last time she had come Kroghstein. Doom had killed King Vladimir, smashed his regime and broken the Kroghs. The walls of the castle had been breached, and the mob rampaged through its halls. Maleva had fled ahead of the villagers' wrath, and she had come to Henry Waldman, the burgomeister, for refuge. He owed her that. He was the authority in the village, her family's deputy. It was his responsibility to act for the rightful hierarchy.

The coward refused to open the doors to her. He betrayed the Kroghs and threw his lot in with the usurper.

Krogh had pounded against the doors, calling to Waldman and looking over her shoulder. It wouldn't be long before someone saw her. In the end, Waldman threw open the shutters of an upper story window.

"You aren't coming in," he had said. "Your time is finished at last. Stay there and be caught, or run away to starve in the forest. I don't care."

"I'll see you damned for this!" she vowed.

Waldman laughed, sounding giddy with anger and relief. "I see you damned now!" he said, and he slammed the shutters closed.

Krogh pounded the doors once more, hard enough to make her knuckles bleed. Then she heard shouting in the streets. The villagers were looking for her.

She had fled then. And now she was in front of the doors again.

She struck the doors, and they shattered as if struck by a battering ram. She strode into the dark entrance hall. The wind and the rain swept in with her.

Lights went on upstairs in the burgomeister's quarters, as Krogh started up the staircase. Krogh squinted, the light painful. She reached the upper floor as Henry Waldman emerged from his bedroom into the corridor.

Waldman was a soft-looking man in his sixties. White hair framed a bald crown like a surprised cloud. When he saw Krogh, he gasped and stumbled back. There was nowhere for him to run, and she advanced on him until he was trapped against the wall.

"Do you know me, Burgomeister Waldman?" She didn't take hold of him yet. She wanted to savor the moment. She wanted him to form this memory, so she could taste the moment again from his perspective.

He was already pale, but when she spoke, he turned sheet-white.

"I think you do," said Krogh. "You forgot yourself, Waldman, fifteen years ago. You forgot to whom you owed fealty."

He was shaking his head in denial of her words, or of her presence before him.

"The true owner of Kroghstein has returned, Waldman. And I am bringing retribution."

The man fumbled at his neck and pulled out a crucifix on the end of a chain. With a shaking hand, he held it out in front of him. "Begone..." he stammered. "In the name of..."

Krogh took the cross from him and held it up to his face. "What did you think to accomplish with this?" she snarled. "What do you take me for?" She hurled the cross down the hall.

Understanding dawned on Waldman's face, and with it, his trembling grew worse. "Urvullak," he whispered. The name had not been spoken aloud for a century.

Krogh nodded, pleased by the sound of those syllables coming from the lips of a man about to die. "Urvullak," she repeated. Then she grabbed his wrist. He jerked in psychic agony. She opened her mouth wide, and plunged into the feast.

Afterwards, when the husk of Waldman scuttled out of the town hall in search of prey, Krogh climbed out of the bedroom window and up onto the roof. She perched on the peak of the gable in the driving rain, and she listened to the town. As the essences of more and more victims flowed into her, she began to hear the screams. They made her laugh.

They only grew worse with the coming of dawn.

TEN

He couldn't go on. He had to rest, though his intuition cried out for him to keep smashing the wall, to break through the wall sooner, faster.

After reading *Phantasmus*, Doom had attacked the barrier again, striking it with all the energy he could muster. With the coming of dawn, he was spent. The premonitions of urgency wouldn't let him sleep, but he had to give himself the chance to recharge psychically.

Doom went topside again and walked away from the dig site, heading up the mountain slope behind his quarters. He tried to keep his frustration at bay. He breathed deeply. The air was fresh, crisp with height. The dawn's light, sullen and gray, did not so much dispel the darkness of the night as reshape the shadows. The pine trees ahead stood guardians over a cache of night that would not vanish with day. It lurked between their trunks, looking out at Doom with knowing intent.

Go back down. Get back to work. Break the wall.

He had to, and he couldn't. Not yet. Perhaps in another

hour or two, he would have the mystical strength to force the breach wider and deeper again.

Gravel crunched under his feet. There was no other sound in the bowl. The workers who were still stationed above ground had not yet stirred. Silence hung over the slopes like mist.

Doom approached the trees. He had no conscious destination. He just needed to walk. If he kept his body busy, that would ease the frustration, and his mind would get a little rest, at least.

He was ten yards from the trees and their darkness when a single raven's caw emerged from the woods. It rang over the bowl, a warning and a scraping toll of mourning. Doom stopped for a moment. He listened. For what, he didn't know.

The silence dropped again.

He started forward, and the trees erupted with ravens. Hundreds of birds flew out of the shadows. They became a chaotic cloud of wings and beaks. Their flapping was the sound of the day being torn. Their cries were a collective scream of anger. The cloud rose higher, spread wider, darkness shrieking with violent laughter.

Doom froze.

Dreamlike in its irrationality, the conviction came to him that while he could see the ravens, there was still a chance of stopping what they symbolized. While they filled the sky above the mountain bowl, if he could break the wall and seize the Devourer he would have his prize and disaster would not come, the disaster he could not divine, but whose premonition tormented him.

And then, their calls turning to mockery, the ravens flew

away. They carried hope with them, a thing turned to carrion in their claws.

Too late! their echoes sneered. *Too late! Too late! Too late!*

Doom turned and raced down the slope. He plunged into the shaft, jetpacks firing on full. He would find the strength. He would find the energy.

The laughter of fate followed him.

Too late! Too late! Too late!

What was worse than the laughter was the realization of just how irrational his conviction had been. There had never been a moment to act while the black cloud circled. It was already too late. It had been before the ravens flew.

Otto Hagen ambushed Kariana Verlak the moment she stepped into the security center of Castle Doom. She hadn't even had her morning coffee yet, and the terrier eagerness on the young man's face was more than she felt up to at that moment. Behind him, shift supervisor Isa Kruger shrugged apologetically at Verlak.

"Monitor Hagen insisted on speaking with you, Captain Verlak," said Kruger.

"If you have something to report, you should go first to Supervisor Kruger," Verlak reminded Hagen.

The junior monitor nodded vigorously, freckled cheeks reddening with anxiety. "I understand, captain, I do. I really do." He looked back at Kruger. "I apologize, supervisor. I mean no offense. I only just realized what I was seeing, and I think it might be very important, and I–"

Verlak cut him off to get to the point. "And you knew that I was due to arrive. All right. Let's see what's concerning you."

She clapped Kruger on the shoulder as she went by. "Thank you, Isa. Go get some sleep."

She followed Hagen down the long rows of monitoring stations. The security center tracked activity in the castle, in Doomstadt and across Latveria. The castle guard and the military were one organization, making Verlak its senior officer, reporting directly to Doom. Following the same principle, the security center of the castle was also the security center of the nation. Much of the heavy lifting of Latverian surveillance was automated, but hundreds of human monitors tracked the data feeds round the clock, trained to watch for the anomalies and subtle hints of sedition that a computer, unable to read the nuances of human behavior, might miss. The front wall of the center was a massive bank of screens, displaying the zones of current interest for the entire hall.

Hagen's station was at the end of a row, and most of the way towards the back of the center's amphitheater. As a junior monitor, he was tasked with the surveillance of a lightly populated sector of little strategic importance. A handful of remote villages in the Carpathians fell under his remit. Verlak liked his commitment to his duty, though his eagerness to please was so earnest that it sometimes had the opposite effect.

Hagen sat down and typed quickly, opening up a number of windows on his screen. Verlak stood behind his seat and watched.

"It's Kroghstein," said Hagen.

"What's happening there?" Verlak asked.

"Nothing, captain. That's the problem. That's why I didn't notice anything until a few minutes ago."

"Why is nothing the problem?"

"It's the kind of nothing," said Hagen. "There has been no phone activity of any kind in the village for the last three hours."

Verlak looked at the timeline in one of the frames on the screen. "It's a small village," she said. "How much phone traffic does it usually have at four in the morning?"

"Very little, if any," Hagen admitted. "That's another reason why I didn't think there was a problem at first. But it isn't just the phones. There's been no internet traffic either. No data usage at all. There's usually a little. Somebody who can't sleep, someone who has to get up very early…"

"Yes. I get the picture. Go on."

"And look, captain." He pointed at a graph. "There *was* some activity during the night. Then it drops to nothing over a short period of time. There's been no resumption."

Verlak looked at Hagen's data. He was right. No usage at all, and it was after eight in the morning. That was unusual. She frowned, feeling the first tingling of concern. "Has Kroghstein lost power?"

"No. It's still on the grid. There is some electrical consumption happening."

"Call the town hall," Verlak ordered. On another screen, she called up the list of the town's authorities. *Show me a sign of life, Burgomeister Waldman. I would be very grateful for that.*

Hagen tapped in the burgomeister's number. It rang repeatedly. No one answered.

"Try some other residences," said Verlak. "Any ones. It doesn't matter." *Come on. Somebody talk to us.*

Hagen tried one home after another. There was no answer from them, either.

Now Verlak was worried. "You were right to speak with me, Monitor Hagen," she said. "You've done well. Come with me." She strode back down the row.

"Where are we going?" he asked, hurrying to keep up with her.

"To Kroghstein. You are its monitor, and that means your duty is in the field as well as in front of that screen."

A Doombot and a squadron of drones escorted the combat helicopter as it flew north toward Kroghstein. The landscape became more and more empty of human habitation. The main agricultural lands of Latveria were already far behind. Once in the Carpathians, habitations became sparse.

Verlak sat in the troop compartment with Hagen and a squad of ten guards. Like the others, Hagen wore body armor and carried a pistol. He hadn't had his full field training yet, but he knew how to use his equipment. This would be good experience for him. He was showing promise.

Verlak willed the helicopter to fly faster. The hour it took to reach Kroghstein was too long. She was growing more concerned all the time. She glanced at her watch. It had been another five minutes since she had last checked with Hagen. "Anything new?" she asked.

He looked up from his tablet. "No," he said. "No data usage. No change, captain."

The helicopter bucked through some turbulence, and Hagen's complexion turned green.

Kroghstein is twenty miles from the dig, Verlak reminded herself yet again. She was worried about Orloff. She was worried about the possibility of a connection between the dig and Kroghstein's silence. A link seemed unlikely. But she couldn't discount it. She knew to be wary of coincidences. She knew they were not to be trusted, and could be dangerous illusions.

And Walpurgis Night was still a recent memory.

This wasn't that, though, she told herself. If Hell had burst from the dig site, she would have heard.

There was smoke rising from Kroghstein when the helicopter drew near. The pilot flew low, and Verlak leaned forward, head out the side door, surveying the village. The smoke was from burning houses. At least three, Verlak judged. It was hard to tell. The smoke was thick, and sat over the entire village, obscuring much of the ground below.

Damn. Damn, damn, damn. She was going to regret waking up this morning. *Please let this just be an attack by Fortunov's partisans.*

But why here? There was no strategic value to Kroghstein.

"Is there any sign of life?" Hagen asked.

"Not that I can see," said Verlak. "No one seems to be doing anything about the fires, at any rate." She tapped the mike on her headset. "Take us down," she told the pilot. "There's room to land in front of the town hall."

There was less smoke in the open space of the square, though it still roiled in the wind from the rotors. Verlak and her squad jumped out as soon as the aircraft touched down. Pistol drawn, she made straight for the town hall. She paused at the entrance, eyeing the smashed doors.

"What would have–" Hagen began.

Verlak silenced him with a look. Signaling quiet to her team, she moved from room to room on the ground floor. They were all empty. The doors to the offices were locked, and had to be forced.

"They don't look as if they've been disturbed," said Hagen.

Verlak agreed. "Still closed up for the night. Even with fires burning in town."

Upstairs, they found the windows of the bedroom wide open. A crucifix lay on the floor at one end of the hall. There were bloodstains at the other.

"No body," said Verlak. "No other signs of violence." The destruction of the doors seemed out of place. It was too much.

And where was everybody?

She headed back outside, then took the squad down the street opposite the town hall. Smoke rolled between the houses. The doors of every home the guards moved past hung open. Verlak split the squad in two, each group entering the buildings on one side of the street. They were systematic, checking every house for an entire block. The lights were on in some. Others were completely dark. Broken windows, overturned furniture, torn scraps of clothing and splashes of blood showed that struggles had taken place. But there were no bodies anywhere.

Verlak turned right at the first intersection, and the next group of houses were more of the same, some with lights on, some with them off. "Whatever happened wasn't instantaneous," she said. "Some people were woken in the dark. Some never woke. Some might have slept until dawn. What happened took some time, but it was still fast." This wasn't the work of Fortunov. He wouldn't wipe out a village. She'd give him that much.

"You think it's over, captain?" Hagen asked.

"I think Kroghstein is deserted," she said. That was what worried her the most. What human agency would kill everyone and vanish without trace?

None that she could think of.

The squad regrouped before moving on. The guards moved past one of the burning houses. All that remained was a charred ruin, blackened timbers sticking out like broken bones. Smoke billowed out of the smoldering center, gray and choking. The rubble cracked and settled, and it was only after the fire was behind them that Verlak realized there was another sound in the ghost village. It was a scrabbling against metal, as if there were a large animal trapped nearby.

Verlak followed the noise. She rounded the next corner. Where this street met another, two cars had collided. One of them had flipped over.

"People were in a hurry to leave," said Hagen.

Verlak nodded. For the impact to be that hard, the cars would have had to be going at a reckless speed along the village's cramped and twisting streets.

The scrabbling noise was coming from the other side of the overturned vehicle. Verlak split the squad again. She and the guards approached the wrecks and circled them on both sides.

Hagen gasped when they saw what was pinned beneath the car. It had been human, Verlak thought. Its features had become rodent-like, and the body, caught at the waist, had the texture of a sun-leathered mummy. It snarled and hissed at them, and dragged its claws on the ground, trying to pull free of its prison. It strained, shrieked in bestial frustration and battered its fists on the wreckage. The hammering and scratching ran up and down the street.

"Doom save us," Verlak breathed. She couldn't look away, yet all she wanted was to burn this thing and erase its sight from her memory.

"What *is* it?" said Hagen, white with horror and revulsion.

The creature snapped at him with a mouth full of needle teeth.

Hagen jerked back, and that only made the thing lunge his way with renewed fury.

"You have a new friend," one of the guards said.

"Don't be afraid. It *does* bite," said another.

They were masking their own terror with bravado, and that jerked Verlak out of her horrified trance. She looked up and saw Hagen blush with anger. He heard only the mockery in the other guards. He was too frightened to see that they were as close to panic as he was. He reacted to his humiliation in the worst way. He tried to prove himself. Verlak realized he was about to do something rash. *Stop*, she thought. *Stop!* She tried to reach out for Hagen. Her body, numbed by shock, was too slow.

"Monitor…" she warned.

Hagen had already stepped forward and aimed a kick at the creature's chin. Its head snapped back, its teeth coming together with the snap of a steel trap. It struck at him with a blur of speed and grabbed his leg with both hands. It yanked back, knocking him down. It ripped his trouser leg open, then seized the exposed flesh.

Hagen screamed. His eyes bulged, staring at nothing. His skin tightened around his skull and began to darken, turning gray. The monster tore into his skin with its teeth.

Shouting in horror, the guards that had teased Hagen

grabbed the monster and tried to pull it off him. They couldn't break its grip, and they couldn't shoot it without hitting the monitor.

Hagen's body shrank in on itself. He stopped screaming. He twitched violently, as if an electrical current were passing through him. He took a shuddering breath, and then his chest was still.

The kill had taken mere seconds.

"Step back," Verlak ordered the guards. There was nothing they could do for Hagen. He was dead. "Stand clear of them." She raised her pistol. She started to pull the trigger. Then she stopped.

Wait. Doom will want to know if this is all there is to these creatures.

If the monster was just a humanoid predator, that was one thing. But the town was empty. There were no bodies. What happened to them? She forced herself to watch.

The monster gnawed on Hagen's leg a bit longer, then released him. It looked at the body with an expression of despairing hunger. It mewled like a cat, pathetic in its need for more of what it consumed.

Hagen started to twitch again. His skin kept shrinking against his bones. His freckles were gone, subsumed by the withered, cracked, thick texture of the flesh. He whipped his head back and forth, jaw working, chewing air. There was a cracking sound as his skull reshaped itself.

He was turning into the same kind of monster. And there was nothing holding him down.

Verlak shot him. The energy blast from the pistol blew his head apart. The body kept moving. The hands with their new claws reached out for prey. Verlak kept firing, pausing between each shot to see how much it took to finally still the horror.

The body didn't stop moving until there was almost nothing left of it.

The other guards aimed their guns at the trapped creature.

"No," said Verlak. "Send for a containment field. We need to capture this one. Lord Doom will wish to examine it."

She thought about the dig, and she wished she believed in coincidences.

ELEVEN

Doom received the message from Verlak at midday. He paused in the middle of gathering more sorcerous energy for another blast at the door. Motionless, arms raised, power crackling around his fists, he listened to the relayed recording. Then, with a hiss of frustration, he dispelled the energy, lowered his arms and ordered the drill shut down.

He examined the wall. The crack in the matter was growing, and it wasn't resealing itself as soon as the drill withdrew. He had no idea how far there was to go. The substance of the wall blocked Zargo's perceptions of the earth. He saw only an interruption of indefinite dimension between them and the Devourer. None of the technological scans Doom had deployed were able to pierce the wall's secrets at all. It appeared as a blank on every reading, an insult to his gaze.

Doom bristled at the idea of stopping the work, no matter how brief the pause was. It would have been easy to dismiss the possibility of a connection between the dig and what Verlak had found in Kroghstein. It would also have been a mistake, and he would permit no error to derail his project. He was so close to the goal, so close to taking the Devourer's power for himself. If he pressed too hard, and fell with the goal in sight, he would have only his own folly to blame.

He took slow and even breaths, calming his fury. He circled the standing stones carefully, ensuring their wards were unbroken. He checked the signals he was receiving from the pyramid. The trap was still ready to spring the moment the psychic atmosphere in the region shifted to a dangerous nature.

"You are held," he whispered to the thing beyond the wall. "Your prison will not release you until I am ready to place you in a new one. Tarry here, then. I will come again soon."

He paused. Calmer, he listened to Verlak's message again. It troubled him. He thought about the energy spikes that had escaped the region of the dig.

Could they be responsible?

Responsible for what?

They were psychic jolts, certainly. But they would have dispersed quickly. There was no way of sealing the Devourer off utterly. As long as there were memories and there was death, all of creation had a link to it. A short spike in the link was not enough for major consequences.

There might be a way...

That was speculation. The odds against it happening were tremendous.

But not impossible.

He would reserve judgment until he saw for himself what was in Kroghstein.

Doom marched out from the protective circle. Orloff and

Zargo were at what had become their habitual observation posts. Orloff was there much less than Zargo. Her work on the helmet was consuming her, and she had not been there when Doom had last paused briefly in the attack on the wall. She was back now, looking tired but driven. Zargo seemed just as tired, lines of strain deepening at the corners of his mouth.

Doom stopped in front of them. "Captain Verlak has contacted me from Kroghstein," he said. "There is a matter there that requires my immediate attention. Doctor Orloff, you will accompany me. The matter is of relevance to your work too, I believe." He looked at Zargo. "Until my return, you will have command of this site."

Zargo blinked. "I will?"

"There must be no further work attempted until I authorize it. The precautions I have put in place will prevent anything from escaping. But that is no excuse for a lack of vigilance. That is something you are not usually without."

"I will keep watch," Zargo vowed. He met Doom's gaze steadily. As tired as the geomancer was, he also seemed stronger than he had been since the night of the demons. "What are the limits to my authority?" he asked.

"In my absence, none. If something must be done, then you will have it done. See that you do not abuse my trust."

Zargo nodded.

Good. We understand each other. Given a free choice, Zargo would have shut the dig down altogether. But that choice was not his, and never would be, and he knew it. Perhaps he sensed, too, that it was too late for any of them to walk away again. The wall was cracked. The prison had weakened. Leaving the Devourer alone was no longer an option.

"Come, doctor," said Doom. "We have a journey to make." He smiled tightly behind his mask. "We have a wonder to see."

The last time Doom had been in Kroghstein had been more than fifteen years ago. His visit had been brief, and savage. He had shattered the defenses of the castle and broken the resistance of the Kroghs. The battle had been a minor skirmish in his destruction of the forces of King Vladimir. If the Kroghs had thought that their low profile would save them, and that they would continue to wield power behind the scenes in the new regime, they learned how wrong they were that day. Their time was over. Their cruelty was over. Doom stayed long enough to see that the people of the village were taking the vengeance that was rightfully theirs, and then departed.

He had renamed many cities and landmarks of Latveria. He had erased every commemoration of the Fortunovs. Vladimir had killed his parents. Just one of the punishments Doom meted out to the Fortunovs was to remove all trace of their memory from the country they had believed was theirs by divine right.

He had left Kroghstein's name untouched. Their name was the most hated in Latveria. Even the Fortunov loyalists feared and despised the Kroghs. The village's name remained as a reminder of the salvation Doom had brought to Latveria. It was a reminder of what might happen without him.

The helicopter that had Orloff for a passenger set down in the town hall square next to the transport aircraft. Doom landed on the other side of the fountain, where Verlak and her squad had established a containment field around their prisoner.

The feral body had lost both its legs. It propelled itself with arms that were longer than they should be, and stronger than they looked, given how thin they were. It launched itself repeatedly at the invisible wall that kept it from its prey and held it inside a square ten foot square. Four energy poles, one at each corner, kept the field charged.

Doom stared at a creature he had only ever seen in the woodcuts of *Phantasmus*. What had brought this out of legends and into existence, and why now? Was this how the Devourer responded to his threat? It was a bad memory made flesh.

Orloff joined the group. She touched Verlak quickly on the shoulder, and they gave each other a quick look of relieved affection. Then Orloff focused her attention on the monster.

"What," she said, "in the name of sanity, is *that*?"

"It is an urvullak," said Doom. It felt strange to pronounce that word aloud. Verlak's description, in her message, of what it had done had told Doom what to expect when he saw the creature. And its appearance removed any doubt as to its nature.

Some of the guards shifted uneasily. One of them made the sign of the evil eye at the urvullak. Verlak repeated the word as if testing its reality.

"You have heard of them," Doom said to her, seeing the set of her jaws becoming tighter.

"I heard some stories when I was little," she said.

"I didn't," said Orloff. "What's an urvullak?"

"An old fear," said Doom. "A very old one. So old that it has faded from much of Latveria's folklore. You are looking at a memory returned, doctor."

"Those teeth," said Orloff. "Is it a vampire?"

"No, though the terrors associated with them are not unrelated. There may be a kind of parentage. The urvullak do not consume blood, though." To Verlak, he said, "That is not what happened to Monitor Hagen, I gather."

"It didn't suck his blood," she confirmed. "It bit into him, but wasn't eating him exactly, either. It was its touch that seemed fatal."

"The urvullaks devour the soul," said Doom. "They have no need of teeth to do that, though their hunger drives them to savage the flesh. That, at least, is what the lore that has come down to us maintains."

"They devour the soul," Orloff repeated, looking thoughtful.

"I can believe that," said Verlak. "It looked like everything that was Hagen was being drained from him."

"That sounds like what I experienced," said Orloff. "The pull of the Devourer."

"Yes," said Doom. "There is clearly a link." The earlier anger he had felt when facing that possibility had melted away. He felt vindicated instead. He was right about the nature of the Devourer. He was right to hunt it. It was now even more urgent that he imprison the being and place it under his control. He would put an end to this threat. However the urvullak had come into being, Doom would break the link to the Devourer.

You don't have it in your power yet, he reminded himself. There was a crisis to be dealt with immediately. The entire village of Kroghstein was missing.

"What happened to Hagen, then, is what happened to the rest of the village," said Verlak. "Is that right?"

"It is," Doom growled. And there would be retribution. The

people of Kroghstein were his subjects. He did not take their annihilation lightly.

Verlak looked grim. "Hagen transformed very quickly. If they reach more populated areas, we'll have a plague on our hands. If we don't already."

"How quickly can they travel?" said Orloff. "Are they traveling on foot?" She gestured at the urvullak. "I mean, *can* these things drive? It looks mindless."

"If the folklore concerning them is to be believed," said Doom, "they have no more than a certain instinctual cunning. What is left of their minds is consumed by the need to feed. Their selves have been taken from them, and that includes their knowledge and memories."

"There are a number of vehicles parked on the streets," Verlak said. "The collision we found looks like it was the result of people trying to flee."

"That's a mercy, then," said Orloff. "Even if it's a small one."

"There is another factor," said Doom. "In the tales of the urvullaks, there is always a ruler. One of their kind who is in full possession of their faculties, and who commands the spread of the plague."

"You believe the legends are right?" Orloff asked.

"Until we know more, they are all we have to go on. For now, then, yes, I believe there is a monarch of the urvullaks. There must be another actor involved. The energy spikes would not have been enough, of themselves, to lead to the spontaneous creation of the urvullaks. There has been an intervention, somehow, by someone." *We are in Kroghstein. That may not be a coincidence.*

"Transport this creature to Castle Doom," he said to the

guards. "Doctor Orloff, though I do not want you to neglect your work on the helmet, it is now your primary responsibility to study the urvullak. I strongly suspect that the two lines of research will be of use to each other. Find out this creature's weaknesses."

"That would be good to know," said Verlak. "It took a lot to stop the one that Hagen became. A shot to the head isn't enough."

"Does the lore help us here?" Orloff asked.

"It does not," said Doom. "At least, not the few tales that I recall. They are full of warnings, and empty of hope.

"Return to Doomstadt, all of you," he continued. "Await my commands. There is something I must learn before we take further action. Captain Verlak, alert me the instant any other villages go dark."

Doom flew south from Kroghstein. He pictured the geography of the region and calculated the distance the urvullaks might have been able to travel, assuming some had left Kroghstein an hour or more before the anomalies had begun to appear on Hagen's screen. He set a mental radius around Kroghstein. South was the easiest direction to travel on foot. Much of the route would be downhill, heading out of the mountains. South, then, would mark the farthest point the creatures could have traveled.

At the edge of the radius was the village of Unterschatten.

The day had begun in gloom, and the afternoon was even darker when Doom descended into the center of the village. October was gathering strength, and a chill wind blew fallen leaves in eddies over the dirt roads of the hamlet.

Unterschatten was a tiny cluster of houses, barely large enough to warrant having a name.

The people in the street fell to their knees and lowered their heads before Doom. Others hurried out of their homes and prostrated themselves as well.

"You," Doom said to the nearest peasant, a man in his fifties who looked much older, aged by the harshness of clawing a living from the land in this region. The man raised his head, trembling. "Have there been any strangers here since last night?"

"No, my lord," he quavered.

"Has anyone gone missing?"

The man looked around, uncertain.

A woman spoke up. "Where is Hilde Murnau? I haven't seen her all day."

"Where does she live?" Doom asked.

The woman pointed to the northwest slope of the mountain flanks that surrounded the village. The forest was thick there, and a shack was just visible within the pines.

"Wait here for me," said Doom. "Gather everyone. I will speak to you all when I return."

The shadows were thick beneath the trees, as if spreading out from their roots. The shack looked back at him with blank windows, its eyes utterly black. Silence coiled within, ready to strike.

There was no need to call for Hilde Murnau. Doom already knew she would not answer. He tapped once on the rough, splintered door.

Something rustled inside.

Doom struck the door, knocking it off its hinges. From the

darkness within, three urvullak launched themselves at him. They grabbed his arms, their claws breaking against his armor. One of them flung itself at his head, wrapping its limbs around him, its jaws scraping madly at his mask.

Doom triggered his armor's electrical field. The air flashed with lightning, and the charge hurled the urvullaks from him. They crashed into the walls and writhed, screaming, on the floor, their flesh blackened and smoking. They scrabbled forward, their hunger stronger than their wounds. They did not fear him. They saw him only as a living being, and they needed the taste of his soul.

Dispassionately, Doom turned the concussive blasts of his gauntlet on each urvullak in turn. The force of the blasts crushed their bones to powder. Even then, their flattened bodies twitched and squirmed. They could not move, but the hunger still drove them. They were almost shapeless. Their teeth were gone. Their eyes were jellied.

Doom walked around them and noted the way the twitches shook the masses of flesh. Something in the urvullaks sensed him and tried to reach him.

He pulled out his blaster from its holster, adjusted its setting to an incinerating charge and fired three times.

He walked out of the burning shack once he was satisfied the cremation of the bodies was thorough.

His mood was grim when he returned to the village. The mind that commanded the urvullaks was cunning and dangerous. It was able to control the creatures, making them hide in ambush rather than run wild through the village. There was thought and planning here.

He had an enemy.

In Unterschatten, the people had gathered outside to wait for him and know his will. They looked at him with fear and obedience – *as they should.*

"There is no one else unaccounted for?" he asked.

There was not. That was a bit of good news. Perhaps he might yet be able to prevent the worst from happening, though the measures he would have to take were drastic.

"You will leave here at once," he said. "Do not return to your homes. Head south, until you are met by the army. Do not stop, for any reason, until then."

They obeyed without question. Because they did, they might survive the coming night and see another day.

Whether they lived to see another day after that was another question. It depended upon the success of what he must now do.

Doom opened a communications channel with the Latverian Air Force base outside Doomstadt.

TWELVE

Doom flew straight up until he was just below the clouds, then headed north until he was over Kroghstein again. He had spoken with Verlak, and she was relaying his orders to the Latverian Army. He had his acknowledgments from the Air Force base. The deployment he had commanded had begun.

It would not be fast enough. And though the checkpoints would be established to deal with the refugees from the Carpathians, there was no way to quarantine the region. It was too wide, and the army did not have anywhere near the troops to cordon it off.

If quarantine was impossible, then sterilization was the one course of action open to him. He grimaced at what lay ahead.

I will not destroy my country. I will not kill those who have not become urvullak.

He had known rulers who, if they had had the power, would not have hesitated to turn the entire mountain chain into lava and glass. He had overthrown one of them.

But he was not Vladimir Fortunov.

Doom looked down at the land below. He was not high enough to see the full region that he had declared infected. Its radius extended a hundred miles from the center of Kroghstein. That was as far as Doom could imagine any of the urvullak traveling in the time since the earliest attacks might have started, with a margin of error built in. He could see a number of the threatened villages from this point, scattered like handfuls of pebbles on the mountain slopes.

The urvullak were down there. They would be in the vicinity of their prey. What he was about to do would destroy most of them.

Not all, though, he thought.

No, not all. He would diminish the threat significantly now. Then he would deal with the new situation. But he had to act decisively in this moment. This was the time for extremity, to prevent total catastrophe.

Doom activated the video communicator in his armor's right wrist. "Evacuation order," he said, and a signal went to the defense infrastructure he had built throughout Latveria. In every town of the infected zone, air raid sirens blasted two short wails and one long one. Every citizen of Latveria knew what that warning meant, and knew to obey it immediately.

"Initiate Damocles," Doom said to the communicator. More than twenty-two thousand miles above, in geostationary orbit, the satellite he had named unfurled its solar panels, powering up its targeting mechanism and emerging from the cloak that had kept it hidden from all observers, human or electronic, on Earth and in the heavens. The screen of Doom's communicator showed the satellite's perspective. The Damocles adjusted its view to match his further commands. The hundred-mile radius of the infection zone appeared in crystalline black-and-white, the villages bright, pulsing scars on the gray faces of the mountainsides.

While he made the final preparations and fed the satellite its targets, Doom waited for the communications the Damocles' decloaking was going to trigger. It was broadcasting its identity, but that would do little to dampen the panicked calls that would be setting digital fires between space agencies and seats of government around the globe.

The panic would be worse if any of them knew the reason for Damocles' appearance.

The world would not learn that reason. He would contain the danger and keep the secret of the urvullak outbreak. The great powers would not have the excuse to look at Latveria as a diseased state. He would not allow them that satisfaction.

The leaders of the United States, Russia and China called Castle Doom. Their demands to speak with him came within seconds of each other. The three calls were transmitted to Doom, and he answered all of them at once.

"I should congratulate you," he said. "The speed of your response and its coordination does you credit. We will therefore be able to deal with our communications more efficiently."

"What the hell is going on?" the American president shouted. "What are you getting up to out there?"

"Is that a weapon?" the Chinese premier and Russian president asked at once.

None of the three sounded interested in efficiency. They sounded terrified, even through the filter of the insta-translator.

"The Damocles is armed," Doom confirmed. "It will be firing momentarily. None of you need be concerned. This is a test, and an entirely internal affair."

"A test that violates every one of our space treaties," the Russian protested.

"You are free to present your objections to the UN Security Council," said Doom. "I repeat, the Damocles is no threat to you. Its position is above Latveria alone."

"Today it is," said the premier.

"If you were willing to consult with us–" the American president began.

Doom cut him off. "I did not accept to speak with the three of you because I wished to *consult you*. I am informing you of two things. The first is that this test is no business of yours. The second is that you are warned not to interfere with internal Latverian affairs."

"But–" said the premier.

"The consequence of interference is retaliation. I trust I am clear."

He ended the communication. The Damocles was ready. It was time.

The Damocles was armed with a cannon. It was an enlarged, amplified version of the antimatter extrapolator, a weapon Doom had first created as a handgun. The satellite's extrapolator was infinitely more devastating, and no less precise.

The first shot of the beam of antimatter particles struck the center of Kroghstein. Shields clicked down over the eye-slits of Doom's mask, protecting his vision from the intensity of the explosion's flare. The village disappeared, atomized. The mountain cracked like glass, and Castle Krogh was gone as if it had never existed. The shockwave raced over the landscape, a foretelling of doom to the other villages in the region. As the mushroom cloud rose to meet the sullen gloom of the sky, Doom flew south, beginning a widening spiral as he redirected the destructive gaze of the Damocles.

Kroghstein had been deserted. The urvullak plague had been total. The other settlements in the infection zone were question marks. Doom put each to the test before triggering the beam. He scanned the villages through the satellite's eyes, looking for survivors.

In the nearest villages to Kroghstein, in every direction, no one emerged from the houses. Doom had the magnification of the image turned up, so he would see any movement in the streets. There was nothing. The villages were lost, and so Doom commanded Damocles to fire, and they vanished too.

He switched the satellite's perspective quickly from village to village, and he dealt with each settlement far faster than he could fly to them. The clouds reflected the nuclear-bright flashes of the explosions, and the terminal booms of matter and antimatter destroying each other reached him long seconds after the act of annihilation was complete. On the screen, each cluster of houses disappeared in a bloom of white followed by the darkness of dust and smoke.

Doom swept the antimatter scythe further out from Kroghstein, and he encountered variations in the reactions to the evacuation order sirens. Where he saw people flee after the alarms sounded, he waited until they were a safe distance before firing the beam. They ran together, some holding hands, some clutching a possession or two that they had grabbed as they left their homes. They were human, and behaving exactly as humans would in the face of a sudden, terrifying event.

Doom watched them, and he pitied them. They were fleeing a war. They were fleeing destruction, like his mother's people had tried to flee the annihilating arm of King Vladimir.

I am sorry for you. Latveria was under his protection. I act as your protector in this moment, but it is not how I would have chosen to do so.

Once the people were out of range, he destroyed the villages all the same. Something might have stayed behind. Something might be hiding that hadn't had the chance to hunt yet.

And there were the settlements where people were fleeing before the warnings sounded. On a different day, with a different threat, he might have been willing to believe that they were running because they saw the flashes in the sky, and heard the blasts, some distant, some drawing nearer.

Doom did not believe that on this day. These people were trying to escape a terror on the ground. He saw the figures in pursuit.

There was no one to save there. The urvullak were fast. The fates of the villagers were preordained.

Doom snarled. *You, who have forced my hand, I will make you pay for these deaths.*

Damocles fired, erasing the living and the husks together.

Doom spiraled further and further out, passing over the sites of devastation. On the communicator screen, the last of the villages in the hundred-mile radius was gone. The clouds of dust rose in monumental columns to the sky. It looked as if the Carpathians had become a chain of volcanoes in full eruption. Outside the blast areas, though, the destruction was minimal. There were no fires. The devastation of Damocles was surgical.

"Sterilization complete," Doom muttered. Though he knew it was not. "Damocles retract," he said. The satellite's image winked out from his video communicator. In orbit, Damocles retracted into its shell, becoming inert and undetectable once more.

By the time Doom had completed his initial overflight of the zone of infection, the drone squadrons arrived. They would begin grid searches across the Carpathians, looking for any urvullak who had escaped the antimatter beams.

They would find some targets. He knew they would. He also knew they would not find all the urvullak.

None of this was enough. He had taken a first step. He had bought Latveria some time. Enough, he hoped, for him to determine what the next step should be.

Doom had to get back to the dig. The wall waited to be breached, and the Devourer to be captured. Once it was in his control, that would bring an end to the urvullak. If the Devourer had brought them into being, and he was certain it had, then it was the key to destroying them. But the wall was strong. It would take time to break through. Doom pictured the pyrrhic victory of reaching the Devourer after all of Latveria had succumbed to the plague of the urvullak. The danger felt uncomfortably close to being realized. He could not afford to make the wrong decision.

Doom dropped lower, flying just above the treetops. He would survey the region for one more hour, then make for the dig. He had to accept that his attention was going to be divided now. That angered him. He despised compromise.

But the demands of the dig and the hunt were both strong and connected. He would have to be present for both at once.

The glow of a fire under the shadows of a wooded slope caught his eye. It was miles from the nearest village, and it was too small to be a forest fire. He flew down, gauntlet ready to launch a concussion blast. He found a campfire, burning low. There was no one around.

There was a boulder beside the fire. One face had been scraped free of moss. On it was a sentence written in charcoal. Doom stared at it in growing rage. The words were a taunt, a challenge, and they mocked the work he had done this day.

The past has returned. Latveria is mine.

THIRTEEN

Krogh knew the destruction would come. Doom would hear of what happened in Kroghstein, and his wrath would fall on the village, and everywhere else where he found signs of the urvullak. She knew it from the moment she began her attack. His retaliation was a given. It always had been.

Krogh had survived fifteen years in the wilderness. So she knew not just to anticipate Doom's attack, but how to counter it. She held the totality of her army in her mind. The stolen identities, lives and memories of hundreds were in her now, and the physical shells the souls had belonged to were as much hers to move as she saw fit as the fingers of her hands. So she moved them, chess pieces on a board that Doom thought he could destroy. He could not. He was opening with a sweeping attack, and forgetting the devastation that pawns and their numbers could wreak.

Once she had taken everyone from Kroghstein, she split her forces into two groups. The urvullak with strong links to other villages, she sent to run down new prey. Those whose lives had been more insular, she sent into the wilderness, spreading them out deep in the woods. They cried out in their hunger, desperate for lives to consume, and though she could perceive the world through the eyes of only one urvullak at a time, she could impose silence on them all with a single thought. It didn't matter how far they wandered, or how many miles any of the urvullak were from her, the strength of her control remained the same.

In the hours she had before Doom struck, she grew her army. The urvullak hit one village after another, and she repeated the pattern of Kroghstein. For every monster she sent to another settlement, there was another she directed into the woods. Her reach spread in every direction, but mostly to the south, towards the more populated regions of Latveria, towards conquest.

The first blast came from the direction of Kroghstein, as she had expected. She was thirty miles away from the village, in a narrow fold of a south-facing slope. Ancient oaks, their trunks thick with history, flanked her, rising from the banks of the rocky gully down which she walked, a perpetually shadowed stream rushing and frothing over the stone. She heard the concussion and did not look back. There would be nothing to see from where she was. The village was gone, but she had already destroyed it. Her family's castle was gone too, she knew. The boom was the sound of it being erased forever, all evidence it had ever existed gone. She wondered if Doom intended the insult. She doubted it. She doubted he suspected she was his enemy. Kroghstein was just the village where things had begun. There were plenty of other hamlets close to other ruined houses in the Carpathians and across Latveria. Many families had fallen with King Vladimir.

Whether he had even thought about the home of the Kroghs or not, Doom had sinned against the family again. Krogh added the destruction of her home to the tally of his crimes. He would pay for them all, with interest.

So, she did not look back. The way forward was the path down which the past would return. And the way to reach it was, right now, through stillness. She commanded her urvullak to hide. There was a half dozen with her in the gully, and they crouched with her against the right bank, dark shapes against dark rock, cold and motionless as death. They did not breathe. Their hearts did not beat. There were invisible to any observer who was not present with them.

Elsewhere, across the slopes of the mountains, the other urvullak obeyed her command in the same instant. They hid in caves, under trees and between roots. Some squeezed into animal burrows, Krogh's will forcing them in as brutally as if she had pushed them in physically. They squirmed into the tunnels, heedless of the dirt that shoved up mouth and nose and eyes, or the biting and scratching from the residents of the burrows. Then they too were as motionless as if they had found their graves.

In many ways, they might as well be in tombs. They were dead by any rational measure. It had taken Krogh almost an hour after her transfiguration to realize that she was only breathing out of habit, and that she had to draw air only if she wanted to speak.

So this is death, she had thought. She was frightened for a moment, and then the fear gave way to excitement. Death had not ended things. It had begun them. She was strong as she had never been in life. There was still destruction to fear, but little else. *And destroying me will not be easy.*

She clung to the rock, a stillness waiting to be released to strike again, and felt the concussions of Doom's rage reverberate through the earth. She knew exactly where each strike hit. She had commanded the urvullak in the villages to continue hunting, if there was prey to be found. Let Doom see some targets. Let him think he was making a difference. Let him think he had not already lost this war. That would make his humiliation and his despair the richer when he faced the truth. Krogh felt the disappearance of every one of the urvullak caught in the blasts. They vanished from her mind, and from her will, scores of sudden amputations.

They were amputations without pain, losses without meaning. She had expected this, prepared for it. The urvullak destroyed were sacrifices to later victory. Even so, her anger roiled. Doom was taking something away from her again. The Kroghs were the ones who took, always. Nothing should ever be taken from them.

She waited impatiently for the blasts to end. There was something she needed to do. She was going to take something from Doom today. He could have his illusion still, but she would give him doubts, too. He thought he would win. She would make him worry about losing, even if he dismissed the concern. She would tell him he would fail.

In the end, she did not wait for Doom's attack to be over. Once the explosions were too far from her to be a threat, she climbed out of the gully. She found a suitable place beneath the trees, one that would be visible from above, and made a fire. Then she used a blackened log to leave her message for Doom, and moved on, swiftly putting distance between herself and the fire. Her escort of urvullak scurried through the underbrush with her.

The past has returned. Latveria is mine.

The simple truth. She might not control Latveria yet. That did not change the fact that it *did* belong to her. And she was the past returned. She was the old order. It would rule again, through her, and it would be greater than before. She had the memories and the power to remake Latveria in the image of that past as it had sought to be.

You cannot destroy me, Doom, because you cannot destroy the past. You destroyed my castle, but not what it represented. It is your present and your future that will die, and be erased.

The explosions ended. Krogh commanded the urvullak to hide again. Doom would be searching for what he had missed. He would know that not all the urvullak would have been in the villages. He would know that they had spread out across the land. She had given nothing away by leaving him the message but hoped she had robbed him of some sleep.

She waited, without moving, for hours. She felt no discomfort, no cramping of the muscles, no need to fidget. She heard the passage of drones overhead, and she gave them nothing to see. She waited, and her slaves waited. The hunger of the urvullak tormented them. She shared their hunger. She also reveled in their pain. It was their punishment. It would be endless. Though they were barely sentient shells of the individuals they had been, they suffered, and suffering was the point.

Once it was fully dark, she put her army on the move

again, staying alert for drones and other surveillance flights. There were hundreds of drones scouring the Carpathians, and they found more of Krogh's army. The harsh whistle and report of blaster fire echoed between the peaks. There were losses.

They didn't matter.

The urvullak spread wider, and found new villages in the mountains and the foothills. Soon, the first city would be in reach. Krogh commanded new attacks, following new tactics. She did not use the sudden, devastating assaults designed to wipe out a village as quickly as possible. That approach had served its purpose, giving her the foundations of her great army. Now she had to be careful. The urvullak had to avoid notice.

Even though she could look through only one pair at a given moment, Krogh had a thousand eyes. She knew all the undead had seen before their transformation, and at will, she could see what each of them saw now. Doom could never surveil the countryside as utterly as she could. She would see more and more as her army grew. And omniscience, the greater promise, waited for her, just over the horizon.

Her eyes saw. And they hunted.

The night bus from Zalbach to Doomsburg was leaving in five minutes, and Jovan Vogel's parents were still refusing to accept that he was going.

"You can't," his mother said. She'd said it a hundred times every day since he had told them he was taking the job in Doomsburg. "You belong here. Who is going to help your father in the bakery?"

They were standing just outside his parents' home. The bakery was on the ground floor, and the few rooms in which they lived were above it. The door was open, and the light from inside seemed to Vogel to be trying to lure him back in. Then the door would shut, and he would never get away.

"Whoever father hires will help him," said Vogel.

"They won't know what to do," his father said.

"Then you'll train them. Like you trained me." He wondered why he was answering them. They'd gone around and around with the same argument for a week. Nothing he said registered. Nothing they said was going to change his mind.

"Why go to Doomsburg to bake when you're already baking here?" his father asked again. "What can you do there that you can't here?"

Everything. That was the truth. The job didn't matter. He just wanted out of Zalbach while he was still in his twenties. Doomsburg was hardly Paris, but it had a population of twenty thousand. By comparison to Zalbach, it might as well *be* Paris, as far as Vogel was concerned. As frustrated as he was, though, he didn't want to hurt his parents. So he trotted out the same reasons he'd been giving them all along. "I'll learn more. I'll have chances I won't have here." That was true enough, if not the reason he wanted out of Zalbach. "I'll be back for visits," he promised. *Just not anytime soon.*

"No," his mother said. "I've had enough of this nonsense." She took hold of his arm. "You come back inside the house at once, and unpack that bag."

He pulled free, and had to pull harder than he would have liked. His physical effort shocked his mother, who stared at him as if he had slapped her. "I'm sorry," he said, and he walked quickly away from the house, the battered old leather bag swinging back and forth with his steps, jouncing against his legs.

The bus stop was just outside the village, at the intersection of the road through the mountains and the dead-end lane that led to Zalbach. The engine was running, and the driver, a middle-aged man with the face of a weary bulldog, gave him a look that told him how close he had cut it. The driver closed the bus door. Vogel barely had time to fall into a seat halfway down the bus before it pulled away.

The bus wasn't crowded. It never was. Vogel guessed there were about a dozen people making the trek to Doomsburg. It looked like the usual mix. People off to visit relatives, others to sell wares, to judge by the boxes they had on the seats beside them. They were all coming back, he thought. *I'm not.* He settled back, relieved to feel Zalbach receding from his life.

The bus rocked back and forth as it took the sharp curves of the road. Vogel leaned his head against the window, looking out into the night. He was glad the thunder and lightning of bombardments had stopped. Midday, when the booms had rolled over Zalbach from the north, he had wondered if he might not be able to leave at all. He had begun to worry that he had waited too long. What if the whatever was happening in the north came for his village too?

He worried, but as long as the explosions stayed far from Zalbach, that was all that mattered. The destruction he was hearing had been commanded by Doom. That went without saying. And it was not his place to know anything more than that.

Late in the day, some refugees had arrived in Zalbach. They

brought tales of evacuation sirens and the annihilation of their homes, but they didn't know why this had happened. They didn't question it, either. It was not their place.

There were drone flights after the explosions, and Vogel had heard them during the evening too. The night was quiet so far, though. Maybe the crisis was past.

The woods grew thicker on either side of the road. The sky was overcast, hiding the moon, and Vogel could see nothing outside. He closed his eyes, and then was jerked forward, banging his head against the seat in front of him, when the driver slammed on the brakes. The bus bumped over something, and there was a scraping sound underneath.

The bus stopped. The driver sat still, clutching the wheel and breathing heavily.

Vogel got up and made his way to the driver. "An animal?" he asked.

The driver gave him a stricken look. "I don't think so." He was ashen.

Vogel swallowed. "We'd better look," he said.

The driver nodded. He opened the doors. "Please wait here," he said to the other passengers, then followed Vogel outside.

As they alighted, there was a dragging sound from under the bus, and then a rough scuttling on the other side of the vehicle. Brush rustled.

"That," said Vogel, "was definitely an animal."

The driver took a deep, relieved breath. "Yes," he said. "Had to be." He turned on a flashlight. "I was so sure I saw a person. But it was just a glimpse."

"I'm happy to tell you that you were wrong," said Vogel.

The driver got down on all fours and shone his beam under the bus. "Whatever it was, it's gone now."

"Any damage?"

"Hard to tell. There might be."

They got back into the bus. Vogel sat down again as the driver tried the engine. Things ground in a disheartening way.

Vogel's heart sank. He had visions of being stuck out here all night.

The driver sighed. "I'm going to have a look," he announced. "See if I can do anything. We don't have the tools for anything major, though, so…" He shrugged, grabbed his flashlight, and went out the door.

"What does he mean by that?" an elderly woman asked.

"He means we're stuck," Vogel told her, a bit more irritably than he had intended.

He heard the driver crawl underneath. There were some clunking sounds, some tapping. Vogel didn't think that boded well.

There was a heavy bump, a grunt, and then silence.

The silence stretched out.

"What's he doing?" a man with boxes in the seat beside him asked.

No one answered. The silence went on. The passengers stirred in their seats.

"Can anyone see him?" someone else asked.

No one could.

"This is ridiculous," said the man with the boxes. He blew air through his walrus mustache in exasperation. "Someone should see if he needs help." The man was speaking loudly, as if to shout down his own unease.

The man looked at Vogel. Vogel looked away. He didn't want to go outside again. The night seemed thicker than it had been, the trees and what they concealed closer.

"*I'll* go, then," said the man. He stood up, and paused for a moment, as if to see if his gesture would shame someone younger into going in his stead.

Vogel stayed where he was. No one else moved.

The man grunted, then stomped down the aisle and out the door.

A few seconds later, he screamed. There was a scuffle, and the screaming stopped.

Vogel lunged out of his seat and down the aisle. He seized the door lever at the driver's seat and yanked it hard. The door slammed shut. Vogel stared out into the dark that pressed itself against the glass of the door and windows.

People were shouting and crying out. Someone was pointing outside and sobbing. Then the monsters came. They scrabbled at the windows with their long claws. Their misshapen faces snarled in abject hunger. One of them leapt onto the hood of the bus and began to pound on the front windshield. Vogel gasped and backed away. The creature wore the clothing of the driver. The shriveled, hairless, rat-like features were still just barely recognizable.

"Urvullak!" the old woman wailed. "*Urvullak!*"

Monsters surrounded the bus. They hammered on the windows. The glass cracked, frosted and then exploded inside. The urvullak hurled themselves through the windows. Drooling, their long tongues licking their rows of dagger teeth, they leapt onto the passengers and tore at them.

The driver crashed through the windshield and reached

for Vogel. In the terrified second before the claws seized him, Vogel had time to wonder how long it would be before anyone even knew that he was missing.

The urvullak had him, and there were no more thoughts, only the horror and the agony of his self's disintegration.

A short time after that, ravenously hungry for the souls he would find there, he was on his way home.

FOURTEEN

Orloff moved into a larger laboratory in the sub-levels of Castle Doom. She needed the space for the number of researchers and technicians she had under her authority, and for the containment of the urvullak specimens. Since her return, more had been spotted by drones and then captured. The lab was a huge, open area, and one half was taken up by a bank of plexiglass cubicles in which the urvullak were sealed. Orloff and her team examined them by means of robotic arms that reached into each cubicle, and were operated remotely by cybernetic gloves. The precision of the arms was remarkable. They felt like extensions of Orloff's body, the metal fingers as responsive as her own. She was able to operate on the urvullak as easily as if she were in the cubicles with them. More easily, because the arms were strong, much stronger than the urvullak. Their strength was unnatural, but still limited by what was possible for the matter of bone and flesh.

Her work was grotesque. Her mission was to find the best way of killing these things. *Destroying,* she had to remind herself. *Not killing – they're already dead.* This was a situation where it was necessary to dehumanize the enemy. To see them as people was a mistake, and a good way of falling victim to them. But they had been people. They had loved and feared and hoped, and they were still driven by hunger and loss, and the remnants of human appearance were enough to make what she had to do difficult.

And what she had to do went contrary to everything she had ever sought to achieve in her life. All of her training rebelled against her actions.

How did I get here? she asked herself again and again.

She knew the answer. Part of it lay on slabs in front of the cubicles. The corpses and their obelisk had been moved into this lab too. The project she had begun for Doom had not been abandoned. It was now part of a bigger, more urgent task.

"You have crossed the veil," Doom had told her before she headed back. "You have experienced the connection between the Devourer and the dead. You are well placed to understand the nature of the link between it and the urvullak, and to learn how to sever it."

She knew all this and accepted it. Yet the question would not leave her alone. *How did I get here?*

The initial stages of testing turned her into a butcher – *Kariana was right, they're hard to put down.* The only way to stop them physically was to make the body utterly non-viable. Anything less, and the monsters still tried to reach her through the plexiglass, claws gouging scars in the walls of their prisons.

The urvullak were always straining to escape. They howled and scrabbled at the walls, going into a frenzy whenever anyone approached the cells. They never let up, though, even when no one was around. Monitors recorded them constantly, and Orloff checked the footage whenever she came back from a restless nightmare-riven sleep. She was running on fumes. She was surrounded by horrors. But the work needed to be done. She reviewed the recordings too, before ending a shift, watching for anything she might have missed when she was focused on another task, and those images followed her down into another night of gasping dreams.

She was going over the third day's recordings with Hans Cass, one of her assistants, when she spotted something that worried her. They were looking at the recording of the robot arms removing the spine of an urvullak in an attempt to find a faster way of immobilizing the body.

"What's that other specimen doing?" said Orloff. "That one, three cubicles over." It was just at the edge of the frame.

"It's watching what we're doing to the other one," Cass said.

The recording played on. The watching urvullak remained motionless until the spinal column of the other had been removed, and the robotic arms withdrew. Then it resumed scrabbling at the walls again.

"Back up," Orloff said to Cass. "Show me the footage from just before we started the spine removal."

Cass did as she asked. The urvullak at the edge of the screen clawed and struggled, consumed by its hunger, until the moment the operation began. Then it stopped as if flash-frozen. The suspension of movement was strange. It made Orloff think of a marionette whose strings had been suddenly yanked upward and then held.

"There must be another actor involved," Doom had said. A monarch of the urvullak.

Orloff looked back at transparent cells holding a dozen specimens. They were all snarling and throwing themselves at the walls. She stared at their maddened, empty eyes, and thought about another, more knowing gaze behind them.

She sent the footage to Doom. A few minutes later, in her private office off the main lab, she spoke to him over a video communicator. She had the door closed, and a steel blind drawn down over the window to the lab. Nothing could see or hear her.

"I agree with your analysis, doctor," Doom said. "Our enemy sees through the eyes of her creatures."

"Her?" Orloff asked.

"I believe our foe is Maleva Krogh," said Doom. "She is a relic of the old regime who has persistently eluded capture. That the urvullak first appeared in Kroghstein is not a fact that I can believe was a random occurrence. And a message has been left for me by our enemy, a message that embodies the ideology of that accursed clan."

Krogh. The name grated. It was one her parents had feared. The Kroghs had been a big part of why they had fled Latveria to keep Orloff safe. "I will do what I can to prevent her from learning more," Orloff said. "We can make the walls between the cells opaque."

"That may not be enough," said Doom. "We will subject them to a test."

He told her what he wanted her to do. It took very little time to set up after she returned to the lab. All the cells except one were plunged into darkness. A flexible arm descended from the ceiling. It held a communications monitor before the cell, so Doom could see how the urvullak responded, and so he would be visible to the creature. He had been emphatic about the need for this detail.

"Approach the subject with a tool you have not used before," said Doom. "Keep it behind your back."

"You want me to conceal the tool in such a way that the urvullak knows I'm concealing something," said Orloff.

"Precisely."

Orloff picked up a vibro-trepanner and walked toward the cell. The urvullak lunged against the wall, drooling in rage and hunger. When she was almost at the plexiglass wall, the creature stopped with a jerk. It shuffled to one side, head cocked, its dead eyes moving as if trying to see past her, to what she was hiding.

"Remain still," said Doom. "Do not let it see."

The urvullak looked up at the screen. It stared at Doom for a long moment, and then, as if a grip on its body had been let go, it went back to its futile attempts to attack Orloff.

"I have seen what I need to know," said Doom.

When Orloff was back in her office, he went on. "The situation is clear. What any of the urvullak knows, their leader knows. I felt her gaze just now, when the wretch faced the monitor. She knew what we were doing, and why. When the urvullak looked at my image, that was a boast. Maleva Krogh defies me, and wants me to know it." Doom spoke with steely, cold fury. Orloff thought she heard an undercurrent of concern, too, and that disturbed her.

"I can see if I can find a way to block the connection between Krogh and her urvullak," said Orloff.

"If you discover that in the process of learning how best to destroy them, then that is well. But destruction is your priority, and your task is more urgent than ever. The urvullak cannot stand before me, but I cannot be everywhere. We need weapons for the Guard. You are in a race against our enemy. She will know much of what you learn. You must ensure that her knowledge becomes irrelevant. Have you tried connecting yourself to the urvullak by means of the helmet?"

The change in subject was so abrupt, it took Orloff a few moments to catch up with Doom's question. "No," she said. It was something she had been preparing to do.

"Then do so," said Doom. "Today."

"I haven't finished working out all the needed modifications yet."

"You have completed the work on some."

"Yes."

"Then begin your tests. What happens will tell you what the other needed changes are. Circumstances have altered since you last used the helmet, doctor."

"They have," she admitted. The thought of using the helmet on an urvullak terrified her as much as it intrigued her. To link her mind to one of them…

"Do what you must," said Doom. "I command it."

She bowed her head. Defiance was more even more frightening.

In the command center of the dig site, Doom killed the communications link and looked out at the pyramid suspended above the shaft.

I am getting the measure of your threat, Krogh, and you are careless in your arrogance. You should not have left that taunt for me. It amounted to your signature.

It was the writing in charcoal that made him certain she was the queen of the urvullak. The past has returned. Latveria is mine. That maniacal obsession with the old order was the sign of the Kroghs and was one of the reasons she had remained high on his list of members of Fortunov's resistance to track down. Her escape from her family's destruction was a loose end that had gnawed at him, as her terrorist attacks had gnawed at the peace of Latveria, for more than fifteen years. That she was the queen now seemed an inevitable working of events.

No. It was not fate. It was a consequence of unfinished business. And now he knew who he faced.

To identify the enemy is to have them in one's sights.

Maybe. But the more Doom learned of the threat, the more he realized, to his fury, there was too much he didn't know.

He had entered into this project so that he might know all. The proliferation of unknowns was an insult.

He was in his quarters here instead of down in the cavern, going over the pyramid's sensors and their readings, trying to find what he had missed, because there had to be something. If his precautions were working, there could not be as strong a link between Krogh and the Devourer as there clearly was.

There had been psychic energy leaking out, but not to this level. If he was wrong, why hadn't the pyramid activated? The Destroyer was still sealed in its vault. Zargo felt its presence, though he could not see it.

Doom went over the geologic and psychic scans again, ones taken before and during the operations on the wall down below. The vault of the Destroyer was a spherical blank spot on all of them. *Is that the shape of prison? Perhaps. The exposed portion of the wall had a slight curve. But that could also be a zone of indiscernibility, concealing the true shape and dimensions of the vault.* Either way, the area covered by the pyramid was greater than the diameter of the blank spot.

Yet energy is escaping, whether I detect it or not. How? Krogh has a link to the Devourer. I will find it and break it. I must.

He couldn't understand how the link could have been established. He still believed what he had said to Orloff and Verlak. The spikes that had escaped were not powerful enough to have created the urvullak. And the protective circle he had created in the cavern reinforced the containment.

Unless…

Driven by uneasy inspiration, he left his quarters and flew down the shaft to the cavern. At the wall, two more immense drills had been set up and were awaiting his command to recommence the work. He had called another halt after receiving the message from Orloff.

He found Zargo in his usual position, just outside the protective circle. "Read the wall again," he said.

Zargo obeyed. He closed his eyes, and his face went slack, his consciousness descending into the rock. He returned to himself in less than a minute and opened his eyes. "What I can see remains the same," he said. "I can't see the Devourer. The wall blocks me. But I can sense how you've weakened it. I can't see the barrier, but I can see the crack in it, if that makes sense."

"It does," said Doom. "How do you approach the barrier?"

"It's hard to explain."

"Your awareness has a direction, though?"

"Yes," said Zargo. "It's almost like I'm swimming through the earth, until the wall stops me."

"Change your approach," Doom told him. "Go deeper, then come at the vault from below."

Zargo obeyed. When he opened his eyes, he looked puzzled.

"What is it?" said Doom.

"I saw the crack again," said Zargo. "The same one, in the same configuration. As if I had come in straight from our position again."

"The same crack," Doom muttered.

"I don't understand. What does it mean?"

"It means," said Doom, "that we are weakening the vault on all sides at the same time. The fissure created here is not a break in a specific portion of the vault. It is a crack in the totality of its being. The Devourer is still contained, but not entirely." His protective circle was shoring up the vault here, but not elsewhere. The flaw extended around the sphere, but not the protection. He didn't know why. The reasons were unimportant, though. What mattered was his response.

Excavate on all sides? Extend the protective ring into a true circle around the vault?

He dismissed the idea. It would take too long. He had bought Latveria some time with the destruction of the infected villages. Orloff might get them a bit more if she was successful in her research. *Not enough time – the urvullak were loose and were spreading.* He had to cut Krogh off from the Devourer. He had to claim it and its power for himself.

"It might not be too late to undo the damage," said Zargo.

Doom looked at him sharply. "What?" he snarled.

Zargo winced, and plunged on. "We must stop while there's still time. Seal the Devourer up again, more fully than before. Seal it forever."

"What lies beyond that wall is *mine*," Doom said. "Once I claim it, the danger will be over. Destroying the urvullak will be a simple matter." *I will know all.*

"But if it should escape…" Zargo protested.

"It will not," said Doom. The words were a vow to himself. "This is not the moment to hesitate, or to stop the work, or to reverse it. We must break through that wall with all speed. There will be a short period during which the danger will increase, and then it will end utterly." *The power will be mine. All doubts, and all uncertainties, will cease. I will have that prize. I will smash through that wall.*

"My lord," said Zargo, "if I could only make you see…"

Doom held up a hand. "It is you who does not see. Since you will not, you must be silent."

Zargo bowed his head.

Doom spent the next hour preparing the drills. He was having to alter his approach to breaking through the wall. *Be accursed, Krogh, for forcing me to deal with you.* He could not stay and control every step of the breaking of the wall. So, he had no choice but to embed powerful enchantments into the adamantium drill heads. This way, the double attack on the wall would continue in his absence. It would involve the application of blunt force, though. There would be less control. There would be even greater risks.

No matter. The greater risk lies in tarrying. Defeat lies in turning away. Zargo was a fool to believe sealing up the vault again would end the threat of the urvullak. *The prison had always been imperfect. The Devourer had always been reaching out. It had always been feeding on the memories of the dead.*

He finished the work, then stepped back to see how the great machines would function in his absence.

"Begin," he commanded.

The drills lumbered forward on their heavy treads, behemoths approaching a castle gate. The heads spun up, surrounded by a piercing violet nimbus. They dug into the wall, and its black substance seemed to scream.

The cavern shook. The tremors were deep, as if the entire world vibrated in pain.

"Good," said Doom.

FIFTEEN

Late at night, in his quarters, Doom consulted the latest reports from Verlak. People were continuing to go missing. And more villages had fallen silent, ones beyond the boundary of the zone Doom had tried to purge. The urvullak were advancing. He was sure he had slowed them down, but it was hard to see what difference he had made. *If I had not acted, the deluge would already be upon us.*

Maybe. The tide was rising fast all the same.

He squeezed the arms of his seat in anger. They cracked.

On the screen in front of him, he called up a map of the region and plotted the pattern of urvullak activity, suspected or confirmed. Krogh's army was about to spread into the lowlands of Latveria, pouring out of the Carpathians like a river of rats. They were about to take their first city, Doomsburg, just beyond the mountains and a hundred miles north of Doomstadt.

No. You will not have Doomsburg, Krogh. You will not take it, and I will not destroy it. This will be your first true defeat.

He opened a communications channel to the command center of Castle Doom. He spoke to Verlak, and explained what must be done.

Dawn broke over Doomsburg with the shrieking blasts of the evacuation warnings. Doom arrived with the first of the siren wails. He flew around the perimeter of the town, watching the streets fill with frightened citizens, all of them making their way south. Squadrons of drones had maintained surveillance of Doomsburg and its surroundings throughout the night. They had picked up no sign of urvullak activity, though Doom did not count on that absence being good news. All it took was a single one of the creatures to reach the city without being seen, and the drones, no matter how many of them there were, could not see everywhere at once. The sight of the population on the move was a good sign, though. Those citizens were still human, still alive. Doomsburg had not fallen yet.

South of the city, flights of heavy transport aircraft arrived, carrying enormous slabs of a prefab structure. Big as freighters, with four engines on each wing, the transports reached a wide, level area a mile south of the town. They rotated their engines to the perpendicular, hovered in place, then slowly descended with their cargo hanging beneath them from huge chains. They came down slowly, in a formation so precise that the segments came together, the building assembling itself as if out of thin air. Automatic mechanisms sealed walls together and welded seams. The last portions to descend were the eight wedges of a shallow dome. Before the first of the citizens of Doomsburg were halfway to the site, an arena of black iron had risen before them, its doors open and waiting.

Doom landed on the roof. Holographic projectors embedded in it mapped him, then projected his figure to a towering height, bright and solid even as the sun rose. Speakers amplified his voice to thunder. At the same time, transmitters sent his image to projectors across Latveria. When he spoke, he was looking at the evacuees from Doomsburg, but he was addressing every one of his subjects.

"Citizens of Latveria," he said, "an enemy has come among us, an enemy from the dark past, before the reign of Doom. The urvullak have returned to Latveria. They stalk our forests and our streets, and they are led by the traitor Maleva Krogh." He had no definite proof, yet, that Krogh was the queen of the urvullak. He was certain she was, though. *Even if I'm wrong, she is a useful symbol to hate. Let her be the face of the enemy.*

"Watch for her," he said. "This is the foe who would destroy Latveria." The hologram changed to become a portrait of Krogh. It was a composite, created from official portraits under the old regime, surveillance footage captured during guerilla attacks, and AI extrapolations. The image changed, undergoing metamorphosis into an urvullak. The end result was speculative, and Doom had the projection transform back into the human, and then to the monster, back and forth, to sear both images into the minds of the people.

"Beware Maleva Krogh," said Doom. "Beware her creatures. Raise the alarm if you see them. Do not approach them. Do not allow them to touch you.

"Be wary, but be without fear. Doom is your salvation. Outside Doomsburg now is a sanctuary. Soon there will be other places of refuge. Go to them when you hear the sirens.

There, you will be safe from the urvullak. There, you will be fed and sheltered until the danger is past.

"Listen for the sirens. Watch for the eaters of souls. Listen for the commands of Doom. Be vigilant and obedient, and you will be saved."

He ended the holographic transmission. By now, much of the population of Doomsburg had gathered in the space before the sanctuary. When Doom finished speaking, they raised a cry of gratitude. They moved forward into the sanctuary, their advance kept orderly by the guards posted outside the massive doors. When the last of the townspeople were inside, the doors closed with clang that echoed across the rooftops of the abandoned town.

Doom descended from the top of the sanctuary and spoke to one of the guards. "What is the tally?" he asked.

"A bit more than a hundred unaccounted for, my lord."

So many. So quickly. So easily.

Anger growing, he turned to face Doomsburg.

That many, but no more from my city, Krogh. I shall have it back.

He flew toward the thick cluster of peaked roofs, where the shadows that had come with the night still hid, and waited.

Orloff gazed at the equipment laid out on the lab table. *It wasn't ready.*

It's as ready as it has to be for now. Doom said use it. So you have to use it.

Some of the modifications to the helmet were complete. There was also a rough prototype of the armor.

Armor was what she now considered the suit to be, though

it wouldn't offer much protection from most physical attacks. It was built out of leather, into which micro circuitry was embedded. The joints were nylon, for ease of movement. Once she had it and the helmet on, none of her skin would be exposed. When she had first conceived of the bodysuit, she had not pictured it as having particular physical requirements beyond what was needed for it to provide embodiment for her beyond the veil. That had changed the moment she had seen the urvullak in Kroghstein. The first requirements she sent to the technicians who had to turn her conceptions into reality were for something that would prevent an urvullak from touching her.

Kariana had, over the years, taught her some basics of self-defense, but that didn't make her a soldier. She could see where events were heading. She would be taking this suit into combat.

And it wasn't ready yet.

It will be. It will have to be.

"Let's get started," she said to her team.

A pair of technicians operated the arms in the chosen urvullak's cell. Four of the robot limbs, flexible tentacles with a grip stronger than steel, held the creature motionless. Two others, with surgical fingers, affixed electrodes to the skull. Hans Cass helped Orloff put the suit on. It was comfortable enough, and she felt that she could move well in it. *That was a good start.* She picked up the helmet. The suit would draw its power from it.

"We'll start with ten seconds," Orloff said to Cass. She wasn't going to depend on her ability to shut the helmet down. Ten seconds was all she was going to risk for the first time she plugged herself into an urvullak, and even that would feel like an eternity.

"Ten seconds," Cass repeated, sounding even more anxious than Orloff felt.

She checked the settings one more time, then put the helmet on and activated the suit.

The storm of the beyond was stronger than before. The pull of the Devourer was more powerful, the rage of its hunger wrapping around her and pulling, riptide and hurricane at once. It would have taken her if she had crossed over as she had before. But her experience of her self was different this time. She had a shape. She had a body, a physical being that anchored her and made her a stone holding fast against the breaking waves of the storm. She was herself, the contours of her identity as firm as they were in the material world, and the Devourer howled in frustration.

She saw the urvullak. It was a shape carved by wind and hollow with hunger. It saw her, too. It answered the scream of the Devourer with a shriek of its own, and the shape launched itself at her.

She reacted as if this were the physical world, raising her arm to block the attack. She moved faster than the material Orloff could have. She moved with the speed of need and thought and instinct. She parried the silhouette of the urvullak, then knocked it back.

And then she was out. The suit had shut down, and Cass was lifting the helmet off her head.

"Ten seconds," he confirmed. "How did it go?"

"It was… eventful," said Orloff. The grin came unbidden, fierce, and Cass jerked back from it.

"Is that good?" Cass asked uneasily.

"I think so. Yes."

"Now what?"

"Now, we disconnect the urvullak." If the helmet was going to lead to an effective way to combat the monsters, it could not be dependent on transmissions sent by wiring up the things. The helmet was already no longer physically linked to its subjects. Now Orloff had to see if the next modifications worked.

She double-checked the readings from the urvullak, and set the helmet's neural pulses to that frequency. "Disconnect the subject," she said.

The technicians released the urvullak from the electrodes. "Should we still hold it down?" one of them asked.

"No," said Orloff. "That made no difference on the other side." *Let's take another step closer to what things are really going to be like.*

She raised the helmet and took a breath. "Twenty seconds this time," she told Cass.

She put the helmet on.

Orloff crossed over, into the maelstrom of streaming memories. She saw the shape of the urvullak again, and more. No longer linked to one specimen, she saw the others in the lab too. Their silhouettes varied in sharpness, depending on how close their physical bodies were to her position. At first, they didn't see her, and she had several seconds to observe them. They were flailing about in the gale, tortured by hunger and unable to sate it. The Devourer screamed, and the nearest urvullak reacted to her presence. It jerked as if shocked, then rushed at her. In the moment before its response, Orloff saw a pulse that flowed against the current of the storm. It flashed out from the unseen center where the Devourer raged, and traveled as if on an umbilical cord to the shape of the urvullak. It struck, and the urvullak, a puppet, twitched and attacked.

Orloff pulled out before the monster could reach her.

"That was less than twenty seconds," said Cass as she removed the helmet. "Did something go wrong?"

"Not at all," said Orloff, heart beating with excitement. The pulse, the link between the Devourer and the urvullak was a blazing image in her mind's eye. *I have you now,* she thought.

Doom flew into the abandoned city. He landed near the northern section and walked the streets, choosing the narrowest and the darkest. "I am here, Krogh," he called, amplifying his voice, his challenge a thunder in the silent town. "Doom is here, and has come for you and your creatures." He strode down the middle of the road, eyeing the darkened windows of the houses. "Do they fear me as you should? Or will they hide, like the vermin you are?"

He picked up movement in his peripheral vision. Shapes scuttled over the gabled rooftops. Doom faced straight ahead, luring them out, daring them to attack.

They took the bait when he turned into a dead-end alley. He was midway down when they came for him. They pounced from the roofs and hurled themselves through windows. They swarmed out of the intersection into the street.

"Vermin indeed," Doom muttered.

The urvullak landed on him, and his armor unleashed a massive electrical charge. Sheet lightning flashed in the street, and the charred husks flew back. They hit walls and cobblestones, and shattered to chunks of brittle ash. The running onslaught crashed into him, and electricity flashed again. In seconds, Doom was moving through a funerary mound of blackened, crumbling bodies.

The urvullak kept coming, shrieking with hunger.

"Behold your fate, Maleva Krogh," said Doom, his voice booming across the whole of Doomsburg. "This is the price of your defiance, and the futility of your rebellion." He held up a hand toward the entrance to the alley. He unleashed a concussive blast so powerful that the rushing horde of urvullak disintegrated as if they had run headlong into a hurtling, invisible locomotive. Skulls and fragments of limbs and torsos flew up into the air, a cloud of death, and then rained down, landing on stone with the sound of falling twigs.

And still the urvullak came. *This was the work of a single night.* The realization was a grim one, and it stoked his anger. It was as if Krogh had command of the ocean tides, and he was alone in the waves, ordering them to stop.

I will stop them. If I must shatter the moon to make the ocean cease its movement, then let it die.

He sent another concussive blast down the street, and the waves diminished. *I am stronger than the tide.*

An urvullak landed on his head, catching him by surprise. It wrapped its legs around his shoulders and its insect-leg fingers grasped the edges of his mask and pulled. With a shout of rage, he grabbed the urvullak by its neck with one hand, and one of its arms with the other. He yanked so hard he pulled the monster's limb out at the shoulder. He hurled the urvullak to the ground and stomped its skull to dust. The body squirmed, remaining arm scratching at his armored leg.

The tug on his mask resonated through his heart, a sick, hateful echo of sensation. Doom raised his arms high. He shouted the words of an incantation, and the air of the street rippled like a mirror about to explode. He slammed his fists down, and a sorcerous firestorm erupted. It swept outward from him in a roar of crimson, incandescent fury. The earth trembled, and the clouds above Doomsburg whirled in rage, and from them came a torrent of black, jagged glass.

The firestorm passed, leaving ruin but no smoke. The shards fell over the city for several minutes more. The alley, the houses that framed it, and everything in a two-block radius was gone, reduced to sinuous, obsidian wreckage in a crater with Doom at its center.

This is the face that you will see, Krogh. There is only destruction for you.

The urvullak were gone. They were ash drifting over the roofs of Doomsburg.

The city is purged. It is mine.

He was not sure he had won anything.

The last of the Doomsburg urvullak vanished from Krogh's mind. The final vision she had of the city was of Doom bringing his arms down as if to hammer open reality itself, and then a flash of light and pain.

Her lips pulled back in a silent snarl.

She was in a cave in the foothills of the Carpathians. She would stay here until it was dusk. She found it more comfortable to move about once the sun had set. Daylight did not hurt her, but darkness nourished her. That was when the fears of the people of Latveria flowed like wind-borne nectar.

The darkness was where they stored their terrors, and where the unseen fed their imaginations. She traveled faster in the dark, and found it easier to hide from drones.

The time of stillness gave her a chance to rest. Her body did not need the respite, but her mind did. The rapidly growing numbers of the urvullak presented her with a challenge as well as greater power. The influx of perceptions threatened to overwhelm her if she did not discipline the stream and impose order on it. She was still an individual. The urvullak responded to her commands like a single mass, and operated on their own residual instincts when she left them to themselves. She could look through the eyes of any of them at any instant. What she could not do was see through the eyes of all of them at once. The multitude of devoured selves pressed in on her, clamoring for her to see them, and it took an effort to avoid being tossed from one to the other like a twig in rapids. She chose where she looked, and she was growing better at flipping from one set of perceptions to another at the speed of will, and in an order that served her. But the greater her army grew, the stronger her grip on her core identity needed to be.

The hours in the cave passed slowly until dusk. Krogh stewed in her anger about Doomsburg while she watched her army grow and gradually spread further into the land beyond the mountains. The loss of the city meant little in the long term. Sooner or later, she would take it back again, and it would be hers forever, along with everything else. But Doom had destroyed hundreds of her urvullak in moments, and pushed her back without utterly destroying the town.

Doom had spoken her name. He had addressed her directly through the eyes of her urvullak. She had expected that challenge. She welcomed it. She wanted him to know who it was who was taking Latveria from him. But he knew more than she had expected. From their hiding places, the urvullak had watched Doom's address to Latveria, and Krogh had seen her transforming images. Doom had not seen her new self. She was sure of that. She was well hidden. Yet he had extrapolated her appearance, and projected it for the nation to behold. *He knows too much. He might find us before we're ready.*

She stayed in the cave, nursing a hardening kernel of anxiety at the center of her anger.

The later afternoon brought a change in her mood. As the hours passed, she became aware of the effect of Doom's address. The entire country feared her now. The country feared *her*. The memories of the Kroghs, long buried, reared out of the collective unconscious, ghosts from the tomb. So did the atavistic terror of the urvullaks.

Latveria began to transform, even in Doomstadt and in all the places she and her creatures had not yet set foot.

Krogh felt herself grow stronger on the resurgence of dark memories. *The past has returned. I have returned.*

At dusk, she strode out of the cave as if to her coronation. Where she passed, the autumn foliage withered and fell. She moved through the forest, a poisonous shade of the past, and closed in on a village at the bottom of the slope, on the shores of a small lake. Mist was rising from the water as she approached, and thickened in welcome, rolling slowly through the settlement's single street to pay her homage.

"I have returned," she said aloud, her voice harsh as chain against bone.

The people of the village heard her, and they saw her,

and they knew who she was. They dropped to their knees in fear. They abased themselves, arms outstretched, foreheads touching the ground. Krogh looked at the symbols of protection hurriedly painted over doorways, the evil eye charms and crucifixes hanging in the windows, and bared her lips in amusement. The wards did not hurt her. She fed on the fear they represented.

She walked toward the prostrate people. She spread her arms, and her fingers flexed in anticipation.

"Take what you will!" a woman pleaded.

"Oh, I shall," she hissed.

And because she was their punishment, she took it all.

She took them all.

SIXTEEN

The wall was growing weaker. The fissure was deeper. Smaller cracks were spreading out from it. The drills were fracturing its integrity. It would break soon, Doom thought.

Would it break soon enough?

No. Any answer that was not now was not soon enough.

Coming back even this once was an indulgence he could barely afford. Krogh was pressing him hard. He did not know how much longer the Devourer's vault would resist him. The drills were doing what he expected of them. He did not have to be here.

Damn you, Krogh, for taking me from this project. You will pay for your interference.

He faced the question of whether she would have been able to mount her campaign if he hadn't weakened the Devourer's prison. He dismissed it. He refused to believe he had endangered Latveria. He was its protector.

The work must be done. The Devourer must be under his control. Its power must be his because the world was in need of Doom omnipotence. These were simple facts.

The fact that its power had been harnessed by someone else, only underscored the necessity that he bring it to heel.

Doom turned away from the work of the drills. He put the wall behind him. *The next time I come here, the vault will be no more. The Devourer will be held in its new chains, forged by me.* He walked to Zargo, who looked still more drained than the last time he had seen him, but as determined as ever.

"You will not see me again until the wall is breached," Doom said.

"What will happen then?" Zargo asked.

Doom noted with approval that Zargo did not try to convince him to stop the work. "The pyramid will trigger automatically. Until then, nothing will be required of you except your vigilance. If anything goes awry, you will contact me at once. Is there anything you do not understand?"

"No, my lord," Zargo said. His distress was clear, but so was his resignation to do as Doom commanded.

You are learning, priest. You are learning that you are not my conscience. That is not your role. You are my subject. Your role is to submit, to be shaped by my will.

Zargo had never defied him openly, but he had been trying to influence Doom, to change his mind. Doom did not think Zargo saw himself as a court adviser. Not consciously, at least. He was still acting as a priest, though, even if he did not realize it himself. *Your role is a different one. You are my geomancer. Accept your destiny. I think perhaps a part of you does. Soon enough, you will fully embrace what you are. Bow to my wisdom, Grigori Zargo. It is greater than yours.*

•••

By mid-afternoon, Doom had returned to the castle for the first time since the discovery of the Devourer's cavern. He met with Verlak in the security center. Her command post was a dais that rose and descended in the middle of the hall according to her needs. It was raised now. Doom and Verlak looked down on the rows of security officers and the banks of monitors. A dampening field kept their conversation private. The touch of a communication panel let them speak to a single officer or all of them at once.

"The reports of urvullak attacks are becoming more widespread," said Verlak.

The primary screen showed a map of northern Latveria. Red lights blinked, marking the sites of infection. The plague was reaching its hand across the land toward Doomstadt. More refuges like the one outside Doomsburg had been set up, but they were a temporary measure at best. If the crisis lasted much longer, they would become prisons. That was not his Latveria. He would not let that nightmare be his legacy.

"We can set up some refuges outside the capital," said Verlak.

"You do not believe that will be effective any more than I do," said Doom.

"No. Not with our population."

"We will not draw lots to select the saved," said Doom. *King Vladimir had amused himself that way. So had the Kroghs. The lotteries of the damned.*

"The drones aren't spotting the urvullak," said Verlak. "Not unless their cameras happen to catch them moving, and they seem to know to stay still. They don't give off any heat signatures, so infrared scanning is useless."

"The drones are a limited tool," said Doom. "If the living can hide from them, the dead can do so all the more easily. We will need other ways of finding the urvullak."

"They'll find all of us soon enough." Verlak looked grim. "My lord, are you sure we should not establish at least a few sanctuaries for Doomstadt?"

"If the urvullak take the city, then the sanctuaries will fall too. They would be giant sepulchers, and nothing more. I will not allow Doomstadt to fall. I will not permit this castle to be taken. Maleva Krogh will not set foot in these halls, unless it be to walk to her execution." *You are stealing what is mine, Krogh. That is why you are doomed.*

Verlak tapped the control pad, and clusters of green lights appeared on the map. "We are setting up checkpoints everywhere we can, concentrating on all roads leading to Doomstadt. We've taken out a few urvullak this way."

"A few," Doom repeated.

"Yes. That doesn't make me feel optimistic."

"They will not be traveling by road," said Doom. "The ones you are finding are just a taunt sent by Krogh."

"That's what I thought." Verlak's face was taut with frustration. She was being forced to take actions she knew were inadequate. She pointed at the line of lights around Doomstadt. "We're trying to surround the city more fully. Between the guards and the drones and the Doombots, the barrier is strong."

"There are still gaps," said Doom. "There always are."

"I know," Verlak sighed. "If only Doomstadt were a walled city." She looked up at Doom. "Can we make it one? How long would it take to construct a wall?"

"For a barrier of iron, a day. Less." He had the means. "But I will not surrender the rest of Latveria to Krogh. The people of this city will not cower behind a futile wall." He thought for a moment. "There may be a wall we can use as a way to hold them back. A measure of containment. Something better than a wall of stone or iron."

"Elsa said she had had a breakthrough."

"She has," said Doom. "I believe she has found us our wall."

In the lab, Orloff brought Doom up to speed. "I can see the connection between the urvullak and the Devourer," she said. "What I don't know is how to sever it."

Doom had said nothing while she briefed him. The impassive mask regarded her from within its hood. When she was done, the slight nod was enough to tell her that Doom was pleased with her work. It was a strange moment to feel pride, when she was caught up in a fight to save Latveria. What mattered was the usefulness of her efforts, not the glow of Doom's approval. She felt it all the same.

"It will take more than science to forge the weapon we seek," said Doom. He turned to the helmet and her prototype armor. "This will need improvements," he said, more to himself than to her.

Orloff watched as Doom examined the helmet carefully and went over the readings she and her team had collected. He was silent the whole time, but the simple act of his focus seemed to change the air, as if the mere fact of his genius focusing on a task was enough to begin altering reality.

When Doom finally stepped away from the equipment, Orloff was startled to see that more than an hour had passed.

"Shungite," said Doom. "In conjunction with black obsidian." He tapped a finger on the work table, then nodded emphatically. "Yes, with the right charge, protection and reflection will become weapons. Then it becomes a question of focus."

"Focus of what?" Orloff asked.

"Of will and of power. In the case of a directed weapon, the two will function synergistically. For a static, defensive barrier, the focus will be different." He waved off difficulties that Orloff wasn't even sure she could articulate. She was hearing a sorcerer and scientist speak at once, and the discourse gave her vertigo. "These are mere questions of refinement," said Doom. "Now that we know what to do."

Orloff wasn't sure that she did. She assisted as best she could over the course of the next few hours, but for the most part she and everyone else in the lab were helping without really understanding what they were constructing. The work spread out from the lab and into other work centers in the sub-basements. Doom ordered materials brought in, and they arrived within minutes. He required the shungite crystals and the obsidian glass to be carved into slices the size and shape of silicon microcircuits, and the machinery, itself a product of his mind, produced what he demanded immediately. One chamber looked to Orloff like a web of tentacles, a hundred mechanical arms all carrying out the work of a single will. She thought of the way the urvullak were controlled, and the comparison gave her hope. *The machines are his slaves like the urvullak are Krogh's. Our wills are the subjects of his. There's a difference.*

The nuance was comforting, though she instinctively avoided examining it too closely.

For a time in the early evening, Doom banished everyone from the urvullak lab. Waiting on the other side of the sealed door, Orloff experienced the now-familiar symptoms of being near an act of conjuring. Her skin crawled, and her heart began to hammer in unprovoked fear. There was no nosebleed for her this time, but a number of her team had red trickling over their lips. A few moaned and crouched, covering their heads with their arms as they tried to huddle closer to the wall.

Then Doom finished his work, and he summoned Orloff back into the lab. "Don your armor," he said. "Your right gauntlet is your weapon now." He explained to her how to operate it. "Do you understand?"

"I do." She was nervous. She was excited. She was ready.

Doom handed her the helmet. "Then it is time for you to take the battle to the foe."

Orloff put the helmet on without hesitation. She went in eagerly, and when she found herself in the storm beyond the veil, she felt strong, ready to shout a challenge in a space where she had no voice. The scanning of the helmet was more refined, and she saw the pulsing link between the nearest urvullak and the Devourer instantly. She pointed her gauntlet at the urvullak, and a psychic shockwave blasted from her palm into the shape of the creature. The pulse flashed crimson and winked out, the link between the horrors severed. The form of the urvullak vanished.

Orloff left the storm and removed the helmet. In the nearest cubicle to her, a pile of ash lay where the urvullak had been. "It works!" she said, triumphant. She could kill nightmares. She held up her hand, looking at the gauntlet in wonder. "How much of a range does this have?"

"In the material world, approximately twenty feet," said Doom. "You will be venturing into combat, Doctor Orloff."

"I know. I'm ready." *How did I get here? How did I come to the point of looking forward to war? What's happened to me?*

Did it matter? She could stop this. She could stop the nightmares. *I can.* This was what she was meant to do.

Doom nodded slowly, as if he could read her thoughts. "Good," he said. "What you must do now is straddle the boundary between this world and the one beyond. If your perception is entirely on the other side of the veil, you will be too vulnerable on this side, and unable to move. You must be able to see your surroundings. You must see the urvullak *here,* but harm it on the other side."

"That should be a matter of adjusting the neural frequencies."

"They will need to be attuned specifically to your own," said Doom. "I leave that in your hands. Become liminal, doctor, and you will strike from their shadows." He gestured to her armor. "This prototype is a sound one. It needs some refinement of the materials. I have sent the orders for a new one to be made for you. It will be ready tomorrow morning."

"Tomorrow," Orloff murmured. *So fast.*

"In the meantime, there is other construction I must oversee. You have given us the key to creating a barrier. You have given us our wall."

The barriers began to go up shortly after midnight. Doom had Verlak accompany him to the site of the first test. He had selected the village of Waldhut, the settlement closest to the most recently detected urvullak movement. The wall was a field generated between cylindrical posts ten feet tall. They were constructed of iron with a core of shungite and black obsidian. A sphere surmounted each, acting as energy source and transmitter. The black orbs received energy broadcast to them from Latveria's solar power satellites. They then sent out a modified version of the frequency Orloff had used to sever the link between the urvullak and the Devourer.

Transport drones flew the posts in, driving them into the ground at predetermined distances. The posts activated as soon as they were in place.

Doom and Verlak took up a position at the top of the steeple of Waldhut's chapel. The village was at the southern edge of a forest, and they could see the line of posts easily in the moonlight.

"What's the radius of the barrier transmissions?" Verlak asked.

"Sixty yards," said Doom. He had commanded that the posts be placed a hundred yards apart, creating an overlap of their fields in the center.

"Does topography matter?"

"Somewhat," said Doom. The land around Waldhut, beyond the forest, was fairly level, making the test easier to monitor. "Significant rock formations will interfere. Vegetation will not."

The drones installed the last of the posts and flew off. Waldhut was surrounded by the invisible barrier.

Silence fell on the village. Its people had come out of their houses when the drones had arrived, and Verlak, over a loudspeaker, had ordered them to go inside and lock their doors.

An hour passed.

"What if they don't come?" said Verlak.

"They will," said Doom. The sounds of the drones carried far in the fall air. Even if the urvullak had not advanced any further than the last sighting, they would have heard the sounds of the work. *What they know, their false queen knows.* "Krogh will want to test her strength against mine. She will want to know what it is that we think we can do to stop her."

"She doesn't care about a few losses, then?"

"The urvullak are dead, and there are always more of them. Sacrifice would be a meaningless concept for Maleva Krogh, unless her losses were so great as to threaten defeat." He thought back to Latveria under King Vladimir, when the Kroghs acted with impunity. "For her family, sacrifice has always been something that has been forced on others, for the pleasure of the Kroghs."

"I would have thought she would have come to understand the concept, and a few others along the way, during her years in the wilderness."

"Perhaps," said Doom. "But I doubt it. I made a study of my foes before I overthrew them. Krogh would have seen her suffering and deprivation as a function of theft, of slights that would require vengeance. There is no room for sacrifice in there." He thought for a moment, and grew troubled. "Yet there is one question. Why is it she, and not another, the queen of the urvullak? What is the link between her and the Devourer?" He felt a certain ease raising questions with Verlak. It was more than the fact that her loyalty was beyond doubt. She understood what Latveria needed. She understood that all he did was necessary.

"You don't think she was chosen by chance?" Verlak asked.

"I do not believe the Devourer is a being capable of *choice* as we understand it. Nor do I believe *chance* could have led to the rise of an enemy such as Maleva Krogh. Her connection to the Devourer must be one of long standing. This is a confrontation forged in the deep history of Latveria."

"A destined one?"

Doom looked at Verlak. "You know what I said to your wife on this subject, I see."

Verlak nodded. "Destiny is something that we've talked about more than once, given the other doctors Orloff."

"Then I say to you what I said to her. Destiny is a product of will. In this struggle, Krogh's will and mine are in conflict. Hers and the will of her ancestors have brought her to this point of power, and Latveria to this crisis." He did not say that his determination to seize the Devourer had a role to play. *What I do is what must be done. So I have always done, and will always do.* "Her will is strong," he said, giving credit to a powerful enemy. "Mine is stronger."

"Do you think…" Verlak began.

Doom held up a hand for silence. He saw movement.

A half-dozen urvullak loped out of the trees. They ran straight for the houses, snarling.

"They aren't trying to hide," said Verlak.

"Krogh has released them to run with their instincts," said Doom. "She knows they will not reach their goals. She wants to see what will happen to them."

The urvullak hit the region of the barrier. They stopped in their tracks, jerking as if electrocuted. One of them screamed, and the sound of mindless despair soared across the night of the village. Then the urvullak fell, twitched once more and crumbled to ash.

"Perfect," said Verlak, sounding excited, like she was already projecting strategy. "We need to weaponize this, make it more than a defense. Rifles projecting this frequency would make short work of the threat."

"They would," said Doom. He liked what he had seen, but he was conscious of its limitations as well. "They are also not possible at the moment. That frequency is extremely dangerous to the living as well as the dead. It is contained within that field, but crossing it would be lethal."

Verlak made a choking sound. "Is Elsa..."

"Doctor Orloff is well, Captain Verlak. The frequency is produced in part by her own neural configuration, which was the model for these generators. Any other human caught within the radius of the effect would suffer extreme, possibly fatal, seizures."

"So anyone who fired a weapon mounted with a generator would incapacitate or kill themselves and anyone near them."

"Precisely. Doctor Orloff, however, can produce a directional beam."

"I see." Verlak's tone was neutral, but Doom knew she was taking in the full implications of what he had just told her. After a moment, she said, with a quiver of pride, "So that's Elsa's mind that is destroying the urvullak."

"In a very real sense, it is." This was what pleased him about Verlak and Orloff. No hesitation, absolute commitment and a sense of honor in serving him and Latveria. "You understand now the nature of the work that lies ahead for her, and for us all. But that," said Doom, pointing at the line of sensors, "is a wall that will serve us well." *Did you witness that, Krogh? I'm sure you did. Take this lesson to heart. Now you will truly feel my grasp around your neck.*

Doom returned to the castle and allowed himself to sleep for a few hours. When he woke, at dawn, the work that he had commanded was well underway. Anti-urvullak barriers were going up around all the principal settlements of Latveria. When he rejoined Verlak in the security center, he envisaged the construction of a wider cordon. If he could deny the urvullak any further advance, then he could start forcing them back too. The production of the barriers was proceeding rapidly. Hundreds of posts were rolling out of the capital's plants every hour.

Verlak had slept briefly too, and she was going over the reports that had come in during the night.

"Some success around Doomsvale," said Verlak. The city was midway between the most contaminated regions and Doomstadt.

"But only some," said Doom.

"I suppose that makes sense," said Verlak. "If Krogh knows what the barriers do, she'll avoid them now." She did not sound convinced.

"Some urvullak destroyed at Doomsvale," said Doom. "Nowhere else? What about the Doomwood Forest line?" That barrier in the thick forest south of Doomsvale was the first step in the broader campaign. Doom had ordered a massive effort to establish a barrier stretching east to west across the forest. By his estimation, there should now be a line a good twenty miles long. The way to Doomstadt was through the forest, and the clusters of urvullak sightings suggested a bulge of Krogh's army closing in on Doomwood.

"The sensors picked up a few scattered hits," said Verlak. "No more than a dozen."

"Not enough," Doom muttered, concerned. Had Krogh countered the barriers already? How? He stared at the center's primary screen. "Where are they?"

"Might Krogh be holding back?" Verlak asked.

"Unlikely. She has been advancing even when we have not seen her forces. *Especially* when we have not seen them."

"My lord," one of the communications officers called out. "Father Zargo wishes to speak with you."

That was not a good sign. Doom wondered what had gone wrong in the cavern. "Put him through."

Zargo's voice came though the speakers in the command platform's console. "*They're in the earth!*" He sounded frantic.

"Where?" Doom asked.

"*I don't know.*"

"Explain yourself," Doom snapped. Zargo sounded like he was on the verge of babbling.

"*I sensed pain underground,*" said Zargo. "*I traveled through the stone, and I encountered disruptions. Hundreds of them. Maybe thousands. I can't really tell. I can't see the urvullak. I don't know why.*"

"They are undead," said Doom, thinking quickly, piecing together what must be happening. It was important to be rational, and not let alarm dictate his actions. "They are a contradiction. Perhaps that is enough to break your perceptions of the earth in their vicinity. Can you tell *where* they are?"

"No. There are so many of them, that there are entire regions of Latveria that I can't see at all. I don't know how they're doing this."

"Because of memory," Doom realized. "The same memories in the earth that led you to the Devourer. Krogh must see them too, because of her link to the Devourer. She knows every cave and fissure."

It took all his willpower not to lash out and destroy the center's useless screens in frustration. How had he not foreseen this? Because, he saw, that his contempt for Krogh meant he underestimated her and what she could do, no matter how much he told himself that he did not.

The barriers would be useless. Krogh had found her way through them.

Doomstadt was open to the plague of urvullak.

SEVENTEEN

"We have until nightfall," Doom told Orloff. "Not much more than twelve hours. It will take that long for the full strength of the urvullak to reach the city. We have less time than that to complete our task here. I will be needed elsewhere before the enemy arrives."

He spoke with a furious intensity just beneath the surface. He radiated an energy of purpose that Orloff thought would burn her if she stood too close. She had not seen Doom like this before. Though he was standing still in the laboratory, he was at war, as fully engaged in combat as if he were blasting a foe's tanks. The eyes behind the mask slits glittered with laser ferocity.

"I will do whatever must be done," Orloff said.

Doom gave her a short nod. He pointed to the upgraded version of her armor that had arrived an hour earlier. "You have familiarized yourself with its functions?"

"I have begun to do so."

"By dusk, it must be second nature for you. You will be needed in the field, Doctor Orloff."

"I understand."

"Good. Then your task now is to assist in the further modification of your work. We can transmit a damaging frequency. What we need now is receptors. A way of detecting the approach of the urvullak."

"Sensors that can pick up the brainwaves of the dead," Orloff said. *Did I really utter that sentence?*

"Precisely. When using your liminal sight, you will be able to see the urvullak through obstacles. That is our starting point. Our end point is the completed distribution of proximity warning devices by dusk."

The size of the task staggered her. But Doom said it must be done, and that meant it was possible. That staggered her even more.

He would make sure they had enough time.

"I assume these sensors won't need to be neurally linked to their users," said Orloff.

"They must sound their warnings whether there is anyone alive near them or not."

Doom plunged into the work, and Orloff followed. There had been urgency in their collaboration on the barrier generators, but that was nothing to what she witnessed in Doom now. This truly was war. He attacked the problem as if it were an enemy. He worked with a speed she would have called feverish if it hadn't been so coldly precise. Orloff assisted. She was, by now, more familiar with the nuances of the frequencies that disrupted and characterized the urvullak than anyone else. In Doom, though, she saw more evidence of a kind of genius she could barely frame. It was more than fiery. It was volcanic. When it erupted, it carried all before it. In the lab, with the task they had, the molten power of his intellect was channeled.

Orloff had a momentary vision of the genius erupting in a very different way, descending upon the landscape like a pyroclastic cloud. The image was terrifying, but passed quickly. She was too consumed by the work for it to linger.

They went back to first principles, to the initial readings Doom gathered from the dead. From there, they compared it to the data collected from the urvullak, and finding the wavelengths that the undead had in common with each other, but were distinct from those of the truly dead.

"None of this is natural," Orloff said at one point. This far down the path of occult research, after everything she had experienced, her rational instincts and her years of medical practice still rebelled at the new realities of her world.

"Of course it isn't natural," said Doom. "But the unnatural and the impossible are not synonymous."

By late morning, a prototype sensor was operational. "It is serviceable," Doom declared. "And it can be produced and distributed quickly."

A technician took the prototype to begin the process of its dissemination. Doom turned to Orloff. "I must go," he said, "and you must train yourself."

"I'll be ready."

"See that you are."

Verlak saw Elsa in her armor for the first time in the great courtyard outside the main castle doors. The gray day was moving towards the grayer dusk and the promise of an oppressive, starless night. In the courtyard, the palace guard mustered. Standing in the center of the space was a self-propelled manufacturing plant. The construct was fifteen feet high and squat. Eight chutes extended from its bulbous mass, and the new sensors rolled down the chutes onto the conveyor belt that ran around the machine's circumference. The sensors were metallic discs with matte black screens, and attached to wristbands. From what Verlak understood, approaching urvullak would trigger a sector of the screen, indicating the direction of the danger. The guards lined up to take their sensors, then took up formations toward the main gate, awaiting their orders for deployment.

Elsa was off to one side of the castle door. She wore her armor, and had her helmet in the crook of her arm. The suit was the same matte black as the sensors. Verlak thought it made Elsa look like she had been sculpted from a block of night.

Verlak checked that the mobilization was proceeding as she had directed, then joined her wife. Doom had not sent the deployment orders yet, so she wanted to use the few minutes she had well.

Elsa gave her a nervous smile. "Are you going to tell me not to fight?" she asked.

"You know I'm not." Verlak hugged her close. She wished Elsa could be home, safe. Except there was no safety there. It had always been Verlak's duty to be on the front lines, to be the protector. Now she was too. "Were you hoping I would ask you to stand down?" she asked.

Elsa leaned her head against Verlak's shoulder. "Yes. No. I don't know." She sighed. "I know you can't."

"I would never tell anyone to turn from their duty. Latveria needs you, Ellie. It needs you for what you know and what you can do." She held Elsa tighter and spoke very softly. "I just wish that it didn't."

Elsa kissed her cheek. "I can't count the number of times I've wished it didn't need you. But you know how proud I am that it does."

"And look at you. Look at what you've already done, and what you're going to do. I'm so proud of you, too." Verlak kissed Elsa, then took a half-step back, holding her wife by the shoulders so she could look at her. "You were born to wear that armor, my love."

Elsa took a shaking, excited breath and smiled. "It feels right. It feels…"

"Like destiny?"

"Yes. Yes, in a good way."

"Good. Just remember that however much Latveria needs you, I need you too. Promise me you'll be careful."

"Only if you make the same promise."

They leaned their heads together. "So we're promising?" Verlak said.

"We're promising."

They kissed once more, and then it was time to think of war.

The Chamber of the Eye nestled inside a spire whose access was forbidden to all. Doom granted no exceptions. No feet except his ever walked the stairs of the tower. It was one of his most jealously guarded sanctums in the castle, and the Chamber of the Eye was its jewel. The psychic atmosphere he had created there would be disrupted by any breath that was not his own.

The room was a perfect dodecahedron, fifty feet in diameter. A thin column rose from the floor, its tight spiral staircase leading to a circular platform in the center of the chamber. Every facet of the iridescent walls was dominated by a silver sigil. The signs regarded one another, amplifying and complicating their effects.

Doom emerged from the staircase. Inside the magic ring of the platform, he turned around slowly, observing each of the twelve sigils on the walls. The only light in the chamber was a sorcerous glow that came from the silver signs. Refracted and reflected by the prism-like surfaces, it seemed to flow like oil along the walls, a mirage and a truth all at once.

There were no windows in the Chamber of the Eye. Doom saw by other means here, and he saw further than he could by any form of optical sight. The Chamber of the Eye was a powerful tool, but he felt a flash of anger to find himself using it, and to be faced with its limitations.

I will see you damned, Maleva Krogh.

The Devourer should be his. Omniscience should be his. They would yet be. Let Krogh believe the gift was hers. Let her think she was using it. She was wrong, because she was not Doom, and so her mind could not be equal to the task. She would surrender what she had stolen from him. He would make her pay for forcing him to use inferior tools. What he had would suffice, though.

I will see you, and I will stop you.

He waited until his anger had run its course. He had to be calm if he was going to succeed in his purpose.

She would not goad him. She could not force him from his path, or the destiny he had forged. She was a delay, an obstacle, and nothing more. He was Doom, and his name was her fate.

This was a step toward omniscience. Every move he made against Krogh hastened the moment of her defeat, and the moment he would claim the Devourer for himself.

Outside the tower, in the courtyard of the castle and in the streets of Doomstadt, his palace guard was gathering, making ready to defend the capital. Drones and Doombots flew overhead, their cybernetic eyes watching for the urvullak. The sensors he had created with Orloff would sense the immediate attack of the foe.

None of this was enough. The sensors would be of little help against a massed attack. The warning would be too little, too late. And the eyes of the drones and Doombots could not see underground. He had to know where to deploy his forces. He had to see Krogh coming.

He needed a sliver of the omniscience he craved.

As he turned around and around in the Chamber of the Eye, he began to intone words ancient as stone, and as powerful as the birth of stars. They gave sound to the shapes of the sigils, and they bent the light in the dodecahedron. It came toward Doom, called by the gravity of his spell. It became more focused, more concentrated, and the chamber walls became darker and darker.

The more concentrated the light became, the less it illuminated physical space. It was turning into something rarer and older than light, and what it illuminated had no material existence.

It had taken Doom hours to prepare the spell, and its casting took time too. During those hours, Latveria would be at Krogh's mercy, and he had not taken this risk before, because there was no point using the spell too soon. It had to be when the urvullak were close to the city. There were frustrating limits to what he could see.

What I see will be enough. I will destroy you, Krogh, you and your creatures of decay.

The light vanished. The Chamber of the Eye plunged into absolute darkness. The transformed light, now an invisible spear, plunged into Doom, and his consciousness expanded, a great sphere spreading over all of Doomstadt. As it grew, it reached into the skies and beneath the ground. It flashed through and above and beneath Doomstadt, and to a full mile outside and above and below its boundaries. Like an omnidirectional sonar scan, it captured everything within its grasp for the brief second of its existence. In that second, Doom knew everything about his city. He knew the location of every inhabitant. He knew whether they were standing or sitting, inhaling or exhaling. He knew how the paint was peeling on the windowsill of the kitchen of an apartment in Old Town. He knew how many vehicles were on the road, and how many of them were running. He knew how and where every insect flew, and how the breeze bent each blade of grass.

Doom staggered under the weight of a tidal wave of simultaneous knowledge. This was a brutal, punishing simulacrum of omniscience. It was an overwhelming snapshot of everything, a filterless onslaught, as hopelessly infinite in scope as it was finite in duration. The Chamber of the Eye was the kind of crude tool he hoped he would never have to use again once he had the power he intended to take from the Devourer, because power was the key to dealing with the overflow of information.

He saw and learned more about his city than he needed. He snarled under his breath as his head throbbed.

But he had what he wanted.

I see you. I see all of you.

He saw the urvullak. He saw them, frozen in that slice of time, closing in on Doomstadt from a dozen different directions, a storm of rats clawing their way through the tunnels and fissures and cracks in the earth. He saw where the greatest concentrations of the enemy were, and he saw where he must go to fight.

Doom left the Chamber of the Eye, taking the spiral stairs three at a time. He contacted Verlak and gave her the deployment orders.

Moments later, he flew out of one of the windows of the tower, jetpacks burning through the new night to take him toward the north of the city, where the horde of darkness would be gathering.

Welcome to Doomstadt, wretches. Welcome to the fury of Doom.

The sirens sounded over Doomstadt with the coming of dusk. They announced the commencement of absolute curfew. Any civilian still on the streets when the sirens ended would be considered one of the urvullak and shot on sight.

This was a battlefield now, Verlak thought. *Like Walpurgis Night again.* There was a difference this time. She had been trapped inside Castle Doom during Hell's invasion. She had been unable to fight in the defense of the city. This time, she was on the front lines.

Doom's orders came. He knew where the urvullak were. He was heading to the largest concentration about to erupt in the northern reaches of the capital. She sent contingents of guards toward the other large groupings of the enemy. She took one last look at Elsa, and saw her don the helmet. Verlak's wife disappeared, replaced by an armored slice of night. *Come back to me, and I promise I'll come back to you.*

Shaking off dread, Verlak took her squad of twenty to head off the next-biggest threat, to the west.

The intelligence Doom gave her was going to change quickly. The longer it took to reach the enemy, the more time the urvullak would have to alter their course and spread out to other avenues into the city.

Verlak acted quickly. She and her guards descended into the sewers of Doomstadt. The last time she had been here, she had been hunting Rudolfo Fortunov. That enemy had been fleeing, craven traitor that he was. This enemy would not retreat. It was coming to feed. It would see her as prey.

"What we are fighting doesn't know fear," she told her troops as they ran down the narrow walkway of the main sewer lines. Her voice bounced off the brick vaults of the ceiling. The lights from the guards' helmets bobbed over the walls and the dark water flowing through the channel on Verlak's left. "They are hunters. We're going to deny them their feast."

She glanced at Sergeant Kurt Genschow, running hard at her side. His face was set and grim. "With me, Genschow?" she asked.

"With you, captain." The words came out choked, like he was having trouble breathing.

"We survived demons," Verlak reminded him. "We can beat these."

Genschow didn't look convinced. "We couldn't beat the demons," he said quietly.

Verlak took a quick look back to see if Genschow had been heard. The troops coming up behind appeared too set on staying close together and watching for the threat to be listening in.

Genschow was right. The guard could not have triumphed over the demons. If Doom had not sent them back to Hell, they would be reigning over Latveria even now.

That he was right about Walpurgis Night changed nothing. "We can destroy these," Verlak said. "I've seen them turned to ash."

Genschow nodded.

Verlak clapped him on the shoulder. "Tell me what you're going to do, sergeant."

"I'm going to do my duty. I'm going to smash the enemy."

"That's right," said Verlak. "You are."

Their target was an intersection of tunnels under Old Town. The fastest route there meant they had to turn off the main channels and take some of the smaller, narrower sewers and accessways. Some of the passages were barely wide enough for one person to squeeze through.

Verlak hated the constricted moments. She dreaded the prospect of the proximity alarm going off when she could not defend herself.

Don't let them touch you. She had drilled that warning into her troops. The words rang like mockery in her head when she had to work her way sideways between damp walls. If the urvullak came for her here, she would have no chance.

The alarms stayed silent, though, until she and her squad

reached their target. They took up position at a major junction. Eight tunnels converged here like the spokes of a wheel. This was a critical access point. From here, the urvullak could move quickly toward any region of the city, and Doom had detected a heavy concentration of the creatures heading in this direction.

Verlak had her guards take up a circle formation in the junction. Their guns covered every approach.

"Let them come," she said. "We're ready for them." She meant what she said, yet it sounded like bravado a few seconds later, when the sensors went off.

"Where are they coming from?" said Genschow. He shook his wrist, as if that would change the reading on the sensor.

"All sides," said Verlak. She accepted the grim reading on her sensor. The entire circle of its screen had lit up. The urvullak had the guard surrounded.

Verlak braced herself, eyes scanning the tunnels ahead of her and the shafts that opened into them at the edges of the vaults. She saw at least twenty avenues of attack without turning her head.

"Come on," Genschow muttered. "Come on."

She sympathized. The anticipation was murderous. She felt hideously exposed. She had to trust the guards at her back, but the need to look everywhere at once was overwhelming. Wherever she could not see, that was where the strike would come.

"Silence the sensors," she ordered. There was nothing more for them to tell the guards. Verlak already knew the worst.

She glanced at the pulsing disc on her wrist. Was it getting brighter as the monsters closed in? No, that wasn't its function.

Still...

The sounds came first. The scrabbling of claws and the snarls of rage and hunger traveled down the tunnels, filling the air with the echoes of the hunt, the hunt that was coming like a surging tide. And the sounds were everywhere, colliding with each other, no one location louder than the other, no way to prepare except to think *everywhere, everywhere.*

The urvullak came. They leapt out of the shafts. They boiled up the wider tunnels, a frothing wave of vermin. There were far more than Verlak had expected. In the time between Doom's detection of the enemy and Verlak's arrival at the junction, Krogh must have redirected a portion of her force, sending a much larger contingent to this point.

How much does she see? Do we have any secrets from her? Any way of getting ahead?

Verlak and her guard were armed with force rifles. They were particle beam weapons, capable of firing in single and burst shots. Their power supplies went for long stretches before needing to be replaced, and slapping in a new battery was as fast as replacing a magazine on an assault rifle. The troops unleashed a withering, sustained web of fire at the urvullak, and the creatures ran straight into it. The will that commanded them had no concern for losses. Krogh's was an army that would replenish itself and grow with every encounter.

"Shoot to immobilize," Verlak ordered. "Finish them off when they're no longer coming at us." She aimed the barrel of her rifle low, slicing off legs and blowing torsos in half with sharp, precise bursts. She slowed the urvullak in the lead down, and shot the arms of the undead that were scuttling too close. Her troops followed her lead. For several seconds, she thought they had a chance.

The urvullak fought in two very distinct ways. Most of them charged forward like rabid beasts. Instinct drove them forward, and nothing else. Some attacks, though, looked more planned. Those urvullak tried to flank the guards and use their kin as meat shields to get closer. There was nothing to distinguish the sentient urvullak from the animalistic ones, and after a few moments Verlak saw that the behavior of any one of them could change, as if an unseen puppet master suddenly seized control of an individual to propel it forward in a more purposeful charge.

Verlak's hope that she and her troops could stop the wave faded quickly. They were barely slowing it down. It took too many shots to stop a single urvullak. The damaged corpses kept coming with just as much fury.

"Retreat," Verlak ordered. They were seconds from being overwhelmed. "Southwest tunnel! Now!"

This was the tunnel with the fewest urvullak. *They could get through these. With a bit of luck.*

A lot of luck, she corrected as she charged toward the cluster of undead, firing as she ran. It wasn't enough to force their way through. *Don't let them touch you.*

And the creatures at their back were pursuing hard, screaming with hunger.

The guards concentrated their fire on the urvullak in the center of the tunnel. The undead fell, thrashing in the fetid water, and in another few moments were still, their bodies burned and shredded by the intense beams. As a small gap opened in the group, Verlak turned her fire to the sides, cutting monsters down and forcing them back.

"Get through them!" she shouted. "We can do it!"

Just get past. Then lure them all into a bottleneck. The dream of a counterattack flashed through her mind as she reached the enemy.

If the guards had been able to kill all the urvullak ahead of them, things might have been different. But there hadn't been time, and so there were still enough of the monsters waiting for them to lunge, attack and break the charge.

Verlak ducked below the slashing arm of an urvullak. She sprinted past the undead, then turned around to strike them from both sides.

She couldn't fire. The urvullak were all over her guards. She couldn't shoot without killing her own troops. The urvullak sank their claws into faces and their fangs into throats, tearing flesh in their frenzy to consume the soul. Guards screamed as they felt their selves torn away. They struggled with their attackers, and the struggles were brief and futile. Bodies went limp and began to change within seconds of falling prey to the ravening corpses.

Some of the guards got through, and they turned, like Verlak, with the thought of helping their comrades.

We can't, Verlak realized. She wanted to scream back at the urvullak in her frustration and anger. *There's nothing we can do.*

Nothing except flee, and avoid adding to Krogh's swelling ranks.

"Run!" Verlak yelled, cursing the day that had forced her to give that command. "Stop for no one! Run! Back to the castle!"

She paused long enough to see that she was obeyed, and then she ran too, even as monsters began to pull away from the scrum of fighting bodies to pursue the escaping prey. Already, Verlak had lost half her squad.

She pounded down the tunnel, leaping out of the water to the walkways, then tearing along the brickwork, shrieks and snarls rushing past her into the gloom.

More urvullak dropped out of shafts above and ahead. They landed on guards and dragged them into the water. The canal foamed with the thrashing bodies, and foamed still as transformed guards rose to add their voices to the choir of despair and thirst, and then joined in the hunt.

The guards' numbers dwindled. Verlak saw them fall, one at a time, sometimes a few at once. She did what she could to provide covering fire to the troops ahead of her, but it did no good.

A blur of motion in her peripheral vision warned her of an attack from above, and she jumped right, off the walkway, into the canal. She splashed across and onto the opposite platform, firing behind and taking the legs out of her pursuer.

She ran on, and there was no one left ahead of her except Genschow. He had crossed to this side as well. He was breathing hard, his face drenched in sweat and drawn with terror. Verlak's own lungs were aching. She was running on the fumes of adrenaline.

"Up," she gasped.

He nodded, understanding.

Fifty yards ahead, there was a ladder of metal rungs leading to a maintenance hole cover. If they could reach the street, they might have a chance.

An urvullak lunged out of the water and seized Genschow. They toppled into the canal. Verlak yelled and tried again to shoot, but it was already too late. Still yelling, alone now with the horror, she hurled herself down the last stretch to the ladder.

She started to climb.

She was halfway up when a monster screamed behind her, and the voice was familiar.

She looked down into Genschow's gray, mindless, distorted, wailing face. He snatched at her leg and grabbed her with elongated fingers. Verlak kicked at him.

His claws tore through her trouser leg. The urvullak made contact with her skin.

A devouring vortex roared into her soul.

EIGHTEEN

Orloff watched Kariana march away. Then she looked down at the helmet in her hands, took a breath and readied herself to put it on. She thought about her encounter with Doom, just inside the castle, before he left, and before she went outside to witness the final muster and see Kariana off to war.

"You haven't told me where I should go to be most useful," Orloff said to Doom.

"I have not," he said, "because I do not need to."

Orloff looked up at the impassive mask. The eyes that gazed back her seemed both knowing and expectant. "I don't understand," said Orloff.

"You will know where to go, or I am very much mistaken in my analysis of your character. And I am not mistaken."

"What is your analysis?" Orloff asked.

"That you are a hunter."

Orloff's eyes widened.

"You are surprised," said Doom.

"I've never thought of myself in that way." Yet the idea

did not displease her. She wanted to understand what she represented in Doom's eyes.

"You have always been a hunter," said Doom. "All that has changed is your prey. You tracked down the conditions that harmed your patients. Your research has been consistently far-reaching. That is another form of hunt. So is everything you have done in my service."

Orloff nodded slowly, still uncertain.

"Go now and hunt the urvullak," Doom told her. "You will know where to find them."

You will know where to find them. The words came back to her now with the force of a command, and of a promise.

She put the helmet on and activated it.

The world turned gray and crystalline. The sense of night vanished. There was no difference between the arc-lit space of the courtyard and the darker region of the bridge over the moat. There was no sense of illumination or shadow. The world had become perfectly delineated, and perfectly ephemeral.

She didn't move, waiting to adjust to the liminal perspective. She felt detached from reality. *Or is it reality that's detached from me?* This was not the unworld of beyond the veil, but it wasn't the world of the living either. It was almost as if the two had become simultaneous palimpsests of each other.

Orloff stared at the castle wall, and it became translucent. She saw through it, down the slope to the rooftops of Old Town. She concentrated, and she began to see through them to the walls and rooms inside.

No. Too much.

She closed her eyes for a moment, then brought her attention back to the courtyard. The castle wall was solid again, or as solid as any simulacrum could be. Orloff looked down at the paving stones. They were little more than a diagram of a surface.

Look deeper, Orloff thought, and she did. She saw beneath the courtyard, into the halls below.

That's enough.

The halls vanished.

Good. You can do this. She could move through this limbo.

Now hunt.

Orloff left the courtyard and marched across the moat bridge. She didn't have a destination in mind yet. She was still exploring the space around her, getting to know how to look at it, how to move through it. And she was letting her mind run free. Doom said she would know where to go. She had faith in what he saw in her.

She reached the streets of Old Town. She turned right, because it felt like the correct decision to make, not because she knew anything definite. She practiced looking through the walls of the buildings beside her, tuning in and out of different levels of clarity, looking for the shapes of the urvullak.

This was what the sensors saw, and what they saw was based on her vision. If the sensors picked anything up, she would too, and better. She was the hunter.

There were no urvullak here. She kept moving, and as she did, she realized why she was walking in this direction. This was the way she had seen Verlak take her squad.

She looked at her wrist. Her body was solid here, the armor as black as it was in the material world. She was not translucent. Her physicality anchored her sense of reality. She felt the wind of the Devourer blowing, felt it like the keen of a winter's grief, but it flowed past her, unable to move the rock of her being.

She tapped the screen on the control panel embedded in the back of her left-hand gauntlet. A map of Doomstadt appeared before her, floating in midair. It showed the concentrations of the enemy that Doom had detected. She looked at the region Kariana had targeted.

Go there.

The need to follow was as direct as a command. There was no question of disobeying it.

Go there. The voice might as well have been Doom's.

It wasn't Doom's, though. It was hers, and it was Kariana's. It was the need to fight for her wife.

Orloff broke into a run. Now that she knew where she had to go, the pull to get there was strong, like the Devourer's vortex had been. *Was this love or destiny?*

Did it matter?

Maybe they were the same. It was love that called, that drove her now to fight for and beside her wife. If it was destiny that came into being because of love, then that felt right too.

Doom had told her that destiny was chosen, was forged, that she was not the passive plaything of tides of events, driftwood on the ocean of fate. *Was this what he meant?*

It's what she chose it to mean.

She headed west. In less than a minute, she reached the sewer access point down which Kariana and her troops had gone. It was a low, concrete building with a sloped back and a dark, open entrance. Guards flanked its iron doors, their force rifles aimed at the interior, waiting for anything that wasn't human and alive to come out. Orloff hesitated for a moment, then hurried on. She didn't know the sewers. She might be able to see through walls, but she couldn't walk through them.

Even with the help of the map, she would be moving through the tunnels much slower than Kariana. She needed to catch up. And she knew her way through Old Town. So she stayed at street level, and hurried to where she expected the battle would take place.

She had a few miles through twisting streets to cover. Her heart needed her to sprint the entire distance, but her legs and her lungs wouldn't let her. She was in decent shape, but she had never run a marathon. The armor took getting used to as well. It was light, but it was still a new weight. It wasn't an extension of her physical self just yet.

Is that what it is for, Doom? It must be. For her, as for every other citizen of Latveria, his armor *was* his physical self. That mask was his face. It was impossible to imagine the human being behind it. She might as well have tried to picture herself with her musculature exposed to the air.

Orloff jogged as much as she could, and walked quickly the rest of the time. Her progress didn't feel nearly fast enough. *How quickly was Kariana going through the sewers? Pretty quickly, if she knew her.* She pictured Kariana leading her squad toward the target like a shark. The guard had a head start of a few minutes on Orloff. She hoped she could make up time on the streets. She thought about commandeering a vehicle, and then dismissed the idea when she looked at a car parked at the side of the road. It was as insubstantial as everything else in her perspective. She pictured herself trying put one in gear while trying not to see through it. She needed to master her shifting perspective, make her new kind of sight second nature before she tried driving and hurled the vehicle and herself into a translucent wall.

Go faster. Go faster.

The further she went, the more urgent the need to reach Kariana became. Instinct, premonition, or irrational fear – she didn't know what fueled the need, but she didn't question it.

Go faster. She needs you.

She started running again. She remembered what Kariana had told her about the night of Fortunov's bombing campaign, when Kariana had seen a truck loaded with explosives pull up outside the hospital. Her voice shaking, her arms trembling as they held Orloff in a tight embrace, Kariana had told her of the terror she had experienced, the terror of being too late, of losing Orloff.

Orloff had that fear now. The command to *go faster, go faster, go faster* alternated with the wail of *too late, too late, too late.*

Almost there. Not far now. She looked down, and focused her sight through the pavement, into the tunnels below. She saw the lines of the sewer canals.

She saw the horde of the urvullak. Angular gargoyles, they swarmed through the main sewer tunnel beneath her. She couldn't hear their snarls, but she could see the jaws snapping at air, and the claws reaching for the relief that would be forever denied them. They were in pursuit of prey.

The prey was Kariana.

It was the first time Orloff had seen Kariana from the liminal perspective. She was more real than anything else in the gray world. She glowed, a being of yellow fire, imbued with the importance she represented for Orloff.

Kariana reached a ladder and started to climb. The urvullak were right behind, and catching up.

Too late too late too late too late!

No no no no no no!

Adrenaline burned away Orloff's fatigue. She sprinted to the access cover a few yards away. She grabbed it, and with desperation's strength yanked it up and to the side.

Below, an urvullak had grabbed Kariana's leg. Her mouth was open in a silent scream.

Orloff cried out, her rage and horror primal. She aimed her gauntlet at the monster, acting on the most ferocious hunter's instinct, and she fired. She severed its connection to the Devourer and it crumbled to ash.

Kariana slumped, her hands on the rungs losing their agonized grip. She began to fall back, and more urvullak were starting to climb. Orloff snapped a hand down and grabbed Kariana's wrist. The tiny sliver of her mind that observed her actions, and wasn't consumed by a desperation every bit the equal of the urvullak's, was startled by the power of her grip, and by the fact that she kept her crouched position and did not fall into the shaft when she took Kariana's weight.

Orloff blasted at the urvullak with her right hand. The disruptive frequency appeared in the limbo as a narrow ripple, a sudden seam whipping through the crystalline air. She had no trouble aiming past Kariana. The ripple even bent around her, driven by Orloff's will to strike at what she intended.

Ash rained down to the bottom of the shaft, and the monsters hesitated, as if they or the power that controlled them sensed the danger that Orloff represented.

Orloff strained, her shoulder flaring with pain, and hauled Kariana out of the sewer. The observing sliver of her consciousness was surprised again at how she was able to do that, at how strong she was, over and over, as the moments demanded.

How was she able to do this?

The question was distant and unimportant. It flicked away, leaf on a wind, and Orloff laid Kariana on the road and turned both gauntlets on the climbing horrors. She roared at them, and she ripped them from existence. She sent the frequency of destruction down in a continuous blast, and the shaft became a killing jar. The urvullak disintegrated as quickly as they arrived at the ladder, and when they began to turn away, called back by their ruler, Orloff kept killing them. She could see them as they fled, and she hurled her rage after them. The horde dwindled, its edges and its center vanishing, annihilated by her gaze. Wherever her attention fell, urvullak ceased to exist. When the last of them moved beyond her perception, only a handful were left.

The struggle had lasted less than a minute.

Orloff pulled the helmet off. Gasping, sobbing, she knelt by Kariana and cradled her head. She spoke to her, calling her back. "Stay with me, Kari, oh my Kari. Stay with me. You're not gone. You're not one of them. You're too strong for that. Please, Kari, Kari, Kari."

Kariana's face was gray, her eyes wide and unseeing. Then her chest heaved, and she took a huge breath, as if she were inhaling her soul and holding it tightly inside her lungs. She howled the wail of the reborn, her body rigid as steel, and then she subsided, her muscles relaxing, her breathing regular again. She blinked. Her eyes looked clearer, and her skin took on color. It was no longer the gray of the limbo world.

Trembling petals of hope unfurled in Orloff's chest. "Do you know who you are?" she asked.

Kariana trembled for a moment, then nodded.

"Do you know me?" The question Orloff was terrified to ask, and the one whose answer she needed so very, very badly.

Kariana raised her arm, the movement so weak, her limb might have been tissue paper in a slight breeze. Her fingers touched Orloff's cheek. "You're my Ellie," Kariana whispered.

Orloff embraced her, sheltering her from any threat that might try to tear them apart, and sobbed with relief.

The urvullak erupted from the sewers the instant Doom landed at the northern edge of Doomstadt. He let them come, defying Krogh's show of force.

"Do you hear me, Krogh?" he boomed. "Do your worst, and learn your fate."

The monsters swarmed over him, a carpet of human-sized rats trying to bring him down. Their claws scratched at his armor, and their weight pressed on him. He remained still, impervious as a mountain peak.

"Is this your grand attack?" he called. "Can you do nothing but the same thing endlessly? Is your imagination so poor?"

He triggered his armor's force field. It erupted against the urvullak at the same time as the massive electrical shock. The creatures flew from him, reduced to charred body chunks.

Still more urvullak were scrambling up to street level. Hundreds already surrounded him. They circled him, growling and screaming, wretched, hideous parodies of the humans they had once been, their clothes hanging in rags, their bodies twisted into jagged, vermin-like expressions of undeath.

They circled, but did not attack.

Doom turned around slowly. *Where was Krogh? Was she here? Wouldn't the promise of leading her creatures into the capital city be too much for her to resist?*

If she was present, he couldn't see her. He wasn't sure he would know her at once, given the extent of the distortions the bodies of the urvullak underwent.

"You aren't here, are you, Krogh? You're a coward. You are hiding. That won't do you any good."

One of the urvullak in the front lines, one facing him directly, jerked violently. It stood still, and its mouth began to work. It spoke, the words coming out in rasping coughs.

"I have no need to hide, usurper," it said.

It twitched again, and resumed its predatory circling. Another, this time on Doom's left, spoke. "I am everywhere."

"Do you think so?" said Doom. "Then you are a fool. You have no conception of true omnipresence, Krogh. You are enamored of its illusion. All it means is you can die ten thousand deaths."

Doom unleashed force blasts. He fired quickly, four times, striking through the mass of the urvullak on the cardinal points of the compass. An invisible scythe slashed through the ranks of the undead, disintegrating them.

A thousand throats gave voice to Krogh's snarl of rage.

Doom smiled tightly. "How can you imagine you can defeat Doom?" he taunted.

The urvullak answered as a disjointed choir, one word at a time from one monster at a time. "I. Will. Take. All. Of. Latveria… You. Will. Be. *Nothing!*" The last word was a scream, and the urvullak charged.

But not at Doom.

They turned from him and loped towards the cramped, ancient apartments on both sides of the street. They crashed inside through doors and windows, vectors of disease in search of more victims. If Krogh could not overcome Doom with the sheer physical mass of her urvullak, she would ignore him instead. She would take his citizens and make them her subjects.

Her strategy was an insult, one not to be borne.

Doom waited until scores of the urvullak had entered the residences. The buildings were empty. He had ordered them evacuated as soon as he had seen where the greatest force of the enemy would be.

Before leaving the castle, Doom had mounted his intensified molecule projector onto his right gauntlet. He aimed it now at the buildings before him, and fired. A stream of intensified molecules burst out of the weapon, instantly expanding into perfect spheres ten feet across, massive as granite. Speed undiminished, they shattered the sound barrier. The sonic boom was the prologue to the explosions when, monsters of mass and velocity, they slammed into the facades. Homes that were hundreds of years old exploded into fragments. Clouds of dust erupted into the street and covered the neighborhood. Doom trained his fire on the other side of the road and leveled another two blocks in an instant. When he lowered his arm, nothing remained. The ruins were a slumped unevenness, nothing more.

Then he fired again, at the urvullak in the street, and the expanded molecules pulverized their bodies to mist.

Doom had added versions of the urvullak sensors to his

helmet. He could not detect them with the same precision that Orloff could. Only she was attuned to their frequency, but the sensors did give him a sense of the direction, movement and proximity of the foe. He detected another change in tactic now. Krogh was sending the urvullak away from him, commanding them to come up to street level further away, and spread out as fast and as widely as possible in the city.

The barrier spell had a complex summons. He had begun muttering the syllables of the conjuring as he had closed in on the target region. He had shaped the words in his mind even while he had exchanged taunts with Krogh and begun his destruction of the horde. He completed it now, and pulled all his concentration into channeling sorcerous energy into its being. For a split second, he lost all awareness of the world around him. His mind existed entirely in the world as it would become. Then he clicked back into the present, and the spell triggered.

An invisible barrier surrounded the district. It rose a hundred feet in the air and descended a hundred feet into the ground. The night smeared around it, as if a slick of oil had passed over reality. The urvullak slammed into it, and could not get past. Nothing could.

Doom flew up until he was level with the limit of the unseen wall. He looked down at the region he had sealed off. It covered a square mile of Doomstadt. He saw the urvullak swarming over it, many scrambling over each other in an effort to push through the thrumming force that blocked them. Many others were hunting.

The evacuation of the buildings in the immediate vicinity of the emergence had been complete. Doom had commanded the entire region be cleared, though, and there had not been time for everyone to escape before the urvullak came and the barrier went up. Krogh's army was growing again.

I am fighting a sea, Doom thought. *And even the sea must fall before Doom.*

It was time for another cauterization.

Doom aimed the molecular projector straight down and fired a sustained burst. He shifted the stream of molecules back and forth, covering the entire area. A meteor storm struck the streets, punching craters deep, and deeper yet, into the city. Doom left nothing standing. When he ceased the bombardment, a lunar valley lay where an ancient neighborhood of Doomstadt had been. The land had changed, collapsing in on itself. No trace of roads or homes or the tunnels beneath them remained. The urvullak were gone.

These ones.

Doom landed, and the momentary triumph of having purged this region of Doomstadt gave way to frustration. *There was no more Doomstadt here.* He had taken thousands of Krogh's urvullak away from her, but at a cost that was not that different from what she promised she was going to do to him.

This is not her victory either. This infestation won't spread.

The smaller ones could, though.

He scanned through the reports coming in from the other regions of the city. His Doombots were hitting the urvullak hard, above and beneath the streets. Their combinations of concussive and electrical blasts were effective at taking out clusters of the enemy. The Doombots operated in groups of three, in conjunction with squadrons of drones, to contain the urvullak and annihilate them.

The news from the Guard was less encouraging, even where they had supporting drones. Their weapons were less effective against the undead. In regions where the guards heavily outnumbered the urvullak, they were able to hold their own and beat the monsters back. There were quite a few squads, though, who had stopped reporting. Verlak's was among them.

That was dismaying. He did not wish that loss to be added to the others this night.

Doom looked through the eyes of the Doombots and evaluated the strength of the enemy. *You are not the only one who has the vision of many, Krogh. She had legions, but he had power and experience. And when the Devourer was his, there would be nowhere for her to hide.*

He retasked some of the Doombots, sending them to reinforce the guards. Then he took to the air again, his flight a streak through the darkness to where the reports showed the greatest need.

The hours passed in a blur of combat. Doom rarely stayed in one spot for longer than a minute. He came, and he unleashed his fury on the urvullak and then he left the Guard to mop up the remains. He did not use the molecule projector again. It was too indiscriminate, too utterly destructive a weapon. Krogh wanted to take Doomstadt from him, one way or another. He would defeat her by keeping it. *The humiliation of this night will be yours, Krogh. You thought the war would end tonight. How does the venom of your error burn in your mind?*

Doom's attacks were surgical now, slicing out the cancer of the urvullak instead of amputating limbs. He fought in a hundred encounters, on the streets, inside buildings, in the sewers. The civilian population cowered behind locked doors.

Many of those doors were forced open by monsters, and Doom saw their splintered remains and the shattered interiors as he destroyed the new additions to Krogh's army. But many other doors remained locked, and the windows unbroken, and he heard the calls of a terrified, grateful populace as the people chanted his name. From behind their shutters, they witnessed the majesty of his fury, and they knew that Latveria belonged to Doom.

Their souls would never belong to Krogh. They were his, by his right and by his duty.

Dawn came, gray and full of smoke, and the urvullak retreated. The proximity sensors no longer wailed. Quiet descended over Doomstadt, but quiet was not the same as calm. The battle had ended, but the war was just taking a breath.

Doom returned to the castle. The main courtyard was full of stretchers, where the wounded of the guard were receiving first aid before being transported to the hospital.

Doom moved to the center of the courtyard. All eyes on him, he announced, "You have fought well. Doom is pleased. Rest, and prepare to fight again."

Kariana Verlak was on a stretcher near the main door. Elsa Orloff sat beside her, holding her hand. He was glad to see them both. Truly, he was.

When Doom approached, Verlak struggled to her feet. Her face was haggard, but her eyes were fierce. Though her leg was bandaged, Doom saw no other sign of physical injury, yet she looked as if she had just stepped away from death's door.

"What happened to you?" Doom asked.

"An urvullak touched me."

And yet you live. Doom was impressed. "How long was the contact?" he asked.

"I don't know," said Verlak. "It felt like forever. Elsa saved me."

"I don't think it was more than a second or two," said Orloff. "It seemed like forever to me too," she added quietly.

"Krogh tried to take my soul," Verlak said. "I owe her for that." Her voice was steel, belying the exhaustion in her face. "This isn't over, is it?"

"It is not," said Doom. "We have repelled Krogh's attempt at a mass assault. In her arrogance, she believed she could take Doomstadt in a single night. She has other tactics at her disposal. I have no doubt that she will turn to infiltration. That will be, in its way, more difficult to counter." He looked at Orloff. "Did you hunt well this night?" he asked.

"I don't know if I would call it a hunt."

"More like a massacre," Verlak said proudly, and squeezed Orloff's shoulder.

"Then now you will truly become a hunter," said Doom. "You can see what the rest of us cannot."

But that will not be enough. I need to see. I need the vision Krogh thinks is hers.

He had to break through the Devourer's vault.

NINETEEN

The sirens wailed again in the morning. It was not the all-clear. It was the reiteration of the command to stay inside. Doomstadt was in lockdown. Food and aid were delivered to neighborhood outposts, and only at the assigned distribution times were citizens permitted to venture out into the street. Guards were on every corner, and tanks rumbled down roads barely wide enough for them to pass through. Doombots were a constant presence, the image of the lord of Latveria visible to nearly anyone who looked outside. Drones passed overhead like flocks of cybernetic birds. The smoke from the fires of the night before drifted over the city, stinging eyes and throats with the reminder of battle.

In the mountains, Krogh heard and saw and smelled all of this. Her awareness leapt between the scores of urvullak lying hidden in Doomstadt. They were crouched motionless in the deep shadows of alleys, beneath the rafters of forgotten attics, in cellars, in storm sewers. Wherever there was darkness to conceal a thing without motion or heat, that was where they waited out the passing of the Doombots and the drones and the tanks and guards. Some would be found and destroyed before they ever had a chance to creep forth. Krogh accepted that. There were always others who would be harder to find, until it was too late.

She was finding it a strain to keep all the urvullak in Doomstadt still until she unleashed them. It was one thing to impose her will on them in the countryside, where their prey was scattered, and often miles away. In the city, their instincts were inflamed by the proximity of so many souls, so many memories to consume. Their bodies cried out to lunge at the nearest passerby. Krogh felt spread thin. It was like pressing continuously down on powerful, coiled springs. A moment of inattention could cost her another of her urvullak, and for the first time since her conquest of Latveria began, she was conscious of having to guard her resources. She still had many hundreds more of the undead in the forests and the hills, but she had suffered heavy losses last night.

Wait just a bit longer. Just a little bit, and it would all have been worth it. Every loss would be a step toward victory. They were almost there. Just be careful now. This was the crucial time.

She skipped from one urvullak to the next, watching and waiting for opportunities. Because she was patient, her patience was rewarded. The eyes of the servants of Doom could not be everywhere. Gaps opened in their vigilance. Some shadows were not searched. Some homes were too far for anyone to notice when something moved.

She chose the urvullak she permitted to hunt carefully, and she controlled their actions. They crawled out of their hiding places silently. Their jaws hung open, and they tried to scream their hunger, but she stopped their voices, and they could give their pain no other expression than their contorted grimaces. They emerged from eaves to scuttle like spiders down walls to shadowed windows. They climbed up from the cellars, quiet as wraiths, and drifted up staircases like cold drafts.

They opened doors to reveal the hidden prey within, and they struck before the people inside had time to scream.

Where the urvullak attacked, they took everyone. The targets were few. Krogh made sure of that. She made certain that after every hunt, silence fell again. Where people had been hiding from urvullak, now the urvullak hid, writhing internally in their agony, waiting for the moment she let them strike again.

Slowly, methodically, Krogh stretched the fingers of her will into Doomstadt. Slowly, mercilessly, undead roots took hold and began to undermine Doom's last solid foundation.

There were no more corpses connected to Doom's machine in the laboratory where he had first set Orloff to work. This time it was Orloff who lay on one of the slabs. She wore the armor and the helmet. They were connected to her neural impulses, and to the machine that read and recorded and analyzed the energies of her brain more deeply than anything that was merely a magnetic resonance imager could do.

"Attack," Doom said.

Orloff's right arm shot up. The weapon in her gauntlet was disabled, but the impulses from her brain still traveled through the mechanism. Doom nodded at the results that appeared on the screen. "Again," he said, and after few seconds, "Once more."

Doom tapped the screen, amending the orders that would flow from this lab to another. When he was satisfied, he shut the obelisk down.

This was very good. She would serve well.

"I have what I need," he told Orloff. There would be new weapons now. Through him, his subjects would fight back. They would destroy Krogh's creatures, and she would know that it was his hand that was crushing her forces.

Orloff sat up and removed the helmet.

"That was fast," she said.

Doom shrugged. "Last night gained us the necessary time. I do not propose to waste it." He turned to another screen. A tap brought it to life, and he showed Orloff what was happening in one of the castle's great arsenal assembly rooms. Out of the maw of a cyclopean machine came a stream of barrel modifiers that would allow the guards to use Orloff's destroying frequency without killing themselves. They resembled silencers, and a conveyor belt took them past an army of technicians who picked them up and took them to work tables.

Orloff looked startled. "Those are going on the force rifles," she said.

"That is correct."

She looked back and forth between the screen and the slab where she had been lying. "That production can't be the result of the readings you just took."

"And yet it is."

Orloff shook her head in amazement. "Is that sorcery?" she asked.

"It is not. It is technology. *My* technology. You will not find the like outside Latveria."

"That, I can well believe," said Orloff, and she sounded proud. Then she turned thoughtful. She drummed her fingers on the helmet. "What I can do," she said, "and what I can see … is *that* sorcery?"

"What is your evaluation?" Doom asked. He watched her think things through. *Go, Doctor Orloff. Show me the depth of your perception.*

"No," she said at last. "It isn't sorcery. That's not something I can do. But what I *am* doing is impossible." She looked frustrated.

"Your uncertainty is understandable. You have arrived at the point where technology and sorcery become indistinguishable. Though there are elements of the sorcerous in the tools you have used, in the weapons you wield, and in what you have witnessed beyond the veil of death, you have traveled to this point on a road that is the one familiar to you, and on which you have spent years honing your skills, and that is the road of science."

"I see," said Orloff.

Yes, she did understand. She was an apt pupil.

Orloff watched the weapon parts pouring out onto the conveyor belt. "How well will those work?" she asked.

"Well enough, though what the modified force rifles will do will be a rough approximation of your capabilities. They will be effective at short range. They will also be just as lethal to living beings as they are now. But then, so are bullets. The frequency they will fire is based on your neural patterns, as they exist when you are severing the connection between the urvullak and the Devourer. The frequency is fired forward, rather than being a field, so the guards are safe from their own weapons. These weapons will help in the struggle. Your mind, however, is far more precise than a simple tool."

"When I attacked the urvullak that had Kariana, I didn't hurt her," said Orloff.

"You did not."

Orloff looked at her palm. "When I fired, the beam, or my sense of the beam, wrapped around her."

"Correct. The suit and the helmet amplify the power of your mind, but you control the direction of the blow. You saw where the attack had to land, so that is where it did." Doom paused. "That is not all your vision can do."

Orloff nodded. "It took some getting used to, seeing liminally."

"You have some measure of control now?"

"Yes. I don't see through things unless I want to."

"How far do you think you can see?"

"I honestly don't know."

"Then it is time you learned," said Doom. "See how a true hunter sees. Put the helmet on."

The neurosurgeon obeyed.

"Choose a direction, and now look. Look deeply. Look past all the obstacles." She was strong. She was skilled. She would be what he needed her to be.

Orloff wobbled for a moment, as if fighting vertigo, then steadied. "I can see a long way," she said.

"As though you were on a high prominence," said Doom. "Because there are no barriers to your sight. Not even the curvature of the Earth can hide things from you now. The only limitation is the strength of your eyes."

"I'm seeing for miles," Orloff said. The awe in her voice was clear even with the mild electronic distortion that came from its being passed through the helmet's speakers.

"Keep looking," said Doom. "Find them," he ordered.

Orloff stiffened.

"You see the urvullak," said Doom.

"Yes," she said. Now it was hatred instead of awe in her tone.

"Where are they?"

"I don't know. Far from here. They look tiny, and like they're floating in the air."

"Alter your vision," said Doom. "Allow yourself to see the contours of the physical world again. If walls appear and block your view, you will remember where they are."

Orloff's breath slowed as she concentrated. After a minute, she took the helmet off. "I know where they are," she said. "In the southern part of Old Town. In the rooms above a butcher's."

"Then you know what to do. And you know that there are others too."

Orloff nodded. She examined the arms of the suit and flexed her fists. "I wanted to ask about last night," she said. "When I rescued Kariana. I was able to do things I know I am not physically capable of. At first, I thought it was adrenaline giving me the boost I needed, but I was consistently strong."

"You were not far wrong about adrenaline," said Doom.

"But is the suit making me stronger?"

"It is. This armor must do more than protect you. If you are in battle, you need physical power. What the suit gives you, however, is fueled by your mental effort. Everything about the armor and the helmet is based around the amplification of what you already are."

"Thank you," said Orloff. "I will use it well."

"Go now, then," Doom said. "Let the hunt begin."

Teach Krogh to fear you. Draw and hold her attention. He did not tell Orloff to be the city's champion. He didn't have to. She knew the other task that needed to be completed.

Kariana was already back in the command center, less than six hours after having been taken to the hospital. She still looked drawn, but much stronger than when Orloff had left her bedside to answer Doom's summons to the lab. Orloff joined her at the back of the center, where they could speak privately while Kariana still kept an eye on the wall of screens and the ongoing hunt for the urvullak.

"Should you be up?" Orloff asked, concerned but also glad to see the fire back in her wife's eyes.

"You're the doctor." Kariana gave her a wry smile. "You tell me."

"I know what I'd say if you were under my care," said Orloff. "But I also know that there's a difference between what you should do and what you need to do."

"And I *need* to be here," Kariana said. "It feels good to be on my feet. It feels good to be fighting back."

Orloff touched her cheek. "You definitely sound like yourself."

"Good," said Kariana. "Good." She expressed a world of relief in that word. "The thing tried to take me, Ellie," she said. "It was stealing everything that is *me*."

"I know. I've felt that pull, too, but not like you did." She wished she had been a bit faster. *I wish I could have spared you that.*

"It was like a ripping," said Kariana. "For just a moment, I was me and I was seeing me torn away at the same time." She put a hand over her heart, as if she were holding herself inside. "I'm scarred inside."

Orloff winced. She put her hand over Kariana's. "Scarred?" she asked.

"That's how I'd describe it. It's strange, being put back together. I worry that there might be pieces missing."

Orloff shook her head, emphatic. "If there are, I would have noticed," she said. "You're still you." That was the most important truth. Kariana was who she had always been. But it had been close. The urvullak had almost taken her. They would pay for that. "You're still mine," she said. "My Kari."

"Good," Kariana said again, with even more relief this time. "Good." Her frame relaxed, and still more color came back into her cheeks. "So," she said, "now it's my turn to send you off to war."

"I'm going after them. I know how to find them."

"Make them fear you, my love. Make them have nightmares about you."

Orloff left the command center and hit the streets. Doom had placed an armored car and driver at her disposal. It and the guard, a white-haired veteran named Hugo Zhenkov, were waiting for her on the other side of the castle's moat. Orloff had considered driving herself, but she saw the wisdom of Doom's arrangements. She could focus on the finding the urvullak without distraction this way. She wouldn't have to split her attention between searching for the monsters and keeping the road safely solid in her view.

Orloff put the helmet on and turned around slowly,

scanning the region, before she got into the car. She saw more of the urvullak this time. Her skin crawled. The effect of peering through the walls to find the horrors was like lifting up a rock to see maggots squirming into the earth.

There were so many.

Orloff felt a spasm of anxiety, and her throat tightened with hate and revulsion. Without focusing intently on each of the urvullak, she only had the vaguest sense of where they were, and she didn't know if the individuals and clusters she saw were about to be found by patrols or not. The scale of the struggle ahead staggered her. It would have been easy to despair.

Do what you have to do, she told herself. *One hunt at a time. Each one would make a difference.*

Make them fear you.

The urvullak she had located earlier were the nearest, as far as she could tell, and she knew where they were. She kept them as her target.

"Kiesche's Meats," she said to Zhenkov. "Stop a block away."

He gave her a sharp nod and a quick grin, letting her know that he was pleased to be in on the hunt. They climbed into the car, and he drove off through Old Town. Orloff took the helmet off for part of the way, seeing Doomstadt the way all the other hunters did, as a maze of infinite hiding places. Every wall concealed secrets. Every alley was a potential ambush point. The full import of what she was able to see sank in. Krogh had turned the very being of the city against its inhabitants.

She was going to turn it back against the urvullak.

Zhenkov stopped the car just down the street from Kiesche's Meats. Orloff got out, put the helmet on and headed down the road. She looked up, through the walls and floors to where the urvullak hid. There were six of them, two stories up. They were motionless.

They were not asleep. They didn't sleep. They couldn't. She wasn't going to surprise them that way.

But she was going to surprise them.

They stirred when she slowed down and stopped outside the shop's door. They unfolded their limbs and moved to the window. Orloff kept her head level, as if she were peering into the store. She was looking up, though, marking the positions of the urvullak. After a moment of crowding, five of them moved away from the window as if a will had yanked them back. One remained.

You can see me. You think that I can't see you.

The lights were off in the store, though in the liminal perspective, the interior was the same clear, precisely limned gray as the outside. The cold cuts in the display case and the sausages hanging above the counter appeared to Orloff like diagrams of meat, rather than the things themselves. The urvullak, though, had reality here. They belonged to the world beyond the veil, and that gave them substance in her eyes. They were the only objects she could not see through. That made them easier to spot.

Orloff tried the door. It was locked. She put her shoulder to it and saw herself breaking through it. She felt the armor stiffen. It vibrated slightly, as if a warm electrical current ran through it and along her limbs. The door creaked, cracked and then broke in half.

Orloff entered the shop. She walked slowly, stopping and turning her head back and forth, as if peering around. *Were they listening? Were they hearing their prey sneaking inside and pausing nervously because she didn't know if there might be danger about? Were they getting ready for an easy kill?*

She looked up through the floor. The urvullak were moving again, taking up positions around the doorway of the room where they hid.

Keep thinking that, you wretches. Keep thinking that you're the ones preparing the ambush.

She knew they weren't thinking. She knew they weren't capable of strategy. If they were reacting carefully to her presence instead of storming down the stairs to attack her, that was because Krogh was controlling them, which meant Krogh was about to get another look at her.

Good. They should be afraid of what she could do.

Even though she knew that Krogh was the true consciousness in the room above, it was still hard for Orloff not to think of the urvullak as individual enemies. She had seen them, and not Krogh, attack Kariana.

Orloff made her way to the back of the shop, and to the staircase leading to the apartments above. She kept up her show of caution, taking the steps slowly, pausing in mock alarm after each creak. She stopped on the first landing just long enough to give the impression of looking down the corridor, then carried on to the second floor above the shop's level.

At the top of the stairs, there was a short hallway with bedrooms on either side. All the doors were closed. The urvullak were behind the second one on the left. Orloff opened the first doors, stopping for a moment in front of each bedroom. All the time, she kept her eyes on the urvullak, watching them tense in readiness.

She was grateful for her liminal sight of the bedrooms. It turned the home into a representation of one, every detail present but utterly without life. She wasn't seeing a real place where people had died. She wasn't seeing the tragic absences. She was moving through a backdrop, a setting for the struggle between herself and the urvullak. It had no more weight or meaning than that.

The impact of the meaning might come later, in her dreams, when her guard was down. She would deal with that then. For now, when it mattered, she kept her focus on the things that sought to make her one of them.

Orloff reached the door. She looked into the room, counting the monsters one more time, seeing how she would have to attack. They were arranged in a semi-circle around the door.

Straightforward, she thought. *Hit them counterclockwise, starting at three o'clock.*

I'm going to make you proud, Kari.

She raised her right hand and took hold of the doorknob with her left. Her gauntlet hummed with the frequency she was about to let loose.

The urvullak tensed.

You can hear me. I can see you. This is what's happening – I'm about to ambush you.

Orloff triggered the weapon and threw the door open. The urvullak leapt straight into the lethal frequency as Orloff swept her arm from left to right. She blasted them to ash, this disease that had tried to take Doomstadt.

She destroyed them, these things that had tried to take her Kari.

•••

Doom circled Doomstadt slowly from the air, taking in the city and its quiet war.

Had he done enough?

The modified force rifles were already being distributed. The Guard would now be far more effective against the urvullak. Orloff was hunting, and he could see in her the rapid development of a new sense of purpose. Perhaps it would grow to an obsession. Either would be useful. She was committed now. She was only one person, but she was a powerful weapon against the urvullak.

Had he done enough? No. Not yet. The war would not be won this way.

Orloff could not destroy all the urvullak in the city on her own. The guards would not be able to find every one of the monsters. Krogh would still be able to grow her forces. It would just take her more time, and more effort.

This was a stalemate at best. But that was enough.

Krogh's attention would be held on Doomstadt. Orloff especially would enrage her. *She can see your creatures, Krogh. She can see you far better than you can see her.*

The stalemate would hold long enough for him to do what was necessary to strike the final blow, and take back everything Krogh had seized.

He was going to break the wall. Then he was going to break Krogh.

Doom flew higher and turned north, towards the Carpathians.

He hadn't even left Doomstadt behind when his communicator buzzed and Zargo came on the line, breathless and frantic.

"*Lord Doom!*" he shouted over a chaos of snarls and explosions in the background. "*She's here! Krogh is here! She's attacking the dig!*"

TWENTY

The monsters poured down the sides of the shaft and into the cavern like a rain of spiders. Guards fired at them, trying to hold the urvullak at the mouth of the shaft, but there were too many. The force rifles shot some of them down. A few lay helpless, spines and limbs pulverized. They twitched and screamed, and they could not move for their prey. Others dragged themselves toward the guards. If all they had was a single hand that still functioned, that was enough to pull them over the mounds of history's debris towards the guards and workers.

Down the walls came hundreds more of the undead. They climbed with unnatural speed and ability, their jerking, insect-like movements speeding them down to the wide open killing below.

Zargo stared at them for a long moment, frozen by disbelief. It was the event, and not the monsters, that his mind refused to grapple with. He was back at Walpurgis Night again. The vast space of the cavern was the nave of St Peter, and the urvullak were the demons laying siege. There was too much repetition, and the horror was once more something he could not stop.

He shook himself free of the moment. *This was not the past. This was now.*

Do something. Save these people.

The urvullak hadn't reached any of the workers or the guards yet. The first casualties were only seconds away, though. Zargo reached into the earth, seeking the ley lines. St Peter had been built over a node of geomantic power, an intersection of ley lines, and on Walpurgis Night he had pulled that power to the surface and turned it into a web of energy that had held the demons back. He tried to do that now.

He failed. There was no intersection of lines here. The currents of the earth were too broken and wounded by the presence of the Devourer's vault. There was only pain here, and the memories of agony. The lines he grasped were too weak for him to drag to the surface and weave.

Despairing, he spread his reach farther, and took hold of the earth itself. Sweating from the strain of keeping himself aware of his surroundings at the same time that he sent his consciousness through the bedrock, he lashed out. He whipped his arms out, hands clawed, miming a strike at the monsters rushing across the cavern floor to the encampment.

A ridge of rock shot up like a whip. It hurled urvullak into the air, then came down with a ground-shaking rumble, crushing more of the undead out of existence.

Zargo yelled and struck out again. A line of stalagmites erupted from the floor, impaling urvullak.

It was like trying to destroy a column of ants with a rake.

He slowed the advance of the enemy down in one part of the cavern. He could not stop them.

He had been in one spot all this time, at his usual post just outside the magic circle. He saw the inevitable coming, cursed his failure, and cursed again when he knew what he had to do.

Scores of urvullak were already on the ground. They were taking the first of their prey. They would overwhelm the encampment in short order. He could die fighting them, and then become one of them. He could make that futile gesture. Or he could flee the cavern. He could warn Doom.

Could?

He *must*.

His hover platform was twenty yards away. He ran for it, conscious that he had wasted precious time already. He sprinted past the hills of artifacts, the shape of the hover platform seeming miles away.

A heap of oil paintings on his right slid down, knocked out of its precarious equilibrium by an urvullak jumping on to them, and then skidding down the slope toward Zargo.

The urvullak leapt at him. He reacted on instinct. He clapped his hands together, and two slabs of flysch slammed up and against one another, a sudden vice that crushed the urvullak's torso to pulp. The head snapped at Zargo twice more before it became still.

Zargo kept running, the image of the urvullak's face seared into his soul.

Its eyes.

He had been ready for monstrosity. He had been ready for the hunger Doom had warned him about. He had not been prepared for the pain and the grief he saw in the monster's face. The urvullak was empty, and what remained of its mind knew that it was. Its eyes were tortured by its experience of the true void.

They were what he thought he was.

Only he wasn't empty. *Not like them.*

He wouldn't be like them.

More urvullak closed with him over the final yards to the hover platform. He snatched at the ground, and his survival frenzy twisted the earth. Fissures opened and swallowed the urvullak. Rock rose and bent like sea waves, and folded the monsters inside its curl. The cavern boomed with the cracks of stone and the raging of the undead.

Zargo jumped onto the hover platform. He grabbed the steering unit, and for a slippery second he couldn't remember how to operate the vehicle. But then he did, and he urged up. He took it above the spreading carnage and aimed it at the shaft.

He paused halfway up to the roof of the cavern. The urvullak were still coming down the shaft. He couldn't risk trying to get past them in the shaft. It was too narrow. He wouldn't last two seconds.

Helpless, trapped, he moved back and forth, avoiding the bodies that fell, staying out of reach, waiting for the invasion to end.

Doom must know.

He still had the communicator bead in his ear. He was about to touch it when a figure caught his eye below, an urvullak, but different from the rest. The other monsters moved around the striding creature as if it were the eye of a hurricane.

Krogh, he thought. *It was Krogh. It had to be.*

She moved with the assurance that comes with the certainty of power. She was the center of gravity for the urvullak. Her will moved them. Their actions were the expressions of her desire.

Zargo reached down with his own will. He tried to seize the earth and surround her with it. He had to stop her. Even as he began his attack, he wondered how far he could take it. He was no executioner, but he did not know if there was any way to stop the horrors Krogh had unleashed except through her destruction.

He was too late. She had already stepped across the barrier of the magic circle. Whether Doom's occult barrier was the sole cause, or the proximity of the Devourer's vault and its unnatural material played a role as well, Zargo could not move the earth inside the ring. Rock slid from his mental grasp, just like the interior of the vault blocked his perception.

Perhaps he made the ground vibrate. Something drew Krogh's attention. She turned around, then looked up. Her gaze met Zargo's. He flinched. She was a monster, distorted in body and soul like the creatures she controlled. She was also majestic in her power. Her majesty was not the same as Doom's. It was rotten. It lay on her like a robe eaten by moths and nibbled by rats. It crawled with vermin. Yet it was also real, and vast, fed by the strength that was now hers, and by the hate that was her birthright. Like Doom, she was an absolute, and Zargo's blood turned to ice under that gaze that saw all the world as a possession to torture.

He couldn't fight her. Only another absolute could.

He broke with her gaze and flew higher, trying to escape her attention. He called Doom now on the communicator, and shouted his warning while, below, the battle for the dig site was lost. Munitions exploded as the last of the guard fought the urvullak, and fell beneath their tide.

"*Where is she?*" Doom asked. "*Where is she exactly?*"

"She's at the wall," said Zargo.

"*Has she destroyed the drills?*"

"No. She's leaving them alone."

The operators of the drills went down too, overwhelmed by the urvullak and then joining their number.

"How long will the drills function without technicians?" Zargo asked, grasping at bleak hope.

"*That problem will not arise for Krogh,*" Doom answered, his anger as cold as it was savage.

"I don't understand." Zargo evaded a monster that dropped down at him from the ceiling. It hit the cavern floor with a loud crack and didn't move.

"*Krogh now has all the memories of the technicians,*" said Doom. "And what she knows, she can command her urvullak to do."

Already, a few of the monsters were heading back to the drills. They moved with sharp jerks, as if their actions went against the nature of their bodies. But they operated the drill controls, and the machines continued their work without interruption.

"She's going to break through the wall," Zargo said, despairing.

"*She faces the same obstacle I have,*" said Doom. "*She is not through yet.*"

"The pyramid," said Zargo. "We must activate it."

"*No!*" Doom barked. "*A trap is futile if it is sprung before its prey is within its jaws. Can you reach the surface?*"

Zargo looked up. There were no more urvullak descending into the cavern. The way looked clear. "I think so."

"*Then go. Protect the control center. Protect the pyramid. That is how best you can delay Krogh until I am with you.*" There was a slight pause, then Doom spoke with the relish of promised retribution. "*And now we know where she is.*"

Doom cut the connection, and Zargo aimed over the platform at the shaft. He understood what Doom meant when he said the pyramid could not be used. He was also troubled by the convenience of that fact for Doom. *Could he not have designed it otherwise? Could there not have been a provision to seal the Devourer away forever by containing the vault within the pyramid's prison?*

Of course there could have been. But that was never Doom's intention. The Devourer was to be his prize, and he would not countenance any other possibility. He would have ruled out any design that could have led to the Devourer being placed beyond his grasp.

How many times will you conjure Hell before it takes us all, Lord Doom?

Zargo entered the shaft and began the climb up. Even at the hover platform's full speed, the distance seemed endless, the time before he reached the surface an eternity. He could already be too late to do any good at all. The longer he flew up, the more he despaired.

Below, the sounds of battle ceased. The cavern belonged to Krogh.

A hideous sound rattled up from the cave and chased Zargo up the shaft. It rang in his ears like the stuttering mockery of a raven's croak.

It was Krogh's laughter.

•••

You will pay, Krogh. You will pay for what you have cost me, and you will pay for this insult. You will kneel, broken, before me, and beg for the relief of your destruction.

Doom cursed Krogh as he flew, and he cursed the events that had conspired to his humiliation.

The land raced by beneath him, a blur of forests and farms and villages and hills. The winds of October seemed to blow in from the Carpathians, and the mountains remained stubbornly distant on the horizon. The sky lowered, darker than before, a storm brewing as if in answer to the tumult of the war.

Doom pushed his jetpacks harder. He flew like a comet of vengeance toward the dig site. *He was coming for Krogh. This was her reckoning at last.*

Except he knew it wasn't. She had fooled him. He thought he had been keeping her attention focused on Doomstadt. The reality was the other way around. Krogh had lured him away from the dig site, had forced him to abandon his quest there in order to defend Latveria.

He should have stayed.

That wasn't true either. If he had, then Doomstadt would have fallen. Krogh had constructed the perfect trap. It was one he could not have avoided even if he had seen it.

But he hadn't. And that compounded the humiliation.

Krogh did not have the imagination to conceive of the debt she had incurred, and that she would be made to pay, with interest. Doom tried to will himself to the dig site. The mountains refused him. They kept their distance.

He could strike now. He could command the Damocles satellite to destroy the site.

It was a foolish thought. An unworthy one. Have it now, expend it, and be done with it. There would be no room for mistakes at the site.

If he fired Damocles, he might unleash the Devourer, while destroying the means of containment. It was even possible that Krogh was trying to goad him into making that error.

No. That was not possible. She would be destroyed too.

Doom cursed her again, furious that Krogh should be taking up so much room in his mind, her phantasm urging him to foolish speculation and reckless action.

He could not act now. There was nothing he could do, except fly and rage.

Doom roared. Above, the clouds rumbled in answer, shaken by his wrath.

Krogh ran her clawed hand over the wall. She savored its growing weakness. "I am here," she rasped. She pressed her ear against the dark barrier, listening as if the thing beyond could respond. "Do you feel me here? I have come for you."

Her losses were continuing in Doomstadt. She could feel her eyes being put out there one by one. They didn't matter. That hunter who could see the urvullak wherever they hid and destroy them with a gesture didn't matter. That woman's little victories counted for nothing, and Krogh would teach her that soon enough, just as she was teaching Doom the folly of trying to defeat her.

He was, she was sure, conscious of his education at this moment.

He was on his way.

Yes, he was. He was on his way to another defeat.

He was still dangerous.

But not for much longer.

Every loss Krogh had experienced, from the day King Vladimir fell until now, was on the verge of being repaid. Every loss, regardless of their injustice and how they had angered her in the moment, now seemed worthwhile. The losses had led to here. The final steps to total victory were before her.

Don't waste time.

There was time. Doom could not stop her now. Doomstadt was too far, even for him.

Are you sure?

The drills were making good progress, but the vault was not breached yet. She had stolen the site from Doom. She must not risk the irony of his taking it back and trapping her here.

Krogh sent her awareness out along the length of Latveria from the Carpathians to Doomstadt. At her command, all the urvullak in the wilds looked up, watching for the usurper. After a few moments she had him located. She watched through different eyes the burning line of Doom's flight.

Krogh's lips pulled back in a snarl's rictus. Doom was coming more quickly than she had thought possible. She struck the fractured wall with a fist. She could not tell how long it would be before the Devourer was free of its prison.

Too long.

The wall might break in the next minute or the next hour, or maybe not then, she realized. She could feel the eagerness on the other side, the inchoate need for souls and the shaped meaning of lives lived. The Devourer sensed its imminent liberation too, but it was a prisoner. It could not help her to shatter the wall. She needed to go faster, to break through the barrier quicker than Doom's tools permitted. They were too slow because Doom and Krogh had not come here for the same reason. Doom sought control. *She sought union.*

The memories of everyone at the dig site but Zargo were hers now. Everything they had worked on, everything they had seen, everything they had heard, and everything they had said belonged to her. She thought through her new knowledge. She examined all the means that Doom had gathered, looking for something she could use.

Her thoughts zeroed in on the pyramid. She found what she needed.

She shifted her awareness from the cavern to the surface. She had left some of the urvullak she had summoned for this battle at the site, and she used them now. She sent them to the control center.

The priest was there, guarding the entrance. He had already been fending off attacks as the urvullak, free to follow their instincts, had tried to feast on him. He had fought them off, and Krogh's contempt for the man grew. She had never known him personally. He had come to St Peter after the fall of the Fortunovs. She had known who he was, during the years she had taken part in Rudolfo Fortunov's useless guerilla war. She had made a point of knowing who all the figures of authority in Doom's regime were, however symbolic that authority. If they did not fight against Doom, then they would be punished when the Old Order was restored. She felt a special disdain for Zargo. Fortunov had tried to use him against Doom, and the coward had gone crawling to the usurper. He was a traitor to the rightful rulers of Latveria, and he was a traitor to his calling as a priest.

The terrain outside Doom's quarters looked as if it had suffered a volcanic eruption. Jagged protrusions of stone and new mounds of boulders blocked access to the quarters, and the smashed bodies of urvullak stuck out, with a hand here and a leg there, from beneath the rock.

The priest was fighting as a geomancer.

You are a traitor to everything but your master, Father Zargo. You are pathetic.

Krogh took hold of the horde and made the urvullak attack in a more concerted fashion. They surrounded Zargo before rushing in. Krogh held the charge back for another moment to strike the priest with the force of her judgment first.

She spoke through the throats of the urvullak. "Is this how you honor your god, Father Zargo? By dying as a lickspittle for the usurper?"

"If I die, I die fighting evil. I am at peace with that."

He sounded calm, and that infuriated Krogh. "You have abandoned the traditions that should have commanded your loyalty. You are a worm, and will meet your end as one."

"I have sinned," said Zargo. "I am fallen. I have many regrets, and I have been weak when I wished I could have been strong. But I do not regret the fact that I have never stood for the traditions you value. I have never acted in the name of those for whom tradition and murder are the same thing."

"You will regret that now," Krogh told him, and she hurled the urvullak at him.

Devour him. Make him ours, but shred his flesh first. Make him the weakest amongst you. His hunger will be all the worse.

The urvullak scrambled over the stone barriers, and Zargo hurled them back with new formations surging out of the ground. He made the surface drop into craters, and then molded their sides to come together, crushing the urvullak caught in the depressions. The earth flowed and changed at his command, and he kept Doom's quarters out of Krogh's hands.

The urvullak kept charging, and he kept blocking and destroying them.

He was tired. Krogh could see that. And he was growing more exhausted with the constant mental effort it took constantly to be shaping stone. She could wear him down in the end, but only if she had enough urvullak to throw at him.

He was whittling down the numbers.

Krogh sent the undead in the cavern back up into the shaft. She had no need of them here now. The battle was over. All of Doom's workers served her.

The urvullak climbed quickly, tirelessly, driven by hunger and whipped by her will. It took time for them to climb, though, during which the standoff at the surface continued. Krogh flicked her consciousness away from the dig site for a moment, and sent it back south again.

How close is Doom? Find him. How much time is left?

She found him, and he was drawing closer, and her earlier confidence wavered.

She could not stop Doom. She had to render his arrival pointless.

She tried to gauge the speed of his flight against the speed of her army's ascent. She could not.

Krogh turned her attention back to Zargo. She would not gaze on what she could not change. What mattered was defeating the priest.

Zargo held the urvullak at bay for a while longer. He even

began to seem triumphant, his eyes bright beneath the sheen of fatigue on his brow. But when the other urvullak reached the surface, his triumph withered. He knew he could not beat her now.

Krogh launched the urvullak at him with renewed numbers and speed. He could not summon the earth to his aid fast enough. They clung to the leaping stones, and scrambled over them. Enough of the urvullak escaped the upheavals to reach Doom's quarters.

Zargo could not strike back at them without destroying the building. He jumped back onto his hover platform and shot up out of the grasp of claws. Krogh made urvullak leap from the top of boulders, but Zargo rose too quickly. Hands and jaws snapped at him, then fell back to Earth.

Let him go, she thought. *His escape was only temporary. He would receive his judgment in due course.*

Urvullak rushed into Doom's quarters and up into the control center. Krogh made them circle the throne and the banks of devices at the edge of the arcane table. Individually, none of the workers at the site knew much of anything about the functions of Doom's machines. Even collectively, the knowledge they furnished Krogh was very limited. This was a place of Doom's secrets. She did not know how to operate the pyramid.

She didn't need to. She had enough knowledge for what was necessary.

Sabotage.

The lights in the chamber flared in anger as the urvullak dragged their claws over the controls.

•••

The storm broke in the Carpathians as Doom closed in on the site. Lightning lit the peaks, flashing them into silhouettes. Rain came down in sweeping curtains.

Almost there.

He was heading for the last ridge beyond which he would find the bowl when the intrusion alerts of his quarters sounded. At the same time, Zargo was calling again, shouting about failure. Doom silenced the priest and the alarms. There was nothing useful they could tell him. He knew what the warnings portended.

It hadn't happened yet.

He was not defeated yet.

How many times had he told himself those lies in the past? How many times had Reed Richards turned those hopes to bitterness?

And now Krogh…

No. She would not have this day. She would not have his prize.

He shot over the ridge and into the bowl. He flew down the slope, his quarters in his sights.

The pyramid groaned. A note, deep as time's voice, sounded. Crimson light smeared across the obsidian and silver of the structure.

No.

It was too late. There was nothing he could do. There was nothing that could stop what was happening. But he could not retreat, and so Doom kept flying down, attacking, because that was all there was left to do.

Violet beams shot out from beneath the pyramid, disintegrating its supports.

The pyramid dropped, slamming to the ground with an Armageddon thunder.

Then day turned into molten night.

PART 3

LEVIATHAN

We are the ministers of pain, and fear,
And disappointment, and mistrust, and hate,
And clinging crime; and as lean dogs pursue
Through wood and lake some struck and sobbing fawn,
We track all things that weep, and bleed, and live,
When the great King betrays them to our will.
PERCY SHELLEY, PROMETHEUS UNBOUND, L.452–457

TWENTY-ONE

The pyramid, activated before its time, its devices turned against itself, exploded. In the cavern, the blast of unleashed, misdirected and conflicted sorcery came down as destruction and liberation. What had been designed as a prison became, in its distorted form, the breaker of prisons.

If Krogh had not been embracing the wall of the vault at the moment of the blast, she would have been annihilated. She felt the exterminating force of the explosion, and she felt what could have extinguished all memory of her being. But the moment that would have been her destruction was also the moment that the wall disintegrated and freed the Devourer.

The difference between Krogh's end and her apotheosis came down to a balance between infinitesimal slivers of time. They were too small to measure with any human device, which would have found only simultaneity. But there was a difference, and in its minuteness was the key to the colossal. With the power she had gathered since her transformation, the power that was hers because of her link to the Devourer, Krogh resisted destruction for that unmeasurable iota of a moment that was world enough and time for the Devourer to emerge from the vault. Krogh still existed when the Devourer erupted in freedom, and so it found her, and they came together as one.

The sorcerous explosion filled the cavern, scouring all its features and all its relics from the face of reality. Krogh's awareness of the blast vanished in her encounter with the Devourer. The plenitude of unleashed energy disappeared before the maw of that which was emptier than nothing. The Devourer was an anti-nothing, a sucking void as powerful as a black hole. It was hunger itself, pure and eternal.

She belonged to it.

It was hers.

It was *her*.

The hunger that had tortured Krogh since she became the queen of the urvullak was insignificant in comparison to the new hunger. She screamed in pain and need, and then she roared triumph at the promise of the feast, because her power to feed was now equal to the hunger. The Devourer craved souls and could never be sated. It also possessed the memories of all the souls it had consumed. It was not sentient. It had not thoughts. It only had need. But Krogh could think, and the memories were hers now too. Hers too were the means to reach out, as the Devourer always had. Its prison had been strong, but it had also been porous. As it consumed memories, the Devourer also created new ones, as death always had. Death came, and on its prey it inflicted scars. To the bereaved, it brought the experience and the memories of absence, of grief and of hunger for what was lost. It brought fear, too, to the dying and to the survivors. As she came into the being of her new self, transformed once more and raised to dark godhood, Krogh exulted in the possibility of the weapon that was now hers to wield.

Her consciousness transformed too. Before, she commanded the urvullak, saw what they saw, and knew what they knew. But her awareness had remained that of an individual, and though she could leap between the perspectives of separate urvullak at the speed of thought, she had still been limited by the singularity of her mind.

No longer. Now she was all the urvullak at once. She saw through all their eyes, and there was no confusion in being everywhere and seeing everything. She was present across Latveria, and there was no need to focus on one event or another. She focused on all at the same time. She could issue a separate command to every urvullak in the same instant. She had become a collective, and it was ruled by a single, monarchical consciousness. She was Krogh, and she held the nation in her hands.

In the cavern, the destruction had passed. The space was an empty one now. There was no trace of the heaped, solidified memories. Not even a scrap of twisted iron remained where the drills had been. She was alone in an expanse of bare rock. But she remembered every object that had been in the cavern. They were all her memories now. They were so many bricks in the edifice of omniscience.

Krogh turned to the gap in the wall, to the hole that had been the Devourer's prison. There was nothing there now, just more bare rock. Who or what had built the prison was a memory that not even the Devourer possessed. Perhaps it was the primal loss, the thing that drove all its hunger because it was the thing that could never be regained. Their work was gone now, scoured from existence by the liberation of the prisoner.

Krogh looked up at the shaft. She smiled as she contemplated what had happened on the surface. She laughed as her legions gathered at her command.

It was time to feast, and to restore Latveria to its rightful state. Time for old memories to reassert themselves. Time for the past to strike down the present and become the unchanging future.

Krogh spread her arms, and she rose into the air. Hunger was a flame, a conflagration that would brook no obstacle. Because she must feed, she must fly.

And so she flew.

When the pyramid erupted, all of the sorcery that Doom had embedded in its constructions came whipping back at him. Disrupted, the spells rebounded on their maker. The initial force and light of the explosion were physical destruction, and they smashed him back through a storm of shrieking, abyssal light. He hurtled into the mountainside, striking as hard as a meteor and punching a crater into the south face of the peak. The mountain trembled, and millions of tons of rock broke apart and swept down into the bowl, only to vaporize when it struck the whirling tempest of the raging sorcery.

Doom's force field triggered automatically and prevented the impact from pulping his body. Even so, a ball of pain squeezed his ribs with a constrictor grip. He could barely breathe, and was struggling to hold on to consciousness when the real blowback hit him.

Shattered, its coherence spewing off into the space over the Carpathians and shredding the clouds with whipping coils of energy, the spell of imprisonment that Doom had woven into the pyramid still retained its function, and snapped back to make him its victim. The rebound fell on him in successive fragments, like a hail of chains. Doom struggled with his own creation, fought against his own power. He had designed the pyramid to be strong enough to contain a god, and that force drove him deeper and deeper into the mountain, wrapping him in layer upon layer of power turned into shackles for the body, the mind and the soul.

Thrice bound, thrice punished, he had to fight for each counter with the knowledge that he was on the brink of destruction, that the slightest mistake or weakness would see him entombed forever.

And the initial blast had weakened him, and every strike by his own power weakened him more.

His frame was in agony, and he could barely think. Only his will was as strong as it ever was. It refused to let him be defeated. It fought back in fury against the imprisonment, fought with even greater anger against every blow.

The interior of the mountain turned to lava. It flowed around him, sealing him in, forming the coffin of eternity. The chains of sorcery wrapped around him, holding his arms at his side, immobilizing his fingers so they could not shape the incantatory gestures of the counter-spells. Other chains held him at a deeper level, locking his jaw, freezing his mind so the words and the mental constructs of freedom could not come.

His will found a way. His will would always find a way. It had freed him from Hell. It would free him from this. It was what made him Doom.

It didn't matter how much he had seen and then lost on Walpurgis Night. It didn't matter what knowledge and the power that came with it had been wrenched away. No defeat he encountered truly mattered, because he would never accept it as final.

It did not end here. The thought was a product of his will, and it was full, complete and strong. It was not a denial. It was a command, one that even the fates had to obey.

It did not end here.

Because this was not the end, he found the broken edges of the chain that bound his thoughts, and he flung it away. And now he could think clearly, even as the other shackles closed around him more tightly, the molten center of the coffin expanded in the heart of the mountain.

Doom used the heat of the lava against the prisons. The thermo-energizer of his armor took in the heat, building up its power until it was supercharged. His armor vibrated with energy, and he held the blast back, gathering the force he needed to smash the chains of his own devising. He focused some of the force into his fists, let one small portion of the power push back against the chains, and he regained the movement of his fingers. Now they could weave the first counter-spells, and with a supreme mental effort, he broke another chain.

Now he could speak.

Now he engaged fully in the mystical struggle. He cast an enchantment to work in conjunction with the thermo-energizer. He absorbed the power that attacked him, took it in repeatedly, building it up until the concentration of physical and sorcerous energy contained within his form was greater than the forces that entombed him.

Then, and only then, did he unleash it.

It was as if a quasar burst inside the mountain. The sudden flash of power was so intense, it was felt around the world. The psychically sensitive everywhere, asleep or awake, winced from a sudden, piercing, third-eye migraine that came and vanished in an instant. In the Carpathians, the effect was seismic. The mountain split from the peak to its core, a volcanic transformation. The sides trembled and parted, and Doom shot up from the interior, the center of a combustion of forces that burned through levels of reality, searing the boundaries of a dozen dimensions. The mountain seemed to scream in pain. Sundered rock heaved back and forth, caught by the rip currents of the impossible, and then its torn halves slammed into each other and collapsed. The peak sank into itself, and tremors shook its flanks, the death rattles of a great beast. Rockslides tumbled down on every side, pushing up dust clouds that eddied violently around the shooting star of Doom.

The echoes of the destruction rolled away over the slopes and valleys. Doom landed on the torn, bare rock of the new peak.

It began to rain.

He murmured quietly, and calmer mystical streams flowed through his body, healing him, while he took stock of the world around him.

There had been no sense of time while he fought inside the

mountain. He saw now that he must have been caught in the shackles for hours. Night had fallen. Some distance away, a few hundred yards down the slope towards the ruins of the dig site, was a ten-foot, spherical shell of stone. It was an unnatural formation, the work of someone else's will.

Zargo, Doom thought. *The geomancer had protected himself. He was learning quickly, and perhaps more deeply than simply how to wield his power.*

That would be a subject of interest to contemplate another time. Doom looked down into the bowl. He was exhausted, drained from fighting himself, and the real foe was before him.

Krogh no longer had any need to hide from him. She had stolen his prize, and Doom stared in hatred as she reveled in her triumph.

During Doom's lost hours, urvullak by the hundreds had gathered in the bowl, called by Krogh to replace the numbers that must have been vaporized by the explosion of the pyramid. The new vermin had swarmed in from elsewhere. Perhaps she had held them in reserve, beneath the ground and inside the caves of nearby mountains. She must have guessed what would happen if her attack was successful. Doom wondered if she had guessed what would become of her when she freed the Devourer, and what she would be able to do. Perhaps her new being was a discovery for her. Perhaps what he saw below was the act of joyful, savage revelation.

The urvullak had come together as one. Linking limbs, crushing each other together as no human bodies could, their muscles moving as a single unit, they created a colossus of flesh. The urvullak were a collective more coherent than any hive mind Doom had seen before. As he watched, trying to find the strength to fight again, the urvullak completed their self-construction, and the giant rose from a crouch to stand fifty feet high. The positioning of each urvullak in the shape was so precise that Doom recognized in the monster the clear image of Krogh. She had been distorted by her transformation, but the cruel lines of her family features were present as if the collective form were the work of a master sculptor. Entire bodies shaped the lips, and the line of the nose, and the thin, vicious arc of the eyebrows. The colossus was Krogh as she knew herself to be, the perfect creation of her will.

The shape turned its head back and forth as if seeking something. Its eyes were urvullak curled into tight balls. It did not see with them, but it did see with the hundreds of pairs that looked out from everywhere on its limbs and torso and head. It saw in all directions at once, and Doom perceived in its vision the symbolic reflection of Krogh's omniscience. She had what he desired and had labored to seize.

I will take it back.

Somewhere inside the giant was Krogh herself. The searching movement of its head was the mimicry of her motions. As she acted, so did the construct. She could not have any need to look back and forth that way. Was that a vestigial habit, an instinct staying on from the human she had been?

Or a taunt?

The giant looked up at the peak where Doom stood. Its false eyes stared directly at him.

A taunt, he thought. *She thought to toy with him. She thought her victory was assured.*

No, he realized. That was wrong. She thought her victory was already accomplished.

"*THIS IS THE HOUR, DOOM,*" said Krogh. "*THIS IS YOUR FALL. THIS IS THE RETURN OF LATVERIA'S GREATNESS.*" Hundreds of throats spoke with a single voice. Doom had encountered Krogh during his overthrow of King Vladimir. He had marked her then as dangerous, and so had kept the memory of her voice and appearance fresh. She had proven him to be correct, escaping his purge of the old order then, and his every attempt to crush Rudolfo Fortunov's rebels since. The monstrous voice that issued from the giant was the booming, grating amplification and purification of the voice Doom had heard more than fifteen years before. It was a purification because it was the distilled essence of what Maleva Krogh had always been. That told him something about the being before him. It told him that in the fusion of Krogh and the Devourer, the nature of the beast was shaped by the character of Krogh. It was impressive that she retained her individuality, and that it was not consumed by the Devourer. That also told him how fully he would make the being his own once he wrenched it from her grasp.

He was not going to fight to destroy the Devourer. He could almost hear Zargo's cries of dismay before his determination. Krogh's momentary ascendancy changed nothing. His goal now was the same as it had been the day before, and in the days before that.

The Devourer will be mine.

All he had to do was destroy Krogh.

A simple purpose. A difficult task. He was exhausted. She was renewed.

"Old, tired words," Doom responded to Krogh. "Is that all you are, a repository for faded memories? Latveria's greatness? What a tired, worn-out phrase, coming from the likes of you."

Krogh's laughter sounded forced, and more like a growl of anger. "*LOOK UPON ME!*" she commanded. She spread her arms wide, inviting the worship of a nation that could not yet see her. "*THIS IS JUST THE BEGINNING. I WILL BESTRIDE THE MOUNTAINS! ALL SHALL KNEEL BEFORE ME AND MY GLORY! AND THE GLORY AND JUDGMENT OF LATVERIA SHALL SPAN THE GLOBE!*"

"Tomorrow the world?" Doom said. He was feeling stronger. The time that Krogh wasted in speech was useful to him. He might yet goad her into recklessness too, if recklessness was still a thing that was possible for what she had become. *It was. She was not omnipotent. Not yet.* "More sad clichés," he said. "More pathetic relics. Your words are the fetishes of armchair fascists who never tire of drooling over old lies."

Krogh shook her massive head. A hand that could grasp a tank rose and waggled a finger at Doom. "*YOU ARE THE PATHETIC ONE. YOUR WORDS ARE A FUTILE DEFIANCE. SOON, ALL DEFIANCE IN LATVERIA WILL END. SOON, YOU WILL BE THE MEMORY, CURSED BECAUSE YOU WILL HAVE FAILED YOUR PEOPLE. I WOULD ALMOST CHOOSE TO KEEP YOU ALIVE, SO YOU COULD WITNESS THE PUNISHMENT COMING TO THOSE WHO THOUGHT THEY NO LONGER BELONGED TO THEIR BETTERS.*"

The colossus began to walk. Krogh started up the slope toward Doom. With each step, her gait became more assured and she climbed faster. She left a track of footprints, wet with smears of flesh and bone fragments. The weight of the great body was crushing the urvullak at its base. At the same time, the form gathered more definition, as if the individual urvullak were melting into each other, becoming a single body.

Doom launched himself into the air. He flew down the mountainside. He aimed a heavy concussive blast at the monster's head. The choice of target was a wild guess. No one part of the thing's anatomy would be more vulnerable than another. He just had to hope that he struck the point where the actual body of Krogh resided.

If she still had a body.

His attack punched deep into the giant's skull. It folded in on itself as if it were dough. Pieces of urvullak body rained to the ground. The collective voice roared in anger, and the head reformed, urvullak shifting position to recreate Krogh's face.

You are vain, Krogh. The form is irrelevant. Except, for you, it is not. Latveria must behold you as you choose, is that it? Your anger is a weakness.

Doom circled at a distance. He knew the giant could see him wherever he was. His position was irrelevant for Krogh. He relied on speed instead to give him another few moments to catch his breath. His injuries were healing. They just weren't healing fast enough.

He attacked the head again, destroying its features a second time. Krogh's many throats shouted in anger again. When Doom pulled away a second time, she made a lumbering turn after him, as if she really did have to face him to see him and strike back.

Did she not have the true measure of her being yet? If Krogh was still adjusting, that gave him a chance. He could finish this now. He angled back for another blow.

The colossus changed its form in a lightning-fast blur. Its frame narrowed, and it reached out with an arm that extended three times as long as it had been a moment before.

The movement was familiar in the worst way.

Richards! Doom thought, hate and surprise jolting him, freezing his responses for a fatal second.

The huge, spindly hand seized him, fingers wrapping around him like snakes.

Doom triggered his force field. Urvullak flew away, broken, from the mass. Others whipped into place so fast that the hand's grip remained strong. Krogh's shape changed again, becoming thicker, the limbs strong, pulling Doom in toward the greater mass.

Richards! Richards! Richards! his mind screamed. The hated man, the nemesis, the arrogant leader of the Fantastic Four, the man responsible for Doom's scars, the man who set himself in the path of Doom's destiny. *Richards Richards! Richards!* Doom could not shake off the outraged chant, and he realized the physical grasp was just one part of Krogh's attack. His memories were in turmoil, the image of his nemesis burning through his rational defenses.

How did she know?

He strained against the grip. He clutched desperately at coherent thought, and it turned slippery on him. Memories came at him, hitting like hammer blows.

They were not his.

He saw himself from the outside in assaults of the past. None of the memories came from outside Latveria. They were collages, composites like the colossus, assembled from the pieces of his past witnessed by all the souls the Devourer had taken.

You do not have me yet.

Doom rejected the tormenting constructs of defeat. He centered himself again, anchoring on the conviction that each defeat was the promise of future retribution.

Before he could fight free of her fist, Krogh altered her attacks. Now she assaulted him with all memories, a deluge of a million pasts, complete in every fraction of a moment, flooding into his consciousness at once.

Doom jerked, the psychic noise overwhelming. Blood streamed from his nose and ears. He lost all sense of time and place. He was tumbling through a chaotic vortex of history. His body was a distant mote, caught in the hurricane winds. He could not find himself in the rampage of memories.

All Latveria shrieked at him, demanding his attention.

All Latveria. Indiscriminate, Krogh hit Doom with everything, and made her mistake. Perhaps it was her own history and her personal hatred for Doom that led her to show him the memories of King Vladimir and the deaths of Doom's parents.

Doom saw his mother, Cynthia von Doom, staggering into the woods, bleeding to death from a guard's sword blow. He saw his father, Werner, freezing to death in the mountains where he had fled with the infant Victor. He saw the blood-soaked retaliation Vladimir visited on Cynthia's clan. He felt his parents' anguish, and he felt Vladimir's sadistic satisfaction.

Krogh's hate revived the sharp edge of Doom's wrath. In

the purity of its light, and the agony of memory, he knew who he was, and which scars were *his*, and he fought back. He put all his strength into a mental shield, blocking the flood. The memories buffeted him, thundering waves trying to break through. He held them at bay and triggered a massive surge in his force field. The electrical blast hit Krogh like a solar flare and disintegrated her fist.

Doom flew out of her reach, gasping. He kept the mental shield in place. Free of the colossus, he felt the pounding of the memories diminish.

Then they stopped. Krogh shrieked at Doom, her hate greater than words. Then the giant collapsed to the ground, a mound of insects turning back into its component parts, a carpet of urvullak spreading out in all directions.

Doom felt an adrenal surge of triumph. Then Krogh's shriek became laughter again, scattering away.

Find her. This is your chance. Kill the body.

But the urvullak were indistinguishable in the dark, and vanishing quickly.

Damocles, he thought.

But it would take long minutes to bring it online and trigger.

Another dark thought occurred to him. If all the urvullak could come together to be her single body, perhaps every body was her now.

And she was everywhere.

Before he could decide on any strategy, his communicator erupted with desperate calls. Across Latveria, the urvullak were attacking with renewed fury and power. They laid siege to every city that had not fallen to them, to every sanctuary Doom had created. The war had dozens of simultaneous fronts.

Krogh attacked all Latveria the way she had attacked Doom. The psychic assault was not as concentrated as it had been on him. But it was universal. In the panicked voices that called to him, Doom heard the symptoms of nationwide mass hysteria.

Cursing, he shut down all the channels but one, and managed to get through to Verlak.

"*We need you, my lord,*" she said, and he had never heard such strain in her voice. She sounded like a woman trying to speak calmly while clinging to a clifftop by her fingertips. "*She is doing something…*" Verlak gasped. "So hard to think… We need you here…"

Doom silenced the communicator. *We need you here. Here* was *everywhere*, because that was where Krogh was. In the midst of his frustration and rage, he had a moment, infinitesimal yet crystalline. In it, he had the space to wonder if his fury might not be even greater if he *had* achieved omniscience. Because true omnipresence would never be his, would he be tormented by the knowledge of where he had to, but could not, be?

If so, let that be my price. The power must still be mine, for Doom, and for the world.

Below him, the urvullak had vanished, shadows draining away in the night.

From north and south, and east and west, out of countless caverns and gullies, rattling over the mountains and from the plains, came the croaking laughter of Krogh.

TWENTY-TWO

The stone sphere cracked like an egg. One side shattered completely, opening it to the night and the storm outside. Doom stood in the gap, looking down at Zargo. "The danger is past," he said, and strode a few yards back up the broken slope of the mountain.

Zargo staggered out of the shell. He had conjured it at the last second, when he saw the pyramid drop. The cataclysm he heard outside its protection was so huge, he was surprised the shell had survived, and him with it. The bowl was almost unrecognizable, and not even ruins remained of the equipment and structures of the dig site.

Zargo moved slowly, learning how to control his body while he protected his mind and his soul. The rock sphere was no protection from the memory assault. Zargo found refuge from it by keeping half his consciousness embedded deep in the earth. There was some peace for him there, among the currents of power running through stone, and a history that was measured in eras. The Devourer left its scars on the memories of the earth too, but there were no human traumas there. The pain was slow. Zargo could exist in its presence without harm.

Doom watched him make his approach, and said, "You are straddling the worlds."

"Yes," said Zargo. There was a slight delay between trying to speak and the words coming out. His lips and tongue felt far away and numb, as if he had been injected with novocaine some time ago and it had not worn off.

Doom nodded. "You too, then."

"Me too?"

"Doctor Orloff is also most effective as a fighter when she is in a liminal state."

"A fighter…" Zargo repeated. The spirit of the Zargo that was in the surface world sank at the word. The Zargo that existed in the stone world cared far less.

"Do not be disingenuous with yourself," said Doom. "I have indulged your self-pity, and your regret that you are not the priest you believed it was your wish to be. I have no patience for that pathetic luxury any longer. And you cannot survive if you give in to it."

"I know," said Zargo. It was easier to let the illusions go while he was in this state. He also felt that he was experiencing a more valid form of his identity than he had before. He was letting the lessons of stone sink in. He didn't feel the need to reject his geomantic powers anymore. It had taken him longer than it should have to come to even this half-measure of self-acceptance, but the process had begun.

And Doom was right. He had fought on Walpurgis Night.

He had fought on this day. He would have to fight again, for as long as Krogh was a threat in Latveria.

"I believe you are beginning to understand," said Doom. "Time is of the essence, though, so let us be clear, and complete your education. You are a geomancer. You must be one. That is the necessity of your being, and that is my command."

"Yes, my lord," said Zargo. He had not been a priest since the destruction of St Peter. He had known that, and he had walled in the mourning of his lost calling. The period of grieving was over. Time for him to be what he truly was.

"Look to the earth," said Doom. "That is your new church. Defend it, and use the transubstantiation of stone to destroy the urvullak."

"I shall," said Zargo. The words were not a vow. They were a simple statement of fact.

"Does your hover platform still work?" Doom asked.

Zargo glanced back to where it sat in the remains of the stone sphere. "I think it does," he said.

"Then use it to go where the war takes you."

"You have no specific task for me?" That surprised him, as much as he was able to feel surprise in this state.

"The war is everywhere," said Doom. "Listen to the earth. It will tell you where your skills are most needed. I must return to Doomstadt. I too, must become legion."

Krogh fought in all corners of Latveria at once. Her army was growing quickly, now that she could be present at every moment of every battle, and she was beating down the resistance with an endless flood of nightmare memories. She exulted in her omnipresence. In the days that had followed her first transformation, she had frequently tried to imagine this state, and in some of those speculations she had wondered if she would lose track of her actual body, and if it would cease to have any importance to her. She discovered now that neither of those things was true. Her core self was stronger than ever, and she was as aware of its location and its presence as she was every single urvullak.

No, not as aware. More aware.

It was the eye of the hurricane that she had become. She was in her body as it flew on the wings of hunger down from the Carpathians and into the more populated regions of Latveria. She took it above the trees, soaring high as often as she dared. The many thousand eyes that were hers also warned her whenever there was a danger of discovery, and she always had time to hide. She did not have to hide nearly as much now. All of Doom's cybernetic eyes were fixed on the battles.

She could fly as much as she wished.

She also had the time and the resources for more than battle. In the regions to the immediate south of the mountains, her control of Latveria was uncontested. Here, the battle was over. Here, she could begin to impose the Old Order.

She chose the village of Doomwinden for the first lesson. The village at the top of hill, surrounded by forest. The urvullak came out of the trees in the night, and they took many of the villagers. But not all of them. Krogh halted the feast while more than half the villagers were still alive.

Then she made the urvullak march down the street and speak with her voices. When she stopped the undead from feeding, she inflicted an especially acute agony on them. Their bodies went against their instincts. The need to devour souls in the false hope of replacing their own became a worse torment. Krogh knew the feeling of that torment. The hunger never left her, and it had become so much greater since she had become one with the Devourer. But it was also being fed. Every soul taken by every urvullak came to her and the Devourer, and she thrilled to the savage, vicious joy of feasting. When she held the urvullak back in Doomwinden, she continued to feed from the street battles in Doomstadt and elsewhere, in so many, many elsewheres.

The pain the urvullak felt in Doomwinden was another experience, another memory to harvest. It made the Devourer restless, as there was nothing real to feed on from those that were already dead. But it also vibrated with the pleasure of their tortured sensations.

The real pleasure, though, came from the pain of the living. That was what Krogh had missed for more than fifteen years. That was her past, her memory, her personal hunger that had gnawed at her through all the cursed days of Doom's rule. Now she could sate that hunger.

And so, the urvullak spoke with her voice, her voices.

"The reign of Doom has passed. The usurper is deposed. The old ways are restored. Gather in the square. This is the command of Maleva Krogh."

The people obeyed. They always obeyed. Under King Vladimir or under Doom, they knew they must obey. They did as they were told in the hopes that they would be spared.

Krogh enjoyed the taste of that hope.

As she watched the people leave their homes and troop into the square, heads down, arms wrapped around themselves, their bodies shaking with terror, she looked at them through urvullak eyes, and she hated them. She knew, from the villagers she had already turned, how many had forgotten the name of Krogh. She should not have been a faded memory after just fifteen years. She had been dead. The older residents remembered her, some of them very well. Others remembered her name. Too many of them despised instead of feared it. Doomwinden had not given up as many of its people to the mercies of the Kroghs during the Fortunov dynasty.

You will now, then. You will learn to fear me as I deserve to be feared, and as you deserve to fear.

When all the villagers were in the square, Krogh sent an urvullak scuttling into the small Guard post next to the burgomeister's residence. The urvullak returned with a pistol. From those already sacrificed to the Devourer, Krogh knew everything she needed to know about all the living residents. She had already chosen her first victims.

"The word of Maleva Krogh is the word of iron," the urvullak declared in unison. "Her will is your will."

The urvullak with the pistol approached a woman with the weapon and put it on the ground before her.

"Pick it up," said Krogh's voice.

The woman did. She glanced from side to side at the two men who flanked her. The man on the right was her husband. The one on the left was her brother. She was looking for reassurance that neither could give.

The urvullak turned to the husband. It reached its hand out to his throat, and stopped a bare inch away from making contact.

"Shoot your brother," said Krogh.

The woman gasped in horror.

"Shoot him," said Krogh, "or your husband joins our ranks." She pulled the urvullak's lips back in a toothy smile.

The woman sobbed. "Please," she begged. "We'll do anything you say."

"This is what I say. Shoot."

The begging went on, and it was good. All three pleaded with Krogh, and it was good. The pain and the terror and the tears were all so very, very good.

There was so much to savor before Krogh forced the moment and took the decision out of the woman's hands. There was even more to savor then, as the screams shook the square.

When Krogh let the villagers return to their homes, the air in Doomwinden stank of fear.

The past had come back to life. It was a very satisfying start.

The flight back to Doomstadt felt almost as long as the flight out. Doom felt the memory assault as a slight undercurrent tugging at his mental shield. It would be a painful emotional drain for all of his subjects, and there was no surcease. It didn't come in waves. It was constant, a tidal surge with no withdrawal. He had to counter it, or before long, no one in Latveria would be able to fight back against Krogh.

The journey back to Doomstadt was frustrating in its length, but it gave him time to think. He saw a possible way forward. *The people must see and hear him.* There was a simple way to make that happen. He could address them as he had a few days prior.

And he would. But there was an order to events that must be followed. His appearance must have the proper weight.

So he made a few rapid stops. The first was at Doomsburg,

where the sanctuary was under attack. Its walls were holding. Its defenders, though, were failing, and if there was no guard outside, it would be easy for the people inside to believe that they had been abandoned, and start to panic. Doom showed them that they had not been forgotten. He landed on the roof, triggered the holographic projectors, and then flew in a wide circle over the roof, hitting the urvullak below with concussion blasts until none remained.

Doom returned to the rooftop, and the guards on the parapet knelt in thanks before him. The strain of the memory tide was etched into their faces. But there was the awe of him now, too, renewed and strengthened, as was the troops' morale.

Doom waited before speaking, letting the power of this moment sink in, and the image, as before, was sent to every holographic projector in the country.

"You shall hear from me soon," Doom told his people. "Look for my coming."

That was enough for now. That was all he needed them to know. *Doom is present, and the urvullak fall before him.* He set the recording to repeat once an hour, and took off again.

He stopped twice more on the journey back to Doomstadt, again in locations where there were lenses to record what he did, and the destruction he meted out to the urvullak. "Look for my coming," he intoned again, and soon those recordings were alternating with the one from Doomsburg. *There will soon be more, Krogh. You can renew your attacks on the sites I have purged. I have no doubt you will. But the people have seen me. They have the expectation of Doom's presence.*

He scanned the combat reports as he approached Doomstadt, and chose the point of his arrival carefully. The fighting was at its most intense on Heroic Andrew Boulevard. One of the principal thoroughfares of New Town, in the south of the city, it was six lanes wide. It was here that Doom's triumphal marches took place. It was lined by twenty-foot statues of hammered brass and gold leaf. They were all automatons, representing the stages of the overthrow of King Vladimir. Their shifting stances marked the hours of the day, and every day they recreated the triumph of Doom.

A fitting target for your hate, Krogh. I am not surprised you have chosen the boulevard for a heavy assault.

Heroic Andrew Boulevard was also one of the more open areas of Doomstadt. More than a thousand urvullak shrieked down its length. The guards had set up makeshift barricades, and fired from behind them with the newly modified rifles. As Doom roared out of the sky, the urvullak were forcing the guards into a retreat toward the north. The rifles were more effective than before. A single well-placed shot could take down an urvullak. The undead were more agile and precise in their attacks, too. They were harder to hit, and smarter in their tactics. Doom saw something much more dangerous than a horde running on instinct. He saw an army instantly obeying the commands of a single will.

Every single one of those vermin might as well have been Krogh.

The other reason for being at the counterattack on Heroic Andrew Boulevard was the sheer number of holographic lenses that would capture Doom's every move. The road was designed to propagandize the glorious near past of Latveria, and its gilded present. Doom put its capabilities to good use.

He began with one well-placed strike from the molecular

projector. The boulder-sized projectile slammed into the middle of the boulevard, into a crowded mass of urvullak. There was one explosion, huge in its thunder and in its blast, the dust cloud rising high, causing the sudden disappearance of scores of urvullak. Doom had placed the shot carefully, and none of the statues were destroyed in the explosion. They stood tall in the dust, their footlights wreathing them in an amber aura. Doom had timed his arrival to coincide precisely with the hour, and the automata turned from pointing south to saluting in the direction of the castle as if in answer to Doom's attack.

The rest of the urvullak retreated at high speed, disappearing into alleys and doorways and sewers, scattering widely before the molecular projector could take out another huge chunk of their number.

Doom descended slowly until he was at the same level as the heads of the statues. He hovered over the new crater. The holographic eyes of Heroic Andrew Boulevard captured his devastating arrival and simulcast the new chronicle of the war to every corner of Latveria.

He wondered how well Krogh was reading him, and reading that moment. Did she think he had seen her retreat as a sign that he had already turned the tide? Was she hoping that he believed he had seen a rout of her forces? Perhaps she did. Perhaps she didn't. Doom did not care. He knew that all she had done was redirect her attack. The urvullak that had fled were claiming more victims with each passing moment. Doom knew this, too. He also knew that the molecular projector was just the preparation for his real attack, which would begin now. He wondered if Krogh would understand that. He almost hoped she would.

"Citizens of Latveria," Doom thundered. "You have looked for my coming, and I am here. The enemy falls before me in Doomstadt. Soon you will see them fall before me in your city, in your town and in your village. Wherever you fight the urvullak, you will know that I fight there too. For I am Doom. I am the present and the future of Latveria. I am the scourge of the dead past. What I have once destroyed, shall never rise again. Look upon me. Hear my words. Hurl away the foul memories that assail you. Take up the fight and tread the foe into the dirt. Doom commands it."

He finished speaking, and the troops below shouted his name and brandished their rifles at the sky. They had seen him annihilate the urvullak at the Doomsburg sanctuary. Now they had witnessed him stop the assault against them with one blow. They were determined again. He had given them the courage they needed to resist the worst of Krogh's memory assault. They were stronger now, and ready to fight harder against the physical foe.

Doom flew away from the boulevard. His holographic image remained, towering a hundred feet high in the night, repeating his call to arms.

"*I AM DOOM.*"

"Now," Doom muttered. "It is time I was in many places." He transmitted new commands to the Doombots. Most of them were fighting the urvullak in the capital city. He kept some in Doomstadt, but now they were to make lighting strikes in as many locations in the city as possible, speeding from one battle to the next. It was not their task to finish the fights. They were to hit hard, spectacularly, and move on. Most importantly, they were to be seen. There was no way to tell them apart visually from Doom himself. The citizens who witnessed them would know the truth of the promise Doom had just made.

He sent the majority of the Doombots away from Doomstadt, to fight in the same way across the country.

Be me. Be me, being everywhere.

If Krogh would have them fight a war of presence, then they would. For the moment. This was not how they would decide the conflict. That would be on his terms.

Doom opened a channel on his communicator. "Doctor Orloff," he said, "tell me where you are."

"*At the hospital. Clearing it.*" Her answer came back right away, and her voice was strong. She did not sound as if the memory tide was weakening her. She *did* sound driven.

Take care that the hunt does not consume you, doctor.

"Meet me at the main entrance," Doom said. "I shall be there momentarily."

"*Yes,*" said Orloff. She paused, and Doom heard the screams of urvullak in the background suddenly go silent. "*Yes,*" said Orloff again. "*I can do that.*"

"I did not ask if you could. I gave you an order. Obey it."

There was a slight pause, and when Orloff spoke next, she sounded like a woman coming back to herself. "Of course, my lord," she said. "I will obey."

She was where he had commanded when Doom landed outside the hospital. There was smoke rising from some of the middle-story windows. The lights were all still on, however.

"Is the hospital clear?" Doom asked.

"It is, for now. I found the last of them as I was coming to meet you."

She had completed her task in time to obey him. That was well done.

New forces of guards were arriving, sirens blaring on their vehicles. Troops took up positions outside the entrances, and others headed into the building to patrol the halls. Orloff took the arm of a sergeant as she led a squad inside. "Remember the patients," she said, her voice a bit less taut than it had been a few moments before. "Try not to frighten them." With her helmet on, Doom could not read Orloff's face. Her body language told him what he needed to know. There was a very slight tremor in her arms, and she held herself rigidly. The surgeon truly had become the hunter. Doom had no doubt that she had not stopped to rest since he had first sent her out after the urvullak.

The urvullak had earned her personal hatred, to their cost. That was well. She would also need to be able to pull herself out of the predator mindset, or she would burn herself out and be of no further use.

It was good, then, that he needed her now for something that would engage her searching mind once again.

"We return to the castle," he said. "There is work to be done. I would change the terms of this war."

TWENTY-THREE

The currents of the earth guided Zargo to Doomhelm. It was a town he could reach easily from the former dig site. It was in a valley near the southern edge of the Carpathians. He felt the tremors of great pain and violence there, thrumming through the ground like the convulsions of prey on a web. He climbed onto the hover platform and made his way there. It took a couple of hours at the platform's full speed. That gave him time to think.

Zargo felt calmer than he had for a long time. Even knowing what was happening to Latveria and feeling the edge of Krogh's psychic assault, he was calm. He knew it was because his mind was half-submerged in the ground, blunting the effects of the memory storm. Yet the fact that he felt no qualms about keeping himself like this was a new state of affairs.

Was this peace? Was it contentment?

He didn't know. He didn't know if he could even recognize them.

He had experienced too many years of internal struggle. All

his adult life had been consumed by it. He had rejected his skills as a geomancer. He had thought his faith demanded that rejection, and he had kept true to that conviction all through his seminary training and his years as a priest. When Doom had compelled him to act as a geomancer once more, doing so had been a torment.

Why was that?

That wasn't clear now. He was no longer certain how he had come to think that one identity forbade the other. He also didn't feel the pain of loss that he had earlier. He would never again be a shepherd to his flock. He accepted that.

Would it hurt when he left the calm of the earth again?

He didn't know.

Did he have to leave?

Maybe not.

Was there any reason to?

Before the attack on the dig site, he would have said yes. The guilt of using his powers still bothered him. He didn't feel the guilt any longer.

Why?

He didn't know. Did it matter?

He was beginning to think it didn't.

Why shouldn't he have peace?

Even when you have to make war?

That gave him pause. Unease wormed its way into his heart. What Krogh failed to do, he was doing to himself.

He laughed. "That sounds just about right, for me," he said aloud.

His body and the words still seemed removed. He could function in the world, though. He wasn't being clumsy with the hover platform controls. So he didn't pull out of the underworld. He would need the calm it afforded him.

Doomhelm was quiet as he approached. He came down the valley from the north. The town, home to two thousand, nestled in the bottom of the valley, straddling the Vergessen river. There were no lights on in the houses. There were streetlights, though, and the holographic image of Doom towering over the roofs. Doom called the people to fight, and showed the urvullak being destroyed.

There was no sign of battle in Doomhelm. It was as if the war had passed the village by, and it slept peacefully, unconcerned with the agony of Latveria. Doom's exhortations seemed hollow here. No one was listening, because no one had to.

This peace was a lie, Zargo thought.

He slowed down and then stopped, a few hundred yards from the nearest houses. He looked down the main street and saw no one.

"Maleva Krogh!" he called out. "I know what you have done here."

There was no response.

Pain in the land had brought him here. It lingered in the stone like a bloodstain. If there had been fighting here, it was over.

"*TREAD THE FOE INTO THE DIRT,*" the hologram boomed. "*DOOM COMMANDS IT.*"

A ley line ran not far from Doomhelm. Zargo held it, as if he were trailing his fingers in a stream and feeling the play of the current. It was the line that had vibrated with the pain in Doomhelm. Zargo kept hold of the ley line, bracing himself. He looked up at the sides of the valley.

There was something that would have to be done.

He couldn't though. Not yet. He had to be sure. To be wrong here would be terrible.

If he was right, all was already terrible.

He moved the hover platform forward again, gliding just a foot above the surface of the road. He eyed the dark windows on both sides, waiting.

"Krogh!" he called again. "I know your work is here. Are you trying to hide from me? I'm not Doom."

Zargo stopped in front of the church. He thought about the people who would have come here for help and comfort, just as his parishioners had done on Walpurgis Night.

Had someone come to help them here? The Guard had. How long did they hold out?

He was making assumptions about the village. They didn't feel wrong.

The hologram of Doom winked out. The sudden silence made Zargo's ears pop.

"No, you aren't Doom." The harsh, sibilant voice sliced through the night from a dozen open, dark windows at once. "Is this your contentment, priest? Do you now live to be his errand boy?"

"I have come to fight you," said Zargo. "I don't need to be told that is the proper thing to do."

"If you had been the priest of my village, I would have seen you burned," said Krogh's voices.

"If had I had been *your* priest, I would have deserved it," said Zargo. "To be faithful to you would mean being faithful to nothing." He took a breath. "If you are holding any villagers prisoner, will you let them go?" The question was a forlorn hope. He had to ask it, though. He had to try.

Krogh's laughter ran up and down the main street and off down the smaller alleys. It echoed in the belfry of the church.

"Am I holding them?" said Krogh. "You could say that. You could say that I am holding them back." The streetlights went out, starting from the outskirts of the village, rings of darkness moving toward the center. "Very well. You may have them." The only light left was the one in front of the church. "I release them."

The light went out. Zargo yanked hard on the controls of the hover platform. He rose quickly, just as a surge of urvullak came leaping and shrieking out of the windows and doorways. Zargo's eyes struggled to adjust to the darkness. There were no stars, and all he could see was a squirming, slashing movement all around. He climbed diagonally, away from the church, and a snarling shadow dropped past him. It had leapt from the church tower, and it came so close that he felt the breeze of its claws as they whipped past his face.

Zargo took the hover platform higher, until he was sure he was out of reach. He felt less distant from this body than he had been. Adrenaline called him home. His heart beat steadily, though, calmed by his spirit's home in the embrace of stone.

Krogh's laughter rose, scratching at him, from across Doomhelm. "Coward!" the voices called. "Run, then. Fly away and hide."

"No," Zargo whispered, looking down into the darkness. "Running away is what I can't do." The Zargo of the recent past might have wanted to. The Zargo of the present did not.

"Can you fly when you sleep?" Krogh asked. "No? Then never sleep. For when you do, that is when I will come for you."

"No," said Zargo. "You won't."

He kept a tiny portion of his consciousness in his body. It was just enough to take the hover platform higher yet, more than a hundred feet up. Zargo's physical eyes could no longer see the town at all now.

They didn't have to. The rest of him perceived the valley and Doomhelm perfectly. He was in the earth. He *was* the earth. The valley became his cupped hands. The village sat at the bottom of the cup, writhing with undead.

There was no one to save here.

His mind grasped the ley line. He wielded it as if it were a power cable. It charged him with energy, energy that built and built until he could not contain it any longer.

Then he sent the power into the slopes of the valley, the valley that was his cupped hands, and he brought his hands together.

The mountains roared and shuddered. A crevasse split the village, and the stream disappeared into its depths. The sides of the mountains split, and fifty million tons of rock tumbled off. The double slide came down onto the village with the clamor of doomsday. The earth shook, an anvil struck by a giant's hammer. Zargo witnessed the fall of every stone. He lived the Earth's fury and its pain as it wrenched itself apart to kill the disease on its surface.

The echoes lasted a long time. The dust would linger even longer.

Erased and entombed, Doomhelm was silent. Now it slept forever.

They were back in the lab. Orloff had removed her helmet, but with some reluctance, Doom noted. Her eyes kept going back to it on the table, and she still wore her armor, as if expecting to be back in the field in minutes. Doom frowned. He needed her full concentration.

"It is in this room that we will win the war, Doctor Orloff," he said. "The war. Not individual battles."

His tone and his words caught her attention. She was present once more, conscious that she should not risk his displeasure. "I'm sorry," she said. "You have my attention."

Doom nodded. He did understand her frustration. Here in the lab, isolated from the battlefronts, it was easy to believe they were not engaged in combat. Doom struggled with his own impatience. The temptation was to be out in the streets, exterminating the urvullak. The reality was that this was where he needed to be if that extermination was really going to occur. And if he was going to rip the Devourer from Krogh's grasp.

"Are you suffering from Krogh's psychic campaign?" he asked.

She shook her head. "No," she said. "I know it's happening, but it's deep in the background. I don't understand why that should be."

"That is interesting," said Doom. "Perhaps useful, as well. What we need to accomplish will be based on the neural frequencies of the living and the dead. We will begin by taking new readings from you."

Orloff nodded and climbed onto a slab next to the obelisk. Doom ran the tests quickly. He nodded to himself when he saw the results.

"Look," he said to Orloff when she joined him at the screen. "Your brainwaves have changed since our last tests. The difference is not great, but it is significant."

Orloff pointed to a pattern of signals. "That's close to what we found when I was in the liminal state."

"Quite. And now we find them when you are not wearing the helmet. Your use of it seems to have resulted in a neural restructuring."

"Permanent, do you think?"

"That remains to be seen. Would it trouble you if it was?"

"No," Orloff said without hesitation.

Good. The unknown presented even fewer terrors for her than he had suspected.

"We have discovered the means of disrupting the urvullak's connections to the Devourer," said Doom. "That is our starting point. Rifles and suits of armor are not sufficient. Not against what Krogh has become."

"So now we need a weapon of mass destruction," said Orloff.

"No," said Doom. "Not *mass*. *Total*."

"Total," Orloff repeated, looking uneasy.

"It is simplicity itself for me to broadcast a signal to all of Latveria," said Doom.

Orloff turned pale. "But if we did that…" she began.

"We would kill the entire population," said Doom. He paused. "You do not think I am willing to make that sacrifice," he said. *She must know that I am not. I am Doom. I walk this Earth to save it, not to destroy it.*

"No," said Orloff, color returning to her cheeks. "No, of course not."

"We seek a means of interference that will affect only the urvullak," said Doom. "We must find what has eluded us thus far."

He plunged into the work, and Orloff did as well. Within

minutes, Doom was consumed by the search. He *was* on the
battlefield. Every step he took was as much a part of the war
as a physical march against the urvullak. He was aware of the
pressures of time. He felt the seconds slipping away, never to
be recaptured, and knew that with them, more of Latveria
fell to Krogh. Those same seconds would be lost outside the
castle, and lost in vain. This was the true front line.

He went back and forth between the results of the tests on
the dead, on the urvullak, and on Orloff. He had new tests
run on Orloff's assistants, as he could no longer look at hers
as representing the typical human's wavelengths. What she
could withstand without effort now might kill anyone else.

Krogh's omnipresence felt like another key. *Turn her strength
into a weakness.* If she could be everywhere, then there had to
be a way of striking her everywhere.

"The urvullak signatures are different than before," said Orloff.

"Yes," said Doom. The change was subtle, but consistent.
"There we see the signature of Krogh's wavelength. She is
present as she was not before. That is what must be isolated
and blocked."

"But anything we use to shut down those neural frequencies
shuts down *all* frequencies."

And Doom saw what needed to happen. "Then we do not
shut anything down. We mask one frequency with another
instead."

Orloff's eyes widened in understanding. "We make the
urvullak perceive each other as living people."

"Precisely. We need a baseline human wavelength, one
common to all, so its transmission will be harmless to the living."

"I know what that would look like," said Orloff. Her fingers flew over her workstation's keyboard, and a new wavelength model appeared on the screen before her. "Will this be enough, though?" she asked. "I don't see how this would affect Krogh or the Devourer directly."

Nor did he wish it to. His goal there was different. He would not destroy the Devourer. It would yet be his. "I will deal with that threat," said Doom. The means to do so were coming together in his mind. "That will be my task alone. You may return to the fray, Doctor Orloff. Hold the urvullak back until I can deploy this new weapon."

He sent the other assistants away as well. He wanted the laboratory to himself. When he was alone, he turned to the urvullak specimens. Except for when he and Orloff had needed to run tests on them, they had been kept completely isolated from each other and from the lab, lead screen surrounding each specimen so Krogh could not see the work being done. Now Doom raised one screen, unveiling a single specimen. Its snarling stilled as he contemplated it, and it stared back at him. This was the first time tonight that Doom had allowed himself to be seen in the lab by an urvullak. Krogh would not have known he was here until now.

"Well," said Doom. "Here we are. Is there anything you wish to say, Krogh?"

"You have lost, Doom. Your efforts are futile."

Doom tapped controls. Mechanical arms seized the urvullak and brought it forward into the lab. They held its limbs and its head. It could only look forward. Behind it and to one side, on one of the work tables, was one of the sensory deprivation helmets that Orloff had had placed over the specimen's skulls before the tests began.

"My efforts are futile," said Doom. "That is bravado, and in a not very convincing form." He stepped out of the line of sight and picked up the helmet. "For you to judge them futile, you would have to know what they are."

The urvullak squirmed, trying to see what Doom was doing. "I don't have to know," Krogh spat with its voice. "Nothing you do can stop me."

"Then you should not be worried about what is happening behind your creature," said Doom. "But I think you are, Maleva Krogh. I think you are afraid of me. I think you fear what is about to happen. You should be afraid. You have defied me, and you have injured my country. Your fall will be a painful one. And it is about to begin."

The urvullak strained against the arms. It shrieked, its instinctual rage fused with Krogh's frustration. Doom placed the helmet over the urvullak's head, cutting off all of Krogh's perceptions of the lab.

"And now to work," said Doom.

What was he doing?

Krogh felt the wounds Doom had already inflicted on her. She saw his image in every village, town and city that she attacked. In some instances, she laughed at the holographic projections. Doom's propaganda was empty when all had fallen. But in other places, those images stiffened resistance, and the living fought back with renewed vigor. And that faithless priest, Zargo, had taken her triumph at Doomhelm away from her.

Then there were the Doombots. She saw them everywhere too. She knew they were not Doom, because they had no souls. There was nothing in them for the urvullak to feast upon. The Devourer recoiled from the unliving weapons, its instincts raging against the things that could not feed its hunger. For the citizens of Latveria, though, they arrived as Doom's promise fulfilled. He said he would fight with them, and he did. They could not tell a Doombot from their real sovereign.

They did not matter. They could not alter the outcome of the war. She kept repeating these truths to herself. The setbacks were temporary. All Doom had managed to do was slow her down. He was still losing.

He had also vanished after routing the attack on Heroic Andrew Boulevard.

Where is he? Where is he?

She could see almost everywhere, but she could not see him.

It doesn't matter. It doesn't matter.

But what if it did?

And then he let her see him in the laboratory. He mocked her. He toyed with her, and then took away all sight and sound again. A few moments later, that urvullak disappeared completely from her perception. He must have destroyed it.

If that was all he had done, why did he taunt her? Why have the urvullak in a laboratory?

What was he doing? What was he doing?

The question became urgent. It tormented her. It seeded the beginnings of fear.

Hurry. Finish the war. Do what you told him you would do. Take all of Latveria. Leave him with nothing. If she did it fast enough, it really would not matter what Doom was doing now. He *could not win when the battles were all over. In a Latveria that was only urvullak, what could he do?*

Except that wasn't the Latveria she wanted either. She wanted a living population too. She wanted subjects who would understand who ruled over them, and what their suffering meant.

She wanted Latveria to be the model for the gift she would bring to the world.

It wasn't enough to take everything from Doom. That was just the first part of the usurper's punishment. He also had to be destroyed.

The Devourer hungered for the taste of his soul. The Devourer was not a being of conscious thoughts. It did not care what she did with Latveria, as long as it continued to feed. It had sensed the strength of Doom's being, though. It perceived in him a feast unlike any other. It drove Krogh toward that goal. She could not have resisted even if she wanted to.

She was pleased by the thought of the Devourer taking Doom. That would be the fitting end.

Hurry, then. Destroy his nation, and then him.

She turned all of her strength against Doomstadt. She pulled the urvullak away from all the other population centers of Latveria. *One great surge, now. One great push to topple the capital. When Doomstadt fell, everything else would too.*

The urvullak sprinted over the land. They gathered in a huge swarm around Doomstadt. They joined all their kin already in the city. Krogh sent the flood directly through the homes within. The urvullak crashed through doors and windows. They rampaged up staircases and down corridors. They burst through every makeshift barricade and into the residences where the people of the city hid and waited. Krogh watched the people try to fight. She listened to them cry out for Doom. Her thousands of voices laughed at them.

"There is no hope for Doom," she said. "There is no salvation for you."

The urvullak fell on their prey. They left no one alive. In every building they assaulted, they came out with their numbers increased. A tide of fear swept the city. As it flowed on, it became a tide of hunger. The Doombots and the guards stopped the wave in isolated patches. Doom's propaganda kept the people fighting. It wasn't enough. Krogh made her legions flow away from the stronger resistance, water foaming around a stubborn boulder. There was always another alley down which to send her urvullak, another building to take instead.

Krogh grew in number. She turned Doom's defiant words into lies. She closed in on the castle.

"None of the lines are holding," Verlak radioed to Doom. "The urvullak are pushing forward on all fronts." She was on the outer ramparts of the castle, directing long-range fire into the streets. To the south, the roads were filling with fleeing, screaming people. Behind them, the urvullak came, an encroaching sea of clawing shapes.

"*Fall back,*" said Doom. "*Call the people to the castle and make your stand. Krogh's defeat is close at hand.*"

Verlak relayed Doom's order to the command center, and a new siren began to wail. It rose and fell, rose and fell without pause. It was the call of sanctuary, going out to all who could hear it and answer.

Elsa joined her, helmet under her arm. "Doom says we just

need to hold them back a little while longer," Verlak said to her.

"Yes," said Elsa. "He's almost ready." She put the helmet on. "We're going to win, Kari." She pointed into the night. From blocks away came shrieks from the urvullak.

"Take them down, my love," Verlak said, going back to her rifle sights. "Take them all down."

"I would if I could," said Elsa. "All of them."

Verlak pulled the trigger quickly, repeatedly, taking down the leading edge of a group of monsters that had just come around a corner and onto the castle's ring road. "I've changed my mind," she said. "Leave some for me." She needed the satisfaction of seeing the urvullak fall. It helped blunt the edge of the psychic assault. Her head pounded with the flood of other people's memories. They went through too quickly for her to grasp any single one. They were a sharp-edged blur of impressions, all of them bad. Tragedy, grief, loss, death, depression, desperation, all merged into a single, unending howl that tried to beat her down and sweep her away in the flood.

Verlak used anger to keep her focus. She hated Krogh for what she was doing to Latveria, for what she had done to Verlak's troops, and for what she had almost done to Verlak herself. An ache ran through her body, and deep into places beyond the physical. She felt like broken porcelain, glued imperfectly back together. She still had her memories, and she still had her self. But there were edges, fault lines that she could almost touch. She believed they would heal. She had to.

She was glad that Elsa was with her. The presence of her

wife was the promise that there was a future, and the warmth of love in the present.

They would see this through.

The thought came easily with Elsa next to her. So did belief in its truth.

Crowds of refugees poured over the moat's bridge and into the great courtyard. The few guards that Verlak could spare controlled the stream as best they could, funneling people off into other regions of the castle grounds as the courtyard filled up. There was room for thousands more. What Verlak feared was that thousands more would not be able to come.

"Maintain covering fire," she commanded the troops that lined the parapet. "Get the civilians through."

The people kept coming, terror pushing them past exhaustion. The main mass of the urvullak was drawing closer too. It would only be a few more minutes, Verlak thought, before no amount of weapons fire would be able to hold them back.

She contacted Doom again. "We may have to shut the gates soon," she said. "Or the urvullak will be inside the castle walls."

"*Keep them open,*" Doom ordered. "*The enemy will feel my hand soon enough.*"

Beside Verlak, Elsa cursed. "Look what they're doing!"

Verlak saw. The urvullak were filling the ring road. The fire of the guards kept an open corridor for the people coming up Vandorf Street to cross the ring road and move onto the bridge. The urvullak had been closing in from both directions of the ring road. Now they stopped trying to break through to the crowd, and threw themselves down the bank and into the moat.

"Can they swim?" Verlak asked.

"They don't need to," said Elsa. "They can't drown. They're already dead."

Verlak looked at the cataract of monsters plunging into the dark waters. She pictured them moving slowly but relentlessly across the bottom of the moat and emerging in an unbroken line at the base of the castle's walls. She had already seen how they could climb.

Verlak looked back and forth between the refugees, the moat and the other mobs of urvullak coming up Vandorf and the other approaches to the castle.

They didn't have enough guns.

"I can hold them off the bridge," said Elsa. "I'll keep the way clear."

Verlak squeezed her shoulder and radioed her troops. "Prepare for an attack from the moat. The enemy will be climbing the walls. Aim down and aim well."

We need Doom. We need him now.

Verlak kept firing at the urvullak on Vandorf, looking down between shots for the moment she saw urvullak emerge from the water.

It came. Hundreds of the monsters, dark and glistening, screaming with hunger, crawled out of the moat and began to climb the walls, a carpet of insects.

It was an ugly dawn.

Then, as Verlak trained her rifle on the monsters below, she heard the clank and hum of machinery from behind and above.

"Here it comes," said Elsa, with savage eagerness.

Verlak gave herself a single second to look back. She

saw satellite dishes, the full arsenal of Castle Doom's communications array, emerge from the reinforced tops of their towers.

Verlak started shooting again, and the monstrous shapes rose higher and higher.

The hum grew louder. Then a piercing whine made Verlak's teeth rattle.

What made her let go of her gun and cover her ears was another sound. It was a scream of maddened rage.

Beside her, Elsa roared with furious laughter.

Verlak laughed too.

And the scream grew until it covered the city, reaching up to claw open the sky.

TWENTY-FOUR

Doom flew out into the dawn. Holographic projectors from within the castle tracked his movements and projected his vast image over the city. His voice thundered over the rooftops.

"I AM DOOM. BEHOLD MY WRATH!"

He hovered over the entrance from the moat bridge to the great courtyard, where the greatest number of people could see him.

"HEAR THE SCREAMS THAT GREET THE DAWN. THEY ARE THE FANFARE OF VICTORY. THEY ARE THE DESTRUCTION OF OUR FOE. LOOK UPON THE WALLS. LOOK BACK INTO THE STREETS. SEE THE FATE OF ALL WHO WOULD CHALLENGE DOOM."

The people did as he commanded. So did the guards, and the cheers that rose were so loud, they were just barely audible over the rage of the urvullak.

The undead had turned on each other. The castle's dish antennae sent Doom's signal up to Latveria's telecommunication satellites, which in turn sent it back down through every transmitting device, blanketing the entire country with the frequency. The urvullak perceived each other as mortal, as prey. And the masking signal blocked Krogh's control. Without her will directing them, their instincts reigned supreme. They turned on whatever prey was nearest.

It was each other.

The urvullak tore into one another, and when there was nothing for them to feast upon, they became frenzied and ripped the flesh they grasped apart as if the sustenance of memories hid beneath it. Doom watched them become a horde of maddened rats. Their howls were beyond desperation, beyond anger. They were the sound of destruction at its most primal, of a hunger that received no relief and became something transcendent. As the gray October day gathered strength over Doomstadt, the streets seethed with the slashing of claws and teeth.

I can hear the sounds of your army's flesh being shredded, Krogh. Can you?

With a brief incantation, Doom triggered the device he had installed on the wrist of his left gauntlet. This was the last weapon of the war, the one he had created after he had sent Orloff and the others away. It resembled a miniature cannon, with a mouth that widened out into a parabolic shape. The first stage of the final attack was a transmission. The second stage used this weapon. This receiver.

As the receiver began to thrum, Doom left the castle, rising high above the city, away from the distraction of the shouts of his subjects. He needed to concentrate, to control the sorcerous forces that controlled the receiver.

The urvullak had no souls. That did not mean that no

psychic energy was released when they were destroyed. Their rage and their pain were as real as any living being's. There was nothing in their ends to feed the Devourer. It had already taken what it could consume from them. But just as something lingered in the dead, something that Doom's instruments could measure, so there was something in the urvullak for him to capture. The receiver gathered the energy of the slaughter below, and everywhere else that the masking signal drove the urvullak to self-destruction. Doom stored the power of a hundred ends, and then a thousand, and soon ten thousand. In Doomstadt, the cries of animal rage diminished quickly. The urvullak slaughtered each other with even greater ferocity than they did the living. Their victims did not satisfy, and fought back, driving them even further into terminal frenzy.

The massacre released a monstrous level of psychic energy. Doom gathered it all. He built up layer upon layer of sorcerous shields around the receiver. Without them, it would have unleashed a nova blast of excess power.

Doom moved north, slowly leaving the city. The choice of direction was arbitrary. Krogh had come down from the north, and Doom flew as if to meet her. He had no idea where she really was. He would soon, though. *Do not keep me waiting, Krogh. Let us make an end of this.*

The stream of energy to the receiver dropped dramatically, became a trickle and then stopped. *So ended the war. Did Krogh feel that abruptness? Had she felt how completely everything had failed? The urvullak no longer fought. They had been destroyed. There was no war for Krogh now anywhere in Latveria.*

Silence fell over the nation. Doom would not call it peace.

The silence was welcome enough. He waited for it to be broken again.

Krogh did not disappoint him. The wait was short.

"*DOOM!*"

The cry traveled on ethereal waves. Somewhere, Krogh's physical body screamed. The howl that came to Doom passed through the veil, reverberating through the limbo of the dead.

It was a simple matter to trace the cry back to Krogh's location. She was not hiding from him now. Doom smiled tightly at the helpless, overwhelming frustration he heard in Krogh's psychic voice. He had taunted her with his images, with each setback, however temporary, and when he spoke to her in the laboratory. Now he had taken her army from her in a matter of minutes. The insult was beyond bearing. She had come out into the open. She had nothing left to lose, and a universe of anger to vent.

Doom found Krogh a few miles to the north of Doomstadt. She was on the top of a bare, rocky ridge that rose out of deep forest. He descended towards her. She was a lone figure, a single urvullak.

You are no colossus now. You are nothing.

"*DOOM!*" she roared again, arms outstretched, clawing at the air. Her physical voice, ragged and croaking, came to him this time.

Doom landed a few yards from her on the ridge. Krogh's body shook with rage as she faced him. She did not look much different from the other urvullak. She had grown larger, her frame perhaps swollen with the power it contained, and was easily eight feet tall. Though her features were still those of a rodent distortion of the human, her limbs were so long, and her frame so thin, the aura of the praying mantis hung around her. In the midst of her legions, she might have carried herself with a false majesty. Alone, she was a grotesque, a ragged incarnation of folklore's nightmares.

"I have come," said Doom. "I come without mercy. But I will end you quickly. You are a distraction, Maleva Krogh. You have something that belongs to me. I have come to claim it."

"What do you think you can take?" Krogh hissed. "The Devourer will never be yours. It is you who are its fated prey. You have come here to die. The Devourer hungers for you."

"Then let it come to me," said Doom. "Perhaps it and I have much to say to each other."

Krogh made a sound in her throat like the rattling of bones. "You are a fool. You revel in a victory that is a lie. I have but to set foot in Doomstadt to begin my conquest again." She raised a finger. "One touch. A single touch on a single human is all it takes."

Doom made a sweeping gesture at the landscape. "Doomstadt is miles away. There is no one here. You are alone, Krogh. You are finished."

So was this conversation. Krogh had cost him so much, he had indulged in this moment before destroying her. It was enough. She was still dangerous.

Doom stripped away the shields from the receiver and aimed it at Krogh. She attacked him at the same moment. She still contained all the pasts that the Devourer had consumed, and she hit Doom with a concentrated blast of memories, more focused, more powerful than any she had used yet. The beam of sorrows slammed through his mental defenses like a hammer through glass.

Doom snarled, staggering under the rockslide of eons. All the past and all its griefs came for him at once. It struck as if to shatter his mind, to turn it to slush under the weight of history.

Doom kept his sense of self afloat. What was the past to him except another means to his ends.

I will know everything soon. This is just a foretaste.

He did not care about the mourning of lives long gone. He cared about his past, his memories, and the Devourer did not possess those yet. They belonged to him.

He was Doom. He was not the sum of other griefs.

He fired the stored energy in the receiver.

Krogh screamed, and the memories cut short. Doom's mind and vision cleared. Krogh's arms were splayed out and vibrating. Energy, crimson and silver, surrounded her, and it mocked her screams with the echoes of tens of thousands of others. Her jaw distended in pain, and then her flesh began to smolder and crisp. Her fangs blackened. Her lips shriveled. Ashes flaked from her, whisked away like insects by an ethereal wind.

Her joints cracked, crumbled, and she collapsed to her knees.

Doom strode over to Krogh as her arms dropped to her sides and her claws broke apart like charred sticks. He placed his right hand over her skull and held it tightly. "The Devourer is *mine*," he said.

He spoke the words of conjuring he had prepared since Zargo had first detected the presence of the Devourer.

The Devourer answered his call. It burst from the crumbling body, hurling its cinders away, and for the first time, the Devourer existed in the physical world. It appeared before Doom as a whirling vortex, a maelstrom whose spiral arms were the color of ash spun around a central maw. Teeth formed, disappeared and re-formed out of psychic storm clouds, gnashing in eternal hunger around the darkness at the center. The Devourer grew and grew. The maw came closer to Doom. He reached up for it, chanting the spells of binding.

The blackness filled his vision.

This is wrong.

Too late, he realized that he was not chaining the Devourer. It was coming to him of its own accord, lunging at its prey. Doom drew back, but the Devourer was faster, and the maw closed around Doom's right hand.

The world around him vanished. He was in the gray limbo that Orloff had traveled. The spiral of the Devourer stretched off to infinity above, below and to the sides. The wind of the being shrieked against Doom, seeking to push him forward in the gnawing jaws.

Cold shot up Doom's arm. It spread down his chest and into his heart. His armor still protected him, but the ethereal teeth of the Devourer were reaching through his defenses, coming closer to taking him. Already, he was almost part of the Devourer, and his folly revealed itself to him in all its scale and horror.

There was no omniscience here for him. There was no repository of all knowledge for him to plunder. There would be no restoration of all memories. For him, the Devourer had only hunger. The void opened in his mind and in his soul. He felt the first touches of the ravening emptiness that would be his forever.

He did not understand how he could have been so wrong.

He knew dread, then, dread that he had truly failed, and dread at the price the world would pay.

The epiphany came with the ratcheting snarl of Krogh's laughter. For a moment, above the maw, eyes formed in one of the gray arms of cloud. Doom recognized the eyes. The Devourer was no longer a being of pure instinct. It had a guiding intelligence now. It had Krogh.

It *was* Krogh.

"We are one," said Krogh the Devourer. "We are the fulfillment of centuries of worship. The prize was never in your reach, usurper. The House of Krogh has worshipped and propitiated us for generations upon generations. Union was ever the goal, and now it has come. Now the past will reign forever over Latveria. Give us your soul, Doom. Give us your surrender."

The voice boomed in his ears and in his head and in his core. It was wind and storm. It was hunger and triumph. The voice was also teeth, and it bit down deeper and deeper into his being. The cold spread. It reached into the foundations of Doom's identity and began to pry him loose from himself.

He fought back. His will hurled the cold away and erected walls of denial between his soul and the Devourer.

Krogh roared in anger. The Devourer pulled him further in, and his defenses began to crumble. His body was a million light years away. All he had was his will.

The will to cleave galaxies asunder. The will to topple gods.

The will to make his body move, to do what he must.

He brought his left hand forward. He reached across the endless distance to make his lips move. He uttered the incantation as he plunged his fist into the maw of the Devourer.

Marvel Untold

"*YOUR SOUL IS OURS!*" Krogh thundered in triumph. The cold squeezed hard around Doom's chest. His being began to crack, pain splintering through it.

It was irrelevant.

"No," said Doom. "I have ended you."

The eyes appeared again, wide now with a sudden uncertainty.

Doom triggered the occult receiver.

The storm of the Devourer poured itself into the receiver. The thing whose entire existence was eating was now eaten. The contradiction in states was irresolvable. The Devourer screamed. Sentient at last, it knew what was happening to it. It felt all the memories it had stored disintegrate. It encountered hunger that was not its own, and it learned, at the last, the agony of its atrocities.

The implosion was a cosmic slamming of walls. The limbo vanished, Doom saw and felt only darkness, and then it too disappeared, swallowing Krogh's final shriek.

Doom was on the ridge once more. The receiver was a charred ruin, the barrel cracked and twisted. He smacked it, and it broke in two, falling off his wrist. It hit the ground with a sullen clunk.

A stiff breeze coiled around Doom once, lifting the edge of his cloak, and then died. There was a faint taste of ash in the air.

Doom looked down at the spot where Krogh had been. Her body was gone now.

On the stones of the ridge, there was not even a memory of where she had been.

EPILOGUE

Past ages crowd on thee, but each one remembers,
And the future is dark, and the present is spread
Like a pillow of thorns for thy slumberless head.
PERCY SHELLEY, PROMETHEUS UNBOUND, I.561–3

It was well past dawn before the worst of the dust settled over the grave of Doomhelm. The earth fell quiet then too, and Zargo knew that the war was over. That was when he pulled himself more into the world above ground. He made himself fully regard his works.

He stood on a boulder in a field of debris. The valley was transformed. There was no hint of what had been here before. Zargo turned around slowly, taking in the miles of dark rubble.

He had done this. No one else. Doom had not ordered him to bring down the mountains. He had made that choice.

It was necessary.

Or was it?

Of course it had been. What would have happened to the next village, or the one after that, if these urvullak had not been destroyed?

He found that question a comforting one.

Besides, there had been no one here to save.

Are you sure?

That question was far less comforting. It came on the heels of an assertion that was too quick, too eager to end the internal debate.

Are you sure?

The question demanded an answer. He thought carefully about what he had seen. Could there still have been living people in Doomhelm?

No, he decided. *It was too quiet. Krogh had made the village hers.*

You're sure?

He hesitated. *He was sure enough. This time.*

This time. What about the times to come, then? Would he be so sure then? Had he truly been sure when he buried Doomhelm, or was he just trying to justify himself after the fact?

He didn't know. He worried about the next time.

The peace of stone called to him. He wanted to retreat back underground, where the meaning of *next time* could be another age.

A retreat, he thought. *Yes.* A retreat from temptation, a retreat to contemplation, where he could properly come to terms with the truths of who he was.

It took Zargo a few days to reach his goal. He traveled east, toward Latveria's border with Romania. He followed a trail of bereavement through the Earth, to where he was needed. He came to mountains again, and to the one that stood alone from its fellows, just west of the chain. He took the hover platform up to the peak of Mount Sivàr.

Maria von Helm had lived here, the reclusive witch of the

mountain. She had come down to work with Doom, and when they had raised Hell, it had taken her. The mountain mourned her. Its peak had collapsed, burying the cave that had been her home.

Zargo took hold of the mountain gently, and with its permission he lifted its head once more and opened up the cave. Then he sat by its entrance and breathed deeply. The air was sharp and cold and pure. It had an edge of peace.

Zargo placed a hand against the mountain's face, where it was warmed by a beam of thin October sun. "You lost your witch," he said. "Will you accept me in her stead?"

He sent his mind deep into stone, and the mountain embraced him.

Orloff and Kariana sat beside each other on the parapet again. It was cold in Doomstadt. The cloud cover was unbroken. Leaves from the trees in the courtyards skittered over the paving stones. The breeze was a leeching keen.

Orloff wasn't cold. The touch of Kariana's shoulder against hers warmed her.

"How do you feel?" Orloff asked her wife.

"Better," said Kariana. "I can still feel where I tore. But a lot better. A good war helps."

"I used to think you were kidding when you said things like that. Then I worried that you weren't joking."

"And now you get it."

Orloff put her arm around Kariana. "I do. It's not the fight, exactly. It's getting through to the right end."

"Yes. It's being Latveria's battlements." She turned to look Orloff in the eyes. "And its hunter."

Orloff kissed her. "I'm glad you get that too. I'm glad you understand me."

"Always."

They touched foreheads. "We're lucky," Orloff said softly.

"No," said Kariana. "We're destiny. The kind we choose."

They stayed like that for a few minutes. Then, when they both knew it was time, they stood up and stretched.

"What now for you?" Orloff asked.

"Work to do. Order to restore. And you?"

Orloff put the helmet on. She looked through the crystal world. In the far distance, she saw the movement of her prey. "The hunt's not over," she said. Anger surged at the sight of the urvullak. So did eagerness. "Is it wrong that part of me is glad?" she asked. "Not that the urvullak are there, but that I'm still hunting?"

"The righteous hunts are never over," said Kariana. "Yours is one of the most righteous. That's a good thing."

They embraced again, and then Orloff left the castle, tracking destiny.

In his study, Doom stood at the window, fists clenched.

Nothing. It was all for nothing.

All the work, all the research, all the hopes. A war, and thousands dead. *All for nothing.*

Below, he saw Orloff take up her helmet again. The work with her, at least, had not been futile. Latveria had another champion now, one as loyal as she was skilled. She had many hunts ahead. The urvullak that had been isolated, with none of their kin to turn on when Doom broadcast the signal, had survived. They would lurk in the shadows, following their instincts. They were few, and they were no longer under a lethal will's control, but they were still dangerous. Their hunger would never end.

Doom's anger deepened once more. This was what he had to show for his efforts. The stain of the urvullak had returned.

Krogh and the Devourer were gone. Their taint remained. The touch of Krogh's foul past would not leave Latveria easily. In the places where mist and shadows pooled, superstition would flourish.

To protect the people against the urvullak, for them to be properly wary, perhaps it had to.

Doom cursed Krogh. He cursed her works. *You harmed Latveria. You denied me what was rightfully mine.*

Power, true, unlimited power, that could not be countered, had been taken from him.

Again, he thought. *It had happened again.*

There was a tingle at the back of his mind, the suggestion of a memory, of a pattern, of a thing that was lost but could perhaps be learned, regained. He reached for it, desperate for its promise. Then it vanished, mocking him.

He closed his eyes hard and took a breath, pushing back against the instinct to lash out, to smash the world in frustration. When he opened his eyes again, he could think rationally once more.

Doom turned from the window. He left the study and climbed the stairs to the Chamber of the Eye. He entered the profound night of the space.

And now?

Fury smoldered, an underground fire. Its fuel never ran out. And it was his fire, deeply and forever his own. It could never be taken from him. It would show him the way forward. He would use it to burn a new trail through the shadows.

Another loss did not mean there was an end to his labors. There were other avenues of power, other darkness to claim.

Destiny is to be forged.

He began work on the next link in the chain.

ABOUT THE AUTHOR

DAVID ANNANDALE is a lecturer at a Canadian university on subjects ranging from English literature to horror films and video games. He is the author of many novels in the *New York Times*-bestselling *Horus Heresy* and *Warhammer 40,000* universe, and a co-host of the Hugo Award-nominated podcast Skiffy and Fanty.

davidannandale.com
twitter.com/david_annandale

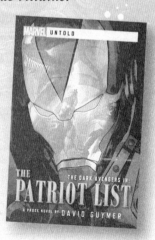

MARVEL

WORLD EXPANDING FICTION

Have you read them all?